HUSH MY DARLING

D. M. HAAS

Cover created by Deranged Doctor Designs.

A Danielle M Haas Publishing Book

Hush My Darling

To anyone who has taken a step outside their comfort zone to try something new.

1

The faint rustling of movement reached Vivian Walker's ears. The baby was waking. She stifled a groan as the sweet oblivion of sleep slipped slowly away. The exact time was unknown, but it was always too early to welcome a new day with false enthusiasm and happiness.

Yet that's what every day had been like since Tabitha's birth two months before. Exhaustion weighed Vivian down day after day, along with the constant fear she was disappointing both her infant daughter and three-year-old son. Each day she vowed to try harder.

Try harder to find joy in the small things, try harder to not let the ear-piercing wails of her baby drive her to the brink of insanity, try harder not to crave crawling back into her bed and escaping into the darkness.

And each day that she tried, she failed.

A soft whimper morphed into an all too familiar scream. A scream that couldn't be ignored. Tabitha needed fed, and her insistent cries made Vivian's breasts fill with milk. She winced as the increasing heaviness became painful.

Vivian sucked back the tears that threatened to break

through as she opened her eyes and prepared to face the day with all the mounting pressures of life.

The bang of a door against the wall erupted into the room.

She shot up, securing the soft sheet against her throbbing chest as an erratic rhythm took hold of her heart.

Her husband, Will, emerged from the en suite bathroom with a scowl etched on his lips. He flipped the end of a blue-checked tie through a loop, securing a thick knot at the base of his neck. "If you aren't going to take care of the baby, why did you want another one so damn badly? Call in the nanny, for Christ's sake."

She blinked, giving herself one brief moment to pull herself together. Words and excuses blurred in her sleep-muddled mind. What was the right thing to diffuse his temper and put their day on a good path? This new version of her once-loving husband had her constantly on edge—another person she couldn't quite get things right with.

Another person she disappointed.

Leaning over to the side-sleeper, she lifted the fussy baby in her arms and snuggled her close before giving the child what she demanded. "I just wasn't awake yet. Took me a second to get to her."

Vivian pressed a kiss to Tabby's forehead, taking a second to inhale the scent that only a new baby possesses—new life mixed with soft, subtle lotions and something unexplainable. Her moss green eyes latched on to Vivian's. A short-lived beat of joy pulsed inside her.

"I've got a lot of meetings today. Not sure when I'll be home." Will crossed the room and ran a hand over Tabitha's soft wisps of hair, jet black like her mother's.

Their son might resemble the other men of the Walker family, but Vivian delighted in the fact that Tabitha looked just like her. Even down to the subtle flash of dimples in her cheeks. If only the baby smiled more and showed them off.

Vivian nodded, biting back a retort about how he was never home anymore. But peeling back the curtains to her real emotions over Will's work schedule wouldn't help anything. The opposite would occur.

She suppressed a sigh. This is what she'd signed up for when she'd married into the Walker family. The plan had always been for Will to take his father's seat in the senate—a seat a Walker man had occupied for the past five generations— until the death of his father years before. Now it was time to reclaim his destiny.

She fixed a smile on her face. "I hope you have a great day, honey."

He paused and moved his palm from the baby's face up to cup her cheek.

She leaned into his touch, yearning for the days when such a simple gesture was a normal part of their morning.

Concern clouded his gray-blue eyes, his brow furrowed creating a ripple of lines along his forehead. "What are your plans for the day?"

Surprise stalled her breath. When was the last time Will cared about what she did with her time—at least time spent away from a camera or campaign events? When was the last time worry shone from those beautiful, vibrant eyes?

Maybe the man she fell in love with was still there, down deep below the family obligations and stress.

"James wants to take a walk around the bluff this morning. I thought I'd take him and the baby. The fresh air will do us all good. Harper might meet us."

Will dropped his hand, straightening to his full, towering height. "You don't plan to drive, do you? And make sure you take Sylvie to help with the children. You can't handle them by yourself. Even if Harper shows up."

The brief moment of intimacy vanished, the familiar pang of defeat taking its place. It never took long for someone to remind her of the things she couldn't do—things her epilepsy prevented her from accomplishing. She'd experienced the same crippling doubt from those she loved since childhood—even her own parents had reminded her daily of her limitations. Especially when she couldn't take the medication that kept her seizures at bay. The dark moments when her body froze and mind went black didn't happen frequently, but often enough to stop her from living her life to the fullest.

She'd never admit it to anyone, but those dark moments sometimes felt like a brief escape from her overwhelming reality.

"Patrick can drive." Driving, especially with the children, was way too dangerous. But she wouldn't mention her plans to have Sylvie stay home. The nanny hovered around her like she was a fragile piece of glass that would break with the slightest gust of wind.

The same way her parents and everyone else had looked at her for her entire life.

James burst into the room with a wide grin on his beautiful face and a smear of strawberry jam along his cheek. "Mama! Dada!"

A wide smile transformed Will into the young man she'd fallen in love with, joy softening the lines of his face and hoarse laughter filling the air. He bent and scooped the little boy into his arms, quickly turning James upside down to hang like a monkey from his forearm.

Giggles reached her ears and transported her back to a simpler time—a time when they were a family of three, when she didn't obsess over her son's inability to say more than the two words he'd squealed when entering the room, when loss hadn't ripped an irreparable hole in her heart.

She wanted to close her eyes and ingrain this moment in her mind to replay during the moments when life seemed too much to bear, but she couldn't take her eyes off the easy fun between father and son.

Tabitha squirmed in her arms then let out an earsplitting wail that halted the carefree moment. Will placed James on his feet. James sidled against Vivian's side of the bed, his little arm wrapped around her waist as if wanting to protect her.

"I've got to run. Be careful today." Will's gruff words were a command, not a note of concern for her safety.

She readjusted Tabitha until the baby was content, eating her breakfast once again. "I'm always careful." The pathetic statement was the best she could do, the only glimmer of rebellion left in her.

Will leveled his stare on her and pressed his lips together. "We both know what can happen. Even when you try your hardest. Make sure Sylvie is with you. I'll let Mother know your plans."

She dipped her head, shielding the expression she couldn't hide. She wouldn't agree to his request or respond to his remark about his mother. Why Lilith Walker needed to know her every move was a constant source of discord between them.

A quick glance out the door showed the nanny exactly where she was every morning. Waiting in the hall, knowing at some point, Vivian would need assistance to deal with her own children.

But not today. Today she would do something she loved with both of her kids. She would take them on a walk to breathe in the fall, Connecticut air and shower them with love and attention, giving them everything they needed.

All she needed was Patrick to get her there.

BEING TRAPPED inside the noisy car on the brief ride to James' favorite walking path would bring grown men to their knees.

The cool air kept the screams and demands of the angry baby from escaping out the closed window.

Vivian sat between the two car seats. Desperation clawed her insides, but nothing she did made Tabitha happy. Frustration tightened her muscles, and it took all her willpower to not lash out.

Giving up, she raked her hands over her face.

"Kids can be difficult, but you got this, Ms. You're tougher than you think." The kindness in Patrick's voice had her dropping her hands.

She locked her gaze with his for a beat in the rearview mirror. "Thank you for that. Sometimes I think I must be the only mother in the world who can't calm her own child."

"Nah. Trust me. We've all been there. My little Tess was a pistol, always hollering and crying about something. My wife and I held on for dear life, just waiting for the day she'd grow out of it."

"And did she?"

Patrick chuckled. "She still hollers, but now it's to demand action in a court room. That little girl of yours will move mountains one day with those lungs."

Vivian settled against the smooth leather of the seat and linked her fingers with James, who sat with his face turned toward the window. His sister's cries never rattled him. Her little boy was always calm—always understanding and full of smiles. Which made dealing with a demanding baby even harder, the expectation being all kids were like her first.

She pressed a hand to her still-soft belly. If she hadn't had her accident, would the second baby she'd carried in her womb have been so high-maintenance?

A burst of guilt exploded in her conscience. Things happened for a reason, and Tabby was the miracle she'd desired for so long. Comparing her to what might have been wasn't fair to anyone.

Patrick pulled into the empty gravel lot just as her phone vibrated in the pocket of her yoga pants. "I'll grab the stroller, Ms."

She gave a single nod and answered the phone. "Hi, Harper. Are you almost here?"

James turned wide, hopeful eyes her way. Her best friend was like the fun aunt Vivian always wanted as a kid. She always showed up with pockets filled with special candy or a fun new toy for James. She brought joy and silliness into their rigid world.

Similar tragedies had brought Harper into her life. Unlike Vivian, who'd never been able to shed the nasty tentacles of depression, Harper worked through her pain and had come out the other side stronger.

"I'm so sorry. My mom fell this morning, and I'm at the hospital with her. I'll have to take a rain check."

"Is your mom okay?" she asked, pushing aside her selfish reasons for wanting her best friend by her side for a quiet walk along the bluff.

"She'll need surgery on her hip. Not sure what happens after that."

"I'm so sorry. Call if there's anything I can do." Vivian disconnected and fixed a large smile on her face as she focused on her son. "Aunt Harper can't join us, but we'll still have fun. I promise."

The disappointment in James's downturned mouth and furrowed brow matched Vivian's reaction. Her days were dominated by her kids and her overbearing mother-in-law, as well as a house full of staff who kept their distance. Time spent with Harper was the one thing that could always lift her spirit.

Tabitha's squeals contradicted her oath of a fun morning, but she was determined to have a good day.

Climbing over James, she slid out of the car then unbuckled him from his seat before helping him down from the vehicle.

Patrick unlatched Tabitha's car seat and settled the bulky carrier on top of stroller, then met Vivian at the side of the car. "Would you like me to walk with you?"

"No, thank you. We won't be long." Patrick's offer was sweet and sincere, probably the only person her husband employed with those characteristics, but she wanted this time with her kids. Even if Tabitha continued to scream and James hadn't gotten over his disappointment of Harper bailing. "Let's go, James."

She sang a little nursery rhyme James loved as they walked along the path, winding upward toward the lighthouse overlooking the bluff. A crisp wind blew through the trees, swirling through the colorful foliage. The smell of the salty sea air filled her lungs, and she could just make out the roar of the ocean crashing against the side of the cliff over Tabitha's cries.

James stayed close to her side, his hand attached to the stroller as they walked. He turned his face toward the ocean, the vast waters stretching for miles.

Vivian kept her pace slow. Her nerves stretched tight, the cries of her baby causing the birds to fly into the clear blue sky. If only she could escape, just for a moment, fly high above and look down on everything below. A bird's-eye view of the surrounding beauty without the gilded cage trapping her beside the things slowly pushing her to her breaking point.

The all-too-familiar guilt swooped in as she watched a seagull dive toward the ocean. She loved her children. She wanted this life. She'd prayed for what she now had. But the harder she tightened her grasp on the things dearest to her, the more they beat her down.

The red and white striped lighthouse grew near, and James shrieked but stayed close.

She smiled down at her perfect little boy. "We can walk a little closer but stay by my side."

The cliff overlooking the bluff made anxiety swell in her

gut. James never tested the limits—never tried to get too close to the edge. But that didn't stop the horrible images of what could happen from invading her mind. Will's words from earlier came back—*be careful.*

Tabitha twisted and squirmed in her seat, straining against the confining straps. Maybe her daughter was just uncomfortable. A quick glance at James told her he was staying right where he was supposed to. She made quick work out of freeing Tabby from her seat. She pressed the baby to her chest and bounced her up and down, whispering soothing noises in her ear.

Nothing calmed her frantic cries.

Defeated, she placed Tabitha back in her seat. She'd cry herself to sleep eventually.

A sense of déjà vu overcame Vivian, stealing her senses. Her muscles tightened, freezing her in place. Panic had her straining against the sensation she was way too weak to overcome. She moved her mouth to yell to James, to make him move to her side, but her mouth refused to form any words. Dammit, she needed to protect him. Make him understand what was about to happen, what she was helpless to stop. She should have listened to Will and brought Sylvie—should have never come alone. Dizziness made her sway along with the wind whipping off the ocean. The explosion of colors on the trees behind her, the jagged cliff looming over the churning sea, and the lighthouse standing tall and proud, a place of safety and warning—these places blurred together in her mind, spinning into a kaleidoscope of colors and sounds, twisting and turning faster and faster until an explosion burst behind her eyes and her world went black.

Fatigue weighed down her eyelids. She struggled to open them, wincing against the harsh sunlight. Time had passed in a blur, as it always did when the seizures invaded her body. Fresh air and the ocean breeze mingled together, and she inhaled deeply to awaken her senses. A heaviness settled on her shoulders, pressing her down, but she fought to release the tension keeping her muscles rigid. She focused on the clear, crisp song of the birds overhead and the almost deafening crash of the water below against the hard rock below.

Sounds clamored together, increasing Vivian's heart rate. The birds, the sea, the rustle of the leaves all competed for her attention.

But no crying.

2

————

She dropped her gaze to the stroller. James stood beside her, blond hair wind-blown and a smile on his cherub face. But the baby was gone. Panic climbed up Vivian's throat.

A strangled sob gurgled from her mouth. She spun in a wide circle, scanning the area for any sign of where Tabitha could be. Seeing nothing but the stupid trees and paths forking out into the forested park, she threw the blankets to the ground, searching the seat.

"Tabitha." The name came out as a plea, a need to see her baby's face. "Tabby. Where are you?"

Terror grabbed her neck and squeezed tight, causing her breaths to come out in short, ragged pants. This couldn't be happening. She dropped to a crouch and grabbed James by his slender shoulders, turning him to face her. "Where's Tabitha? What happened?" She couldn't keep the fear from her voice, causing each syllable to climb higher and higher until the last word was nothing more than a screech.

James winced, rearing back. His eyes widened to saucers, and his bottom lip trembled.

Vivian tried to reign in her spiraling emotions. She didn't want to frighten James. But how could she control the sick sensation bubbling in the pit of her stomach when it felt as though someone had ripped a limb from her body?

Closing her eyes, she counted to ten and steadied her breath. She needed to stay calm and figure out what happened. A two-month-old baby couldn't just climb out of her stroller and walk away.

Someone took her.

The queasiness in her belly erupted, flooding her mouth with the acidic taste of bile. She swallowed it and opened her eyes, refocusing on James with an unsteady smile. "Everything's okay, baby. Mommy just needs to know what happened to Tabitha. Did you see anyone? Did a stranger come and grab her? Maybe they saw Mommy was having a hard time and wanted to keep Tabby safe?"

Her seizures had always made people uneasy. The blank expression that overtook her face and the uncontrollable movements of her body scared others more than concerned them. When she was younger, she'd been grateful she didn't fall to the ground and flail about the way most people envisioned epileptic seizures. But as she got older, it was clear that because her seizures didn't align with people's expectations, it made her even more of an oddity. The girl who stared into the void with no control over what her body did.

Just like before. When her feet moved of their own will, sending her spilling down a flight of stairs. Ending the life of her unborn baby.

Shaking away the horrible memory, she refocused her mind on the current crisis. She had to think. Maybe a hiker had stumbled upon them and thought the baby was in danger because of her inability to react to anything around her while her mind was trapped in the darkness. But if that was the case, why wouldn't they have taken James?

James shook his head, fear shining from his tear-filled eyes. He took a step back in retreat and shifted his face toward the ocean.

A shiver ran down her spine, and she rose on trembling legs. No, she couldn't have. Tabitha's constant fussiness might drive her crazy, but she could never hurt her child. But she had to be sure. Shivering, Vivian edged closer to the cliff and peered out into the open sea. Steeling her resolve, she roamed her gaze over the jagged rock that forged a path down the side of the cliff until it met the violent waters below.

No blood, no scraps of Tabby's little pink sweater, no sign of her daughter.

She pressed the back of her hand to her mouth as heat engulfed her, the bile demanding to slide up her esophagus and be expelled. Vivian turned to a cluster of bushes in front of the lighthouse and dropped to her knees. Her belly heaved as she emptied the contents of her stomach. A constant mantra beat against her head: *I didn't hurt my baby. I love my baby. I didn't hurt my baby.*

She turned in a circle, scanning the area. "Hello? Is anyone there?" She screamed the question against the wind, waiting and willing someone—anyone—to answer.

Nothing.

She yanked out her phone and called 911. Will wouldn't be happy to have the police involved, but she didn't have a choice. Tabitha was missing and she didn't know what else to do.

"911. What's your emergency?"

"My baby, my little girl, she's missing." She forced a calmness to her voice, needing to express what happened as clearly as possible. But her heart pounded along with the rhythm of the waves smashing against the rocks. Sweat moistened her palms despite the blanket of gray clouds hiding the sun.

"What's your name, ma'am?"

"Vivian Walker." She grabbed James' hand and hurried to

the surrounding area, searching for any clue of where her baby could be.

"Where are you, Vivian?"

"Lighthouse Point. At the top of the bluff."

"And how long as she been missing?"

"I... I don't know." Crap. She didn't check to see how long her seizure lasted. "What time is it?"

"11:23 a.m." The dispatcher couldn't hide the suspicion in her voice.

Vivian pinched the top of her nose and replayed the morning in her mind. "Twenty minutes. I was out for twenty minutes."

"Excuse me? What do you mean 'out'? Did you leave your baby alone?"

The accusation raised the hairs on her arms despite the long sleeves covering her skin. She hadn't left Tabitha's side, but she'd left her alone. Gone to the far reaches of her own mind where no one was able to get to her. That's why Will insisted she bring Sylvie on her walk. That's why no one trusted her to do the most common tasks.

She pushed aside the guilt that would plague her until Tabitha was found. What she should have done was of no concern. At least not right now. "I blacked out. I get seizures. When I woke, she was gone. I can't find her."

A brief pause sounded before the dispatcher said, "Okay. I am sending officers to you now. Just stay where you are. Help is on the way."

"I need to call my husband."

"That's fine. Just don't leave the area."

Vivian disconnected and called Will. As the line rang, she studied James. He stood tall, still focused on the blue waters ahead. She tapped her sneaker against the ground. *Come on, Will. Answer the damn phone.*

His voicemail picked up, announcing he was unable to come to the phone.

Tears burst from her eyes and ran down her cheeks. She needed her husband, now more than ever, and he couldn't be bothered to answer her call.

Will's steady voice on the recorded message ended and a beep followed.

"Will. Call me. Now. It's important." A quiver sliced through her words, and she disconnected. She couldn't tell him their daughter was missing on a voicemail, but she prayed her message would be enough to make him call her back.

There was only one sure-fire way to get a quick response from Will. Resentment slid over the fear and guilt battling for attention as she placed one more call.

The line picked up right away. "Hello, Vivian. Have you enjoyed your walk?"

"Lilith, Tabitha is missing. I need you and Will to get here. Now."

The scream of sirens drawing near echoed the wails of her mother's heart. Her baby was gone, and she'd do whatever she had to in order to get her back.

After explaining the situation to her mother-in-law, Vivian disconnected and studied the surrounding area for footprints, broken twigs, anything that told her someone had been close by while she'd been lost in oblivion. Nervous energy bounced around her body like a tiny rubber ball, gaining speed and pinging around her organs. The crunch of gravel and fast-paced footsteps caught her attention. She grabbed James, pulling him close to her side.

Patrick's familiar face poked through the trees. Worry shone from his brown eyes. His cap of snow-white hair flopped in the breeze as he ran to her side. "Are you okay, Ms.? The police are here. I was so scared you were hurt."

Vivian released a pent-up breath and held out a hand to

Patrick. She needed an anchor, someone to tell her everything would be all right.

A flicker of surprise crossed his face, but he grabbed hold of her hand and squeezed.

"Tabby's gone. I don't know where she is or what happened. If someone took her or...hell, someone had to have taken her, right? I mean, what else could have happened?" Her breath hitched, and she tightened her grip.

Patrick closed his eyes for a beat, and his chest lifted on a deep breath. "Everything's going to be fine. The police are here. They'll find Miss Tabitha. Why don't we have a seat?" He led her to the wooden bench off the path.

She collapsed onto the hard wood. How had her legs managed to hold her all this time? Her body trembled, a constant quiver vibrating her core. Pressure mounted in her chest, expanding inch by inch inside her aching body. Everything hurt as her heart raced and a million different scenarios played in her mind.

James sat beside her, his hand finding hers.

Two officers hurried up the path toward her. She straightened and wiped the moisture from her face. She had to hold it together long enough to get out every single detail she remembered. Tabitha's life depended on it.

"Mrs. Walker?" A middle-aged man in a crisp blue uniform hurried toward her. The serious set of his square jaw and narrowed green eyes trained on her.

She stood and wrapped her arms over her middle. "Yes. I'm Mrs. Walker."

"I'm Officer Daniels, and this is my partner, Officer Scott." He tilted his head toward the younger woman by his side. "Can you tell us what happened?"

"My children and I stopped at the top of the bluff to enjoy the view. While we stood there, I had a seizure. I woke twenty minutes later, and my baby was missing from her stroller." The words were like a punch in the gut. They couldn't be true. Someone else had to be standing here telling the police her child was gone. Soon, she'd wake from this nightmare. "When I couldn't find her, I called 911."

"How old is the child?" Officer Scott kept all traces of emotion from her face, but something familiar danced in her eyes. Something that told Vivian this woman didn't believe her.

"She's only two months. Just a tiny baby. She could be hurt or need to be fed. She needs her mother. She needs me to take care of her." The tears came back with a vengeance, and Vivian pushed her fisted hand against her mouth to keep a sob from escaping.

"Was this gentleman with you during your walk?" Officer Daniels asked with a quick glance aimed at Patrick.

Vivian shook her head. "Patrick is my driver. I don't drive because of the epilepsy. He was in the car until he saw the police arriving and became worried."

Officer Scott dipped her chin and dropped her brows so low they almost met above her hooked nose. "You don't drive because you're afraid you may have a seizure, but it's safe to take your two small children for a walk along a cliff? Overlooking the ocean?"

And there it was. The judgement. The insinuation. The assumption that Vivian made a mistake, and it was somehow her fault that some crazy person snatched up her baby. "I refuse to not live my life because of what might happen. My seizures are not frequent, and my children have never been harmed while under my care." She tightened her jaw to keep her voice from shaking, hoping the officer didn't hear the fib in her tone. But what had happened to James was different.

"I didn't mean any offense." Officer Scott held up her palms, but not even a flicker of remorse skittered across her face.

Patrick placed a palm on Vivian's shoulder. "Mrs. Walker is

very careful, but I don't think that's our main concern right now. We need to find the baby."

"I agree," said Officer Daniels. "More officers are on the way. We will canvas the area. We won't stop looking until we've found your daughter. But we do need to ask you some more questions. Who all knew where you were today? How long have you been here? Did you see or hear anyone while walking or when you pulled into the parking lot? Any bit of information can help us as we move forward."

A scurry of movement caught Vivian's eye, and she glanced beyond the police for a clear view of what was happening. A group of officers scattered around them, fanning in all directions. Dogs strained on their leashes as they charged through the trees and off into the woods.

Fear twisted every piece of her. This wasn't a nightmare. It was really happening. Her baby was missing.

"Vivian!" Will's voice broke through the commotion. He stormed to her side, his face a mask of hard lines and hidden emotions.

Lilith made her way behind him, the black kitten-heels slowing her pace.

Relief crashed against Vivian, so swift and strong it almost dropped her to the ground. "Will! Thank God you're here." She fell against him, wanting nothing more than his loving embrace and comforting words.

He wrapped an arm over her shoulder, squeezing her bicep a little too hard.

"We both are, dear." Lilith pressed a quick kiss to her cheek then perched on the bench beside James. Her perfectly straight gray hair swept the tops of her shoulders and not a drop of dirt dared to mar her pressed black skirt and matching jacket.

For once, Vivian was glad for her mother-in-law's presence. James had to be scared, and she couldn't give him the attention and comfort he needed. Lilith might not be the warm and cozy grandma who baked cookies and sang songs, but she loved her grandchildren in her own way and would make sure James was taken care of.

Will extended a hand to the officers. "I'm William Walker. Thank you for getting here so quickly. As you can imagine, my wife and I are beside ourselves with worry."

Vivian flinched at the bland statement that oozed politician.

Recognition dawned in Officer Daniel's eyes as he shook Will's hand. "I understand, sir. It's a scary situation, and please rest assured that we will do everything we can to find your little girl."

"I have no doubt, but if you'd please give me a moment. I'd like to speak with my wife. Alone." He flashed a smile then turned Vivian and took a few steps in the opposite direction. He pressed his mouth to her ear. "What the hell happened?"

His grip tightened even more, but Vivian knew enough not to try and break away. Especially with prying eyes aimed on them. "I told your mother. I blacked out and when I woke up, Tabby was gone."

"And what did you tell the police?"

Her jaw went slack. Anger heated his words, not fear or panic or any normal response to his child being taken. "Exactly that."

He brought her closer to him and pressed his lips against her ear. "That's all you're going to say until our lawyer gets here. Our family can't take this kind of scandal."

Her world tilted, the truth of her husband's reaction more than she could handle. Not only did he not care that their baby was missing, he thought she was responsible.

3

D etective Ellen Olsen hurried up the inclined path, ignoring the bursts of colorful leaves rustling on one side and the roaring waves pounding against the shore on the other. The salty air slapped against her cheeks, reminding her that the crisp days were about to turn downright cold.

At the top of the hill, she found herself at an all-too familiar scene. A scene that punched her in the gut and brought a fresh wave of grief every single time. She beat back the anguish that never went away and focused on the reason she was here.

The disappearance of Tabitha Walker.

A cluster of people huddled together. A woman with jet-black hair sat on a bench and wept while clutching the arm of a small boy. A tall man with blond hair rested a hand on her shoulder, his lips pressed into a tight line and hard eyes screamed of a brewing storm. A second woman, older and smaller than the first, stood beside the man. Her rigid posture spoke of control, her face giving no clue as to what simmered under the tough exterior and well-pressed suit.

The Walkers.

You couldn't live in Hollow Cove without recognizing the powerful family. A family that kept themselves mostly secluded in their large estate tucked in the woods, keeping their distance from the common folk of the small town. Until the perfectly polished William Walker needed votes and everything became an opportunity for publicity.

Or until their daughter went missing and they needed to depend on the local authorities to locate her.

Ellen tore away her gaze and focused on the uniformed officers searching for clues. Speaking to them was her first priority. Then she'd concentrate on the interesting cast of characters whose lives had just changed forever.

"Officer Daniels." She lifted a hand in greeting and made a beeline for the weathered policeman she'd met at countless crime scenes.

He pressed his mouth in a grim line and waited for her to approach. "Olsen. I'd say it's good to see you, but it never is in situations like this."

"Likewise." She scanned the area. An empty stroller sat abandoned on the grassy patch of land by the edge of the cliff. Officers scoured the scene, no doubt searching for any clues to tell them what had happened to the missing child. "Tell me what we've got."

"Mrs. Vivian Walker was out with her two children. She claims to have suffered from a seizure brought on by her epilepsy, and when she came to her baby was gone. No witnesses, no camera this far up the trail, no idea what happened to her daughter."

Ellen glanced over her shoulder, noting the small boy clinging to the dark-haired woman. "What about the boy?"

"James Walker. Three years old." His lips twitched and a touch of sadness darkened his irises.

The same age her Sara was when she went missing two years before. Ellen absorbed this information like a blow to her temple and moved on, pretending not to notice Daniels' reaction to the boy's age. Everyone on their police force knew about the tragic turn her life had taken the day Sara was grabbed from their neighborhood park and never returned. But she couldn't dwell on it when their focus needed to be on Tabitha Walker.

"Can the boy talk? Did he see anything?"

Officer Daniels shook his head. "Can't say much. Gave no indication to us, or the family, what happened to his sister."

"Anything of interest found I should know about before I talk to the family?"

"Nothing yet." His gaze flickered over her shoulder for a beat. "But I'm sure the captain told you who we're dealing with."

Irritation crawled over her skin. Captain Marther made sure she understood the importance of the man she would be interviewing as well as how sensitive the situation was. Any negative publicity on a family as powerful and influential as the Walkers was to be avoided at all costs.

An order that made Ellen bristle with contempt. How could anyone care more about reputations and political clout than the life of an innocent child?

"Marther explained, not like it should matter. Everyone has the same goal here."

Daniels gave a brief nod. "Agreed. But that's not always the case. And this bunch is tight-lipped. The husband's pissed we asked them to wait for you to arrive on scene before leaving. He wants his lawyer present for all interactions with law enforcement."

Ellen raised her brows high. "Interesting." She'd put that piece of information in her back pocket. In her experience, family didn't hesitate to tell the detective in charge of searching for their child every little piece of information they could. The insistence of a lawyer present usually meant guilt—

or at least more knowledge than the family was willing to divulge.

"Excuse me."

Turning at the gruff words, Ellen found herself staring into those storming eyes she'd noted when she got there. The infamous William Walker stood close, towering over her. Was he trying to intimidate her by pushing into her personal space with his hard scowl and narrowed gaze?

No, he was a distraught father who was looking for the person in charge. She couldn't let her disdain for what he represented cloud her judgement of him or the case. Just because his family had dominated their little coastal town for years instead of migrating to a more high-profile part of Connecticut didn't mean he was a bad person.

Just a nuisance who demanded more attention than most—attention she'd never been forced to give until now.

She extended her hand and waited for him to take it before introducing herself. "Mr. Walker, I'm Detective Olsen. My sincerest apologies for what you're experiencing, and for making you wait for my arrival. I got here as soon as I could."

He stuffed his hands in the front pockets of his trousers, angling his head to meet her gaze straight on. "We've waited long enough. I need to get my family home. My wife has already suffered one seizure today, which takes a lot out of her physically. And the added stress and fear over our daughter is too much for her to handle. Whatever questions you have, they can wait until a better time."

"I understand your need to protect your wife and make sure she's okay, but it's important I speak with her now." She didn't step away, didn't back down from his glowering stare.

"She's already told the other officers everything she can. She can answer anything you ask at home, after she's rested, just as easily as she can here."

Ellen raised a hand, halting any further opposition. Maybe

her initial impression about this guy was spot on. William Walker played the part of pompous asshole extremely well, and he might have finally met his match. She didn't give two shits about his name or status—even if her captain had told her to step lightly. All she cared about was the lost little girl who needed to be brought home.

"Mr. Walker. I've worked more missing child cases than I care to count. There is a procedure to follow. A procedure that has proven successful more times than not. If you want the best shot at figuring out what happened to your daughter, I suggest you let me talk to your wife. Now."

The older woman came up behind Mr. Walker and placed one hand on the small of his back, offering Ellen the other. "Hello, Detective. I'm Lilith Walker, William's mother. Thank you so much for getting here. We're all just completely distraught. My son is beside himself about our dear Tabitha, but also worried about his wife and son. I'm sure you under-stand." She clasped her hands together, keeping them in front of her tiny waist.

Ellen smoothed her mouth into a well-trained smile—the one she used when dealing with people who thought they knew more than her. "I understand this is difficult for all of you. As soon as I speak with Mrs. Walker, you may take her home to rest."

Lilith's lips twitched a bit, but she nodded and led the way to the young mother.

The weeping woman rose. "Do you know anything? Has anyone found my baby?" Red-rimmed eyes lit with hope.

"I'm sorry, ma'am. Nothing yet."

The hope faded, replaced quickly by despair.

Ellen wanted to look away. She saw so much of herself in this other woman. Not the striking good looks and delicate features. She was light-haired and plain where the other woman was sculpted from marble with raven hair. But the vision of a mother with a broken heart and fear gnawing her from the inside out mirrored back at her.

She'd stand and ask questions and do her job. It was all that she could do. "I just need some information. Then you're free to return home. Even after that, I'll be in contact with you frequently until we find Tabitha. Okay?"

"Okay."

Ellen grabbed her notebook from the suit jacket. "Mrs. Walker, is there anyone that has threatened you or your family recently? Anyone who wishes to do you harm?"

"Please. Call me Vivian. And no. I can't think of anyone." She wrung her hands together and glanced up at her husband, as if answering questions involving the family was something she'd rather not handle.

"Not that I'm aware of," Mr. Walker said. "Or not anything that anyone has taken seriously."

Ellen stopped scribbling her notes, needing to focus on the exact way the Walkers phrased their answers. "What does that mean?"

He shrugged. "Any family with money or status will get letters or emails from people who feel wronged or entitled to something owed them. My assistant goes through any flagged correspondences and is tasked with informing me if anything alarming arises."

"Have any red flags emerged lately?"

"None."

She retrained her attention on Mrs. Walker. "What about of a personal nature? Someone you angered or someone who felt wronged?"

Vivian shook her head then stared back up at her husband.

Ellen bit back a sigh. She wouldn't get any information out of the wife while her husband was present, and the husband already spoke of wanting a lawyer. Asking questions now was a waste of time. She flipped her notebook closed and put it back in her pocket. "Is there anything at all that's seemed off to any of you? Any tiny piece of information that could help?" She locked eyes on all three adults, wanting any of them to give her something to work with.

"We've already been over this with that officer over there." Mr. Walker flicked his hand toward Officer Daniels. "I'm taking my family home."

Vivian's green eyes got impossibly larger and she darted her gaze from her husband to Ellen, her hands moving in a continuous circle. "How can I just leave? Tabby might still be here. I can't go home without her. I have to stay."

A crack of emotion broke through Mr. Walker's stoic expression, and he pulled his wife against his side. "We need to let them do their job and search for Tabitha. If we think of anything else the police should know, we'll call. But you need rest. You always do after a seizure. And all the emotion and stress might cause you to have another. We can't risk that."

"Do you take seizure medication?" Ellen made a mental note to research epilepsy. She didn't know much about the disorder but was sure most people carried medication to stop seizures in their tracks. It made no sense a mother of two wouldn't carry the medication if it would ensure the safety of her and her children.

"I'm breastfeeding. I can't take my usual medication."

Mr. Walker's pissed-off sneer came back in full force. "What does that have to do with anything?"

Ellen ignored him. "There aren't any prescriptions that can help you now?" She didn't want to say it out loud, but she found it hard to believe modern medicine couldn't give her something, even while breastfeeding a child.

The moisture in Vivian's eyes grew then fell down her face. "I refused to take them this time."

"This time?"

Vivian dropped her gaze and squeezed her hands together so hard Ellen feared she'd break a bone.

"I've suffered miscarriages in the past. I can't take any chances. Not anymore." Her voice was so low, Ellen barely made out the sad words over the growl of the ocean.

"I'm very sorry. Please. Go home. I'll be in touch soon." Sympathy softened her tone.

Vivian rested a hand on Ellen's. "You have to find her."

"Trust me," Ellen said. "I will do everything in my power to bring your little girl home."

Her promise rang in her ears as she watched the Walker family make their way down the path toward the parking lot. Turning, she marched toward a group of officers lingering near the lighthouse. Ellen stopped beside the empty stroller and stared down at the pretty pink blanket. She grazed her finger against the soft cotton. The ache in her heart intensified. Sometimes, no matter how hard she tried, little girls never made it home.

4

Vivian sat in the rocking chair in Tabitha's nursery, clutching the white teddy bear with purple wings she'd bought the day she'd discovered she was having a girl. After years of loss and suffering and sadness, she'd have two children to love. A son and a daughter.

Now her little girl was gone.

Pain so swift and sharp slammed against her, stealing her breath. Her body ached, something she was used to after having a seizure, but this was different. The ache started in a cold place in her soul, gushing out like water until she was drowning in despair. Numb almost, as if shock had settled into her bones, not allowing her to move or think or accept the truth.

She drifted her blurry gaze around the sweet room she'd painstakingly put together. Shadows covered most of the space —the ornate crib with the cream-colored quilt draped over the side, the decorative wall hangings she'd spent hours toiling over, and the bookcase she'd brought from home after her parents had passed, filled with all of Vivian's childhood books.

But she wanted to escape into the dark, away from the curious eyes of the household staff and police lingering downstairs.

A light knock sounded at the door, and Harper rushed inside. "Oh, Vivian. How is this happening?"

Unblinking, Vivian met Harper's sad, brown eyes. Her brain was unable to form words as she stared at her best friend, her number one supporter over the last few years. She wanted to cry, to scream, to yell out to God with anger and fear, but it was all too exhausting.

"Oh, honey." Tears spilled down Harper's high cheekbones. She gently scooted Vivian over in the wide chair and sat beside her, pulling her close—cradling her like a child.

Vivian rested her head on Harper's shoulder, finally getting the comfort she'd craved all day. Not once had Will held her in his arms or Lilith pressed a reassuring hand to her back. No one had told her everything would be all right or that Tabby would come home soon. Instead, Will had ushered her into their room the second they returned and ordered her to sleep. She wasn't sure if he was concerned about the toll the seizure had taken on her body or wanted her where she couldn't talk to anyone about what had happened on that cliff.

What she might have done while no one was around to see.

She shook her head, willing the thought to leave. No, no, no. She didn't do anything. Tabby might be a handful, but she'd never hurt her sweet, innocent baby. She pressed her fingertips against her closed eyes. Just because Tabby hadn't been found and no evidence to show who had taken her uncovered, didn't mean Vivian had done the unthinkable. *I love my baby. I didn't hurt my baby. I love my baby.*

Harper grazed her palm up and down Vivian's arm. "Everything's going to be fine. The police will find Tabby, and she'll be home before you know it."

A shiver shot down her spine. "She's been gone for so long.

They still haven't found her. How can that be? Who'd do something like this?"

Harper lowered Vivian's hands, clasping them in her own. She dipped her chin, leveling a calming stare directly in Vivian's eyes. "Listen to me. You need to be strong. For Tabby. The police will find her and she will come home. But you need to do everything you can to help them. Do whatever they ask, even if Will doesn't agree."

Vivian flinched. She hadn't needed to tell Harper about Will's insistence on keeping a lawyer by their side or not wanting her to speak to anyone about what happened. Harper knew enough about Will to understand his reluctance to open their lives to anyone, no matter the reason. "I told the police what happened. I shared everything I remembered."

Harper nodded up and down several times, as if the constant motion would give Vivian the courage she needed to stand up for herself. Something she'd never been able to do. "Good. Did they ask anything else? Want to know any other information?"

Vivian fought through the fogginess of her brain to search her memory bank. "The detective in charge asked about anyone who'd been unhappy with us. Anyone who'd want to hurt us by taking Tabby."

"And?" Harper asked, her voice low.

"No one." Vivian pushed back the long sweep of hair matted against her moist cheek. "No one came to mind for Will either."

"What about your family back in Ohio? Are there any cousins or distant relatives who'd want to try and get money from you?"

The shiver from before came back with a vengeance, making her whole body shake. "You think someone from home could have been following me, waiting for an opportunity to take Tabby just so we'd pay them?"

Harper winced and pulled her closer. "I'm just trying to think of every possibility, no matter how small."

Vivian sighed. "I never thought about anyone from my hometown being responsible. I haven't spoken to anyone from there in so long."

Unable to sit still, she pushed to her feet and crossed the room to Tabby's crib. She placed the teddy bear she still held inside then ran her finger along the delicate slope of the wood. "I can't wrap my mind around any of this, let alone think of all the different reasons why this could have happened. I'm still hoping the doorbell will ring and someone will return her safe and sound. That everything's a big misunderstanding." Her stomach pitched, and she clutched the side of the crib to keep herself upright.

"I'm so sorry, Viv. Is there anything I can do?"

She turned and faced her friend. Even through the poorly lit room, Vivian made out the bags under Harper's eyes. Her normal bouncy, ash-blonde curls were pulled away from her face in a messy bun and her jeans and long-sleeved t-shirt were a far cry from the business attire she wore for her job as an events coordinator at the local hospital.

The same hospital they'd met at when both attended a grief support group for women who'd experienced the loss of a miscarriage.

A bolt of realization struck through Vivian's shroud of haziness. "How's your mom? I completely forgot about her hip surgery."

"She'll be fine, but we don't need to talk about her. You have bigger things on your mind."

Vivian wanted to argue, to find out what happened to Harper's mom and how her recovery looked, but she didn't have the energy. At least not now.

"Mama!" James ran into the room and wrapped his chubby arms around her legs.

She bent and cuddled him close, inhaling the scent of his freshly washed hair. "Did Sylvie give you a bath, little man?"

He nodded and swung his gaze toward the doorway.

Vivian forced a smile and followed his line of vision. Her heart lodged in her throat. "Detective Olsen." Her pulse pounded and sweat gathered on the back of her neck.

Sylvie stepped into the room and took James, swinging him onto her hip. The twenty-year-old looked impossibly young with her dark hair pulled into a ponytail and not a lick of make-up covering her smooth, bronzed skin. "She was looking for you downstairs. Said she wanted to speak with you. I hope it's okay I brought her up."

Harper rose and placed a hand on Vivian's arm. "Why don't I help Sylvie get James down then we can finish talking after."

Vivian pressed a kiss to James' forehead. "I'll be in to tell you goodnight soon. I love you."

Sylvie carried him out of the room, Harper following behind.

"Did you find her?" Vivian held her breath as her gaze searched for any sign of what the detective wished to speak to her about.

Something flashed across Detective Olsen's face as she stared into the room from across the threshold. Hungry eyes devoured every part of the nursery, as if answers to some unknown question would be found inside.

"Detective?" Vivian's heart crashed against her rib cage. If the detective sought her out, she had a reason. Especially since Will had made it very clear he didn't want any members of the law enforcement to leave the study downstairs. He might have cracked enough to let officers inside the house, giving them a space to gather and work together where the family was easily accessible, but that didn't mean they had free rein of the property.

Rapid flutters closed and lifted Detective Olsen's eyelids

and she cleared her throat. "I'm sorry. No. We haven't found her, and no one has contacted the family for ransom. I just wanted a chance to talk with you. Since you slept most of the afternoon, we didn't have a conversation. I'd like to do that now, if that's okay?"

Disappointment stung Vivian's eyes. "Yes. Of course. Why don't we head to my office?"

Dipping her head, she walked out of the room and led Detective Olsen down the hall to the office she barely used anymore. She pushed the door open wide and flipped on the light, wincing at the sudden burst of brightness.

Detective Olsen entered behind her. "Wow. This room is very different from the rest of the house I've seen."

Vivian motioned toward a pair of light gray chairs in front of a bay window, waiting for Detective Olsen to take a seat before falling into the adjacent chair. She let her gaze linger on the subtle floral pattern of the wallpaper and travel to the distressed antique desk that had once been her favorite place in the house. "This is the only one I was given complete control over decorating, aside from the kids' rooms."

"It's lovely."

Vivian shifted, straightening her spine and placing her clasped hands in her lap. "So, no ransom note, no Tabby, no anything. Please. Tell me there's something you've found that will lead us to my daughter. I can't take it...can't take the not knowing." A hard knot formed in her throat, making it difficult to breathe.

"Not yet. But up until now we thought the kidnapping was money-related. They usually are when a high-profile family is involved."

Vivian squeezed her hands together, trying not to let the impact of the word—kidnapping—turn her stomach over and over. "What now?"

"I keep digging." Detective Olsen pulled out the same

notepad from earlier. "I want to talk with you about a few things."

Vivian swallowed hard. Will wouldn't like her speaking with the detective alone. Spilling secrets about their family. "I'm sure you've gotten all the information you need from my husband."

Detective Olsen pressed her lips together and tilted her head to the side. "I don't want to talk to your husband, Mrs. Walker, or his mother. I want to talk to you. Is there a reason that makes you uncomfortable?"

She pressed her teeth together to keep from shivering. "Not at all. I'm just not accustomed to speaking about family affairs. Not to mention my mind is spinning with all the horrible things that could be happening to my child right now. Excuse me if I seem a little out of my element." Tension made her words come out heated, louder than she'd intended. She sucked in a deep breath. "I'm sorry for my outburst. I just..." The tears came back, sliding down her cheeks. She let them fall. Let them speak for the misery stewing inside her.

"You have nothing to apologize for." Detective Olsen leaned forward and rested a hand on hers, giving a brief squeeze before settling back against her chair. "And I don't want to pry into your family affairs right now. I just want to talk. To get a better sense of you and your life and how you spend your days with your children. Is that all right?"

Vivian nodded.

Detective Olsen glanced around. "Do you spend a lot of time in your office? I've got to say, it's a lot cleaner than mine. I have papers everywhere and clutter I never seem to get under control."

"I used to. Before the kids. I don't have much time anymore." A vise tightened her gut. There was a time when she'd spend hours in here, getting lost in the worlds she created in her imagination. For a girl growing up wanting to escape the lonely life of an only child with over-protective parents, creating stories filled with exciting places and interesting people was the best medicine. Medicine she continued at college and into the first years of marriage.

"I'm sure your days are pretty full with two little ones. Have you always wanted children?"

"Yes. More than anything."

"You mentioned before you'd suffered from miscarriages. I imagine that must have been pretty difficult. Were your epilepsy medications responsible for all these miscarriages?"

Vivian rested a hand on her stomach, wincing when flashbacks of her accident morphed inside her head. "No."

Detective Olsen leaned forward. "I know this is painful, but can you elaborate?"

"Before I had Tabitha, I had a seizure while standing near the top of the stairs in the foyer. Everything went black, and when I woke, I was laying on the floor. Blood pooling between my legs."

Something flickered behind the mask of professionalism keeping Detective Olsen's features unreadable. Something Vivian had witnessed countless times before.

Pity.

She sniffed, pulling herself together. "That was the furthest along I'd been. The other losses were in the first trimester."

"Is it normal for you to move while having a seizure? If you fell down the stairs, that would mean you either lost your balance or walked off the edge. Do you know which happened?"

Her body swayed with the horrible memory. "I walked. Tripped on one of James' toys. Then fell."

"Do these seizures happen frequently when you're not taking your medication? Have the children ever been present before?"

The truth squeezed her chest. Detective Olsen was fishing

for information regarding her seizures to determine if Vivian could have hurt Tabitha. Her heart raced, and she forced lungfuls of air out her mouth to keep her breathing steady. "My seizures come in threes, with months in between cycles. Tabitha doesn't sleep well, so I'm sure the exhaustion triggered my episode today. I wouldn't be surprised if I suffer two more seizures in the coming days. I will make sure to stay safe, and keep James from harm during those times. I have never knowingly placed them in danger. I love my children. I'd die for them. I would never hurt them."

She rose to her feet, balling her hands into tight fists at her sides. She should have listened to Will and not spoken to anyone without him, or a lawyer, present. This *conversation* was nothing more than a witch hunt.

"I didn't mean to upset you. I'm just trying to line everything up, get a clear picture so I can figure out what happened to your daughter." Detective Olsen stood, a frown on her thin lips. "We can talk more later."

Vivian didn't answer, just watched as the detective made her way to the door.

Detective Olsen halted and turned to face Vivian. "I just have one more thing."

"What?" The word came out harsher than Vivian intended, but she couldn't bring herself to care.

"How long have you and your husband been married?"

"Seven years. We met in college." She tapped her bare toe on the soft carpet. Patience for the other woman wore thin.

"You seem close with his family."

Vivian shrugged. "They're all I have."

"Were you aware that your husband had a sister? She went missing when she was four years old. No one has ever figured out what happened." Detective Olsen hooked a brow, waiting for a response.

Vivian covered her mouth with her hand and took a step

backward, bumping the backs of her knees against the plush chair. She lowered herself onto the seat, her shaking legs unable to support her. Her mind spun. Neither Will nor Lilith had ever mentioned a lost sister. "I had no idea."

"Interesting."

Vivian's eyes flew up to meet Detective Olsen's. "Why wouldn't he tell me?"

Detective Olsen shrugged. "Some people never want their secrets unburied." She gave one short nod then left.

A chill swept over Vivian. She couldn't be sure if the detective's parting words were aimed at her or Will. But either way, the dropped bomb left a gaping hole in the picture Vivian had created of their family. And if Will had kept her in the dark about his sister, what else could he be hiding?

5

For the first time since Ellen's daughter went missing, she was happy to wake up in her home. Instead of dreading the empty, quiet house with reminders of the life she once cherished, she yearned for the simple luxuries of comfortable blankets thrown over the sofa for easy access and pictures of happier times cluttered on the walls. Sara's smiling face beaming down from photos might always cause sharp jabs to pierce through her, but this house also held memories that kept her moving through life, seeking to reunite loved ones in a way she'd never experience.

Unlike the grand house the Walkers occupied, her home was warm and inviting where theirs was cold and unyielding. She turned on her back and stared at the ceiling. The shadows morphed into the many faces associated with the case. Each with their own secrets.

With a sigh, Ellen glanced at the clock on her nightstand. She had an hour left before she had to get up, but going back to sleep wasn't possible. Not with all the voices clamoring in her head. Might as well get up and face another day of questions. Pushing her matted hair from her eyes, she slipped into her warm cotton robe and made her way to her office. She'd had just enough energy the night before to put up her board—the one she used to sort all the different angles of an investigation.

The soft hues of pre-dawn whirled outside the windows. Ellen wanted to grab a cup of coffee and sit on her porch swing, admiring the view from her two-bedroom cottage. But the faces on her board demanded her attention—even before her morning caffeine fix. She swiped her notepad from her desk and flipped through her notes, darting her gaze between her messy handwriting and the pinned-up pictures.

So many different actors. So many ways this could have played out. But what made the most sense? Where did her gut lead her?

William Walker. Something about the guy made her skin crawl. His polished responses and lack of emotion toward his missing child. Something didn't add up.

But she couldn't dig her heels in one direction. She was aware of the similarities between William and her ex-husband. That alone was enough to warn her against trusting her instincts.

Yet what if her instincts were right? Whether William Walker and her ex both were grade-A assholes who were born with a silver spoon in their mouths didn't matter. She'd bet money William was hiding something from her.

Hiding something from everyone.

She shoved her hand through her hair. Her thoughts stayed focused on the politician and what secrets he kept, but she couldn't focus all her attention on only one player. Even if she'd already pegged him as a snake. Maybe Officer Daniels would meet her for breakfast. He was a good cop. One she'd depended on countless times before. Getting his take on the family was crucial, and what better way to do that than over a plate of bacon and eggs?

CRADLING a warm mug of coffee in her hand, Ellen scoured over her notes. She wished she could have brought her entire board, filled with faces and connections and insight, to the diner in downtown Hollow Cove, but not only would people question her sanity, she couldn't give away details to a case where anyone could be a suspect. Even if the crowd was thin so early in the morning.

"Olsen. Morning." Officer Daniels slid into the booth across from her and lifted a finger to signal the server. "Early start today, huh?"

She dropped her notepad on the table and took a sip of piping hot coffee. The dab of vanilla creamer took away the harsh bite of the coffee, but left enough bitterness to coat her tongue. "Thanks for meeting me. Hope I didn't get you out of bed when I called."

"Nah. My wife is an early riser, making it impossible for me to sleep in. Breakfast will be nice before my shift starts." He paused when Stewart, a man who had one foot in the grave and who'd owned The Hollow House for as long as Ellen could remember, stopped by their table to take their orders. "Waiting tables today, huh Stew?" Daniels asked.

Stewart scowled, causing the cascade of wrinkles on his face to gather like the skin of a Shar Pei puppy. "Short staffed. Don't mind though. Keeps me young. What will you have?"

Ellen smiled, but kept her ideas of Stewart staying young to herself. "Scrambled eggs and bacon, please."

Stewart nodded, wrote her order, then aimed his hooded eyes at Daniels.

"Coffee, black, and a stack of pancakes."

Ellen watched the old man shuffle toward the kitchen for a beat before focusing on Daniels. "I want your thoughts from yesterday. On the family, the situation, the whole damn thing.

I'm getting sucked into my own bullshit with this one, and I don't like it. I need another person's perspective to keep me in check." She might have a lot of faults—just ask her ex—but self-reflection wasn't one of them. And she wouldn't let her own hang-ups get in the way of doing her job.

Daniels ran a hand over his square, stubbled jaw and leaned back against the vinyl seat. "I think there's more going on than the Walkers will ever tell us. I've been around awhile, and the ones who are so hellbent on privacy usually have a reason other than not wanting to expose their personal lives."

"Agreed. Do you think any of those reasons are related to the missing baby?"

He swung his lips to the side. "Hard to say. The thought of one of them being responsible makes my stomach turn. But if money isn't an issue in the disappearance, usually someone close to the family is involved. The odds of some random stranger stumbling upon Mrs. Walker and taking her child are pretty low."

"Again, I agree. What is your impression of the family?"

"William Walker is a dick, his mother is creepy as hell, and the wife seems...fragile." He ticked the people, along with his thoughts of them, off on his fingers.

Ellen ran a fingertip along the rim of her cup. "Fragile. Yeah, I can see that. Protected, sheltered. I just don't know if I'm buying the in-the-dark act. Like she doesn't have a single clue about what goes on in her own home—in her own family."

Daniels shrugged. "Could be shock. Her world changed in an instant. Not knowing what's happening with her baby—a child who was in her care when she went missing—has to take a lot out of a person."

Ellen drew in a large breath. "No feeling in this world is worse. No pain more unbearable. And I've seen enough struggling family members in this exact same situation. Everyone reacts differently. But I don't know. Something about Vivian just seems off, but I can't put my finger on it."

"We need to talk to the household staff," Daniels said. "They employ quite a few people who would have a pretty good gauge on all three of the main players. But mainly Vivian Walker, since she's the one who spends most of her time at home. Especially the driver and the nanny. Those are the two who spend the most time with the kids and their mother."

Stewart reappeared at the table with a large circular tray, two plates and a carafe placed on top. The contents shook from the tremble in the old man's skinny arm.

Ellen bit into her bottom lip and strangled her mug to keep from helping dish out the breakfast. She's spent enough time in the diner to understand Stewart would be more offended than relieved at her assistance.

Stewart slid a plate overflowing with fluffy eggs and crisp bacon in front of her, and her stomach growled. He lowered Daniels' breakfast onto the table, then flipped a white ceramic mug and filled it with coffee. "Refill?" he asked, hoisting the carafe in her direction.

She smiled and released her grip on her cup now that all the glassware had safely made it to the table.

He filled the mug to the brim then tipped his head. "Enjoy."

Ellen waited until Stewart was out of ear shot then grabbed a piece of bacon. "You talked to the driver before I did. What was your sense of him when you first arrived on scene?"

Daniels took a sip of coffee then drizzled syrup over his stack of pancakes. "Protective over the wife. Didn't like it when her choices were questioned by Officer Scott."

"What do you mean?" She took a bite of bacon and the salty goodness nearly made her groan.

"Scott didn't like the fact that the wife took her kids to stand near a cliff when she suffers from epilepsy. Didn't think it was safe, and she did a poor job of hiding her opinion when questioning Mrs. Walker."

"I'd be lying if I said the same thought hadn't cross my mind. Why go alone? Why choose that particular spot? And what are the chances of a seizure happening in that exact moment?" She let the questions simmer in her brain as she finished off her first strip of bacon. "Word around the house is the baby never stopped crying. That can be hard for a young mother to handle."

"We searched the water, the rocks below. No blood or an indication the baby was thrown in."

Her stomach rebelled against the image of an unsteady woman tossing her infant into the ocean from a towering cliff, and she pushed her plate aside. But she had to explore every single option, no matter how difficult. "If a woman is desperate enough to kill her child, she'd have no qualms regarding lying about where she was when the baby disappeared. Maybe she didn't walk directly up to the top of the cliff. Maybe she stopped near a different ledge and disposed of the child before hurrying up to the lighthouse and calling the authorities, claiming to have lost time because of a seizure. Something that's happened before and no one would question."

Daniels wiped a heavy hand over his mouth. "Well, shit."

"Just one more avenue to look into. I want her medical records. I want to know more about her epilepsy or if she has a history of depression. Anything that could make her snap."

"Postpartum depression could be at play as well." Daniels lowered his chin, inching closer to her from across the table. "You need to tread lightly. The Walkers won't just hand over that kind of information. And if there's any wind of scandal, there's no telling the lengths they'd go through to make you pay. Make sure your career is finished."

Resolve anchored her spine. "I could give two shits about what they'd do. This isn't about me, dammit. It's about an innocent child who deserves to be brought home. If I have to ruffle a few feathers and piss off some people to do that, so be it."

She took a swig of coffee, trying to wash down the disappointment of Daniels' reaction. It was no secret the police tiptoed around the Walkers, never wanting to earn the wrath of one of the most powerful families in the state—hell, probably in the whole damn country. But she thought Daniels was different. Thought he cared more about the job than the bureaucratic bullshit that tried to tie their hands and keep them from uncovering the truth. No matter the cost.

"All I'm saying is there's a way to get the information you need while keeping the peace. No need to sabotage your entire career by storming the castle with guns blazing."

She snorted. "You'd have more luck breaking into a castle than that fortress they're holed up in."

Daniels picked up his fork, pointing the jagged prongs her way before diving into his breakfast. "You've got a point. That place is depressing. Antiques that can't be touched and everything dark and gloomy. Even with the sunlight pouring in all those damn windows. Not a place I'd want to raise a family."

"Have all the Walkers always lived under one roof? I mean, I get the place is enormous and there's plenty of space, but have all the generations always lived together?" Living with her mother-in-law, no matter how much space existed between them, would have been a deal breaker for her.

Daniels dabbed a napkin against the side of his mouth. "William Walker's father died quite awhile ago. Not sure if William was even out of the house yet or not. So I guess it made sense for the mother to continue living there. Not sure before that."

Ellen brought to mind an image of William's mother. "She's the gatekeeper."

Daniels scrunched up his face, bringing together the leathery folds of his skin. "What do you mean?"

"She's the one in control. Every time I saw her, she was poised and polished and always at the ready for any questions that came their way. William is the one running for the senate, the face of the family to the public. But Lilith Walker is the one who makes sure everything is in its proper place. That everyone toes the line."

"I can see that. So how do we get her to cooperate when she's the one calling the shots?"

"I throw something at her she never saw coming." Her gut twisted. Lilith Walker might be a powerhouse keeping the Walker family going, but she was also a mother who'd lost her daughter. And Ellen understood better than anyone that time didn't do a damn thing to lessen the pain over the loss of a child.

But if bringing up a painful past was the only way to get answers for the present, Ellen would do just that. Even if it meant using the disappearance of a little girl from long ago to help bring another one home.

6

Vivian's mind churned through a constant haze as she lingered in the study, waiting for William to leave his office. She hunched against the armrest of the leather sofa, using her fist to keep her head propped up. Sleep hadn't come easily the night before. Not when every time she closed her eyes images of Tabitha stole her ability to breathe.

Finally, around three in the morning, she'd taken a sleeping pill to knock herself out. One blissful night of dreamless sleep where the world was black and nothing haunted her. Nothing hurt her.

But she paid a heavy price this morning. Her body was heavy, her mind muddled. And there was nothing she could take, no pill she could swallow, to ease the agony in her heart or stop the questions piling up.

Questions she needed answered.

She'd debated all morning on the best way to approach Will. Demanding anything from him was never a good idea, and if she asked questions about his missing sister, a topic he'd avoided for eight years, he'd most likely brush her aside. Claiming the disappearance of his sister was none of her business. So, she'd slowly dip in her toe, not giving away what she knew while also gauging his response.

Because if nothing else, the odds that two Walker children could be ripped from their homes without a trace were pretty darn low. Maybe a connection could be made between the two kidnappings. Maybe some lunatic with an axe to grind against their family had waited years between acts in order to inflict the most amount of pain when the family least expected it.

She squeezed her eyes shut. She had to stop spiraling. Stop fixating on the worst-case scenarios bombarding her.

The door to William's office swung open, and she perched on the edge of the couch.

He stepped out and landed his gaze on her. "What are you doing in here?"

She seldom spent time in the study. The hard lines of the masculine furniture and priceless leather-bound books lining the walls never made her feel comfortable. Then there was the fact that Will's office was only accessible through the large, pretentious room. He claimed to need two spaces—one to close off the world and work, the other to smoke a cigar and throw back a tumbler of whisky after a rough day.

What he didn't need to say was he preferred the study as a way to block off anyone from gaining access to his office. Even with the police the day before, he wanted to keep an eye on them while he sat at his giant desk with his door open and continued to work, as if nothing had happened to uproot their lives.

She spied his computer bag draped over his shoulder. "I wanted to talk to you. Are you leaving?"

"I have to go to work. I need to speak to the team about how to handle this situation. We're too close to the election to just throw it all away." He crossed the intricately designed rug and placed a hand on her shoulder.

She stood, anger swelling inside her. "Your daughter is

missing, and you can't be bothered to take the day off work? Hell, bring your team here. You can talk about the stupid campaign and election all you want *here*. But be close. Stay home. There's no telling what the day might bring. I need you. With me and James."

She hated the tremor that shook her voice. But she couldn't do this alone. Couldn't face the questions and the police and the unknown of what was to come without someone by her side.

Emotions warred in his misting eyes, and he swallowed hard. "There's nothing I can do for Tabitha. Sitting here being upset won't fix anything. Not showing up to do my job won't bring her home. All that will do is cause me to lose something I've worked my whole life for. I can't throw away my other responsibilities. Please understand that."

Tears clouded her vision, but she lifted her chin and bit the soft skin inside her cheeks to keep them from falling. Standing up for herself didn't come easy, but this was ridiculous. She and Will should be together, keeping up their spirits and figuring out what had happened to their baby. "What about James? He can feel the stress. See the worry and fear. We need to support him. Show him he's safe and loved, even with the chaos around us."

He gently squeezed her arm than lifted the black leather strap of his laptop bag higher on his shoulder. "James is fine. He's strong. He's a Walker. He doesn't need us coddling him and changing his schedule."

She shook her head, unable to believe the man who stood before her was the same man she'd fallen in love with. "Do you even love Tabitha? Even care that she's gone and could be scared or hurt?"

A flash of anger tightened the lines of his face. "Don't you dare act like it matters how I feel. You were the one who insisted on having more kids. You're the one who whined and cried over and over when your pregnancies failed. It never mattered to you that I was happy with James. That he was enough. Enough to continue the long line of Walker men. Enough to love and care for. So don't go sniveling at me because *you* messed up. *You* weren't careful and now I'm cleaning up *your* mess. Just like I always do."

Pausing, he winced. He sucked in a large breath. "I'm sorry. My emotions are out of control and there's no need to be nasty with you because I'm upset. But I need to go. I'll be home as soon as I can." He placed a rough kiss on the top of her head and strode out the door.

Vivian stared through the paneled glass of the closed doors, watching Will hurry down the hall. Her body shook, her mind spun. William was a stranger.

She fought against the overwhelming desire to curl into a ball and cry. Nothing would be solved that way. Instead, she'd push aside the stinging rejection she'd come to expect and do what she'd set out to do. The ancient grandfather clock ticked out the seconds, announcing how much time had passed since Will left. She waited, needing to make sure he hadn't forgotten anything—or even come to his senses—and returned.

Five minutes passed by like hours. Her pulse beat against her temples, but she willed her feet to move toward the door. Wrapping her hand around the brass handle, Vivian held her breath and turned. The handle moved. She exhaled. She'd half-expected the door to be locked.

But Will would never imagine she'd go where she wasn't wanted. She'd always known her place. No reason to assume she'd step out of line. Light pooled in through the floor-to-ceiling window facing the backyard, highlighting the paintings mounted on the walls.

She made a beeline for the walnut desk in the middle of the room. She had no idea what to look for, or even if there was anything about the missing girl for her to find. Will was far from sentimental, but would he erase everything about his sister? The idea sat like a boulder in her gut.

Would he do the same thing if Tabitha was never found?

Pushing the bleak thought to the far corner of her mind, she crouched in front of the desk, beside the two large drawers on the side. Sliding them open, she sifted through the file folders. Nothing but financial statements, political strategies, and other paperwork she didn't take the time to study filled the overstuffed files. She scooted to the other side of the desk, her heart dropping. More manila folders stuffed to the brink.

The clock in the study continued to tick, making her nerves jump with each second. Going through these files would take too much time, and chances were slim Will would stuff something related to his sister in with important documents. She closed the drawer, placing all her hopes and desperation on the middle compartment. She tugged on the handle, but the drawer didn't budge.

Locked.

A beat of frustration passed through her, but she stomped it down. If he locked the drawer, something important must be inside. She just needed to find the key. She searched the top of the desk, checking the inside of the little container full of pens and behind the computer monitor.

Nothing.

She tuned to the credenza behind the desk, skimming her fingers along the shelves only to find a few specks of dust. Frustrated, she took in the whole of the office. Unlike most of the rooms in the house, Will hadn't stuffed his office full of unnecessary knick-knacks and frivolous displays of wealth. Yes, the fancy desk and credenza were family heirlooms, but everything in the room had a purpose.

Except the art lining the walls.

Most of the pieces were of vibrant landscapes surrounded

by ornate, gilded frames. Precisely placed with the same amount of space between each picture.

Then there was the portrait of Will's father. A man she'd never met—passed before she'd met Will at Yale—but who still dominated the house she lived in. She stepped closer, studying the way the gentle slope of his nose matched both Will and James. He was so familiar, his features on display in the generations that followed him.

Except the eyes. The twinkle in the elder Mr. Walker's bold, blue eyes were no longer present in his son's.

Vivian approached the wall and ran a finger over the plain, wide frame holding up the picture. So different than anything else in the room—in the entire estate for that matter. The wood was thick, a slight edge of material poking around the picture, making Mr. Walker appear as though he sank into the wall itself.

She studied his face as she continued to skim the pad of her index finger along the bottom of the frame. His gaze seemed to follow her, his wide smile encouraging her to continue in her bold attempts. Her finger grazed something, and she flicked it forward. A small key clattered against the wooden planks of the floor.

Excitement curled her toes, and she swooped up the key and hurried back to the desk. She slid the key in the hole and turned, clicking the lock. She pulled back the key and the drawer opened with the motion.

A prick of shame made her hesitate. This was her husband's personal space. A place where he shouldn't have to worry about people breaking in and searching through his things.

The glossy matte of a photo caught her eye and all traces of shame fled. Curiosity moved her hand, grabbing the edges of the picture and freeing it from the drawer.

A woman perched on top of a hill, bright green trees full of color and life surrounded her. Her face was turned away from the camera, but her strawberry blonde hair billowed in the breeze.

Vivian rubbed a palm over her tight chest and sank into the desk chair. Who was this woman? And why did her husband have a picture of her locked away in his desk? The bent edges and smudged prints made it clear it was a picture he handled often, but why? Flipping it over, she searched the back for a name or date, but nothing marked the photo.

Urgency rushed through her veins, and she riffled through the rest of the drawer. Matchbooks and scraps of papers and receipts littered the drawer. No other pictures. Nothing related to the mysterious sister.

She slammed the drawer closed and studied the picture again, taking note of the view from high above whatever hill or cliff the woman was seated on. Something pulled at her memory. The area was familiar. A piece of a memory she couldn't pull forward. Closing her eyes, she tried bringing the image into focus. Figure out the lay of the land. The dip of the valley shielded by trees. She'd been to this place before, but when? Where?

The pictures in her head blurred together, the vibrant trees changing into the jagged front of a cliff. The faceless woman with flowing hair melted away, replaced by a stroller and a lighthouse. James stood beside it. A hand appeared in the stroller beside her, fingers gliding against Tabitha's smooth head.

Her hand?

She squeezed her eyes together tighter, trying to remember, a desire to know what happened sucking the air from her lungs. The colors swirled, the picture changed. She fisted her hand, wanting to keep hold of the moment and figure out the who's hand reached out to touch her baby—who'd taken Tabitha.

Then it was gone, the patterns morphing into blood. A

memory she couldn't quite recall replaced by one she'd never forget. The trees no longer towering above her, but Will. His face a stone mask. No concern. No compassion. Even then, at the lowest moment as she bled on the marble floor in the foyer, he hadn't cared about her. About her unborn child.

But did that mean there was someone else he cared for? She opened her eyes and stared at the photo clutched in her fist.

"And what exactly do you think you're doing?" Lilith stood in the doorway with her hands clasped in front of her and a frown etched on her thin lips.

Vivian's muscles tightened, and she searched for a good reason as to why she sat at Will's desk. Folding the picture into her clasped hands, she rose and faced her mother-in-law. "I wanted to speak with Will, but he's already left for the office."

Lilith tilted her head to the side. "Of course he has, dear. He's a busy man. But that doesn't explain why you're sitting in here. We both know William wouldn't like it."

Vivian squeezed her hands tight to keep her mouth in check. She needed to come up with an excuse. One that Lilith might keep between them. She couldn't let her know about the mysterious woman in the picture. Better to stick with the original reason she'd come into the office. Maybe Lilith would finally confide in her. Especially in light of Tabitha's disappearance. "I wanted to find out about your daughter. The one who went missing."

A vein ticked at Lilith's temple and she widened her eyes, her mouth pressed tight, before smoothing out her facial features. "Why on earth would you want to bring that up to William?"

Desperation urged her on. "Because I'm shocked he never told me he had a sister. Because there could be a connection between her disappearance and Tabitha's."

Lilith held up a hand. "Enough. William and I both worked

hard to keep the pain of losing Daphne in the past. Bringing it up now won't do anyone any good."

"But—"

"No. She was lost to us then, and we moved on. Like we had to. Remembering the horror is of no use. Unlike you, we didn't have the luxury of escaping into our minds and conveniently forgetting everything that happened. Not remembering can be a blessing. Now, it's time for you to leave William's office."

Vivian tucked her chin and crossed the room, halting beside Lilith. "Not remembering has always been a curse. One I'd do anything to stop. And I will never push down my memories of Tabitha or live my life as though she never existed. No matter what happens. Forgetting her would be the biggest sin I could commit."

She rushed through the study, the picture burning a hole through her palms. She might be aware of what her biggest sin could be, but she couldn't help but wonder what sins her husband had committed.

7

A light breeze rippled through the air as Vivian watched James play outside with Sylvie by his side. The sun beat bright in the late morning sky. A morning Vivian would have called beautiful on any other day. But not today. As she sat in the white Adirondack chair at the shady base of the deck stairs, only the unknown dangers lurking in the shadows beyond the fenced-in property took her mind off the agony of missing her baby and the picture of the mysterious woman she still clutched in her palm.

She wanted to take James inside and shield him from whatever prowled in the expanse of trees and forest that surrounded their house. Anyone could be among the thick trunks or behind a cluster of golden leaves. Just like at the lighthouse. When someone had emerged from the woods or the path or God knew where to snatch Tabitha. But he'd wanted to climb on his wooden play set on the patch of land just down the stairs from the massive deck that jutted off the back of the house.

At least she was away from the prying eyes of the police— the suspicious eyes of the staff. Questions floated in the air whenever she walked by. Each minute made it harder to lift her chin and move forward, refusing to give in to the bubble of anger ready to pop at the base of her throat so she could scream and yell and tell the world she wasn't to blame.

But it wouldn't change a damn thing. Professing her innocence never helped her cause. So, she'd sit and watch James play, with Sylvie close by, and split her focus between her son, the fear of what lay in the unseen thicket of woods, and the emptiness swallowing her whole as she waited to find out if Tabby would ever come home.

"Sylvie." Lilith's voice called out from the deck above, weaving through the wind.

Sylvie tilted her face toward the house, squinting against the harsh light. "Yes, Mrs. Walker?"

Vivian tensed, her fist curling around the photo still in her hand. She lowered her arm to the side so Lilith couldn't see what she held, even from the towering height above. Another encounter with her mother-in-law was the last thing she wanted.

"I need you to come inside and answer some questions, please. Bring James in as well."

Vivian gritted her teeth. She could take care of her own son. Turning, she locked eyes with Lilith. "James is fine outside. I'm here."

Lilith raised penciled-in brows. "Are you sure?"

"Positive." She waited for Lilith to step away from the white-washed railing of the deck, her clipped footsteps hurrying toward the house. "Go on, Sylvie."

Sylvie cast a quick glance at James, mounted on a tiny rock wall with a wide smile, then back at Vivian before nodding and running up the deck stairs.

A vise loosened around her lungs and allowed her to take a deep breath of the crisp, fresh air. As much as her soul ached for Tabby, it was the quiet moments alone that she yearned for. When no one watched her every move, waiting for her to mess up. James only ever looked at her with love and kindness, not understanding the things that made her different—or the actions she couldn't control.

Even if those actions had resulted in his pain.

Heavy footsteps clomped down the stairs. Not the delicate heels Lilith always wore. Vivian groaned, lacking the energy to face whoever made their way toward her.

Detective Olsen emerged beside her, hands jammed into the pockets of her loose-fitted gray slacks. "Hello, Vivian."

And just like that, the crushing pressure on her windpipe was back. Vivian stayed seated and offered the detective a quick glance before returning her attention to James. He'd moved to the miniature monkey bars and laughed as he moved his hand from bar to bar, his little feet still on the rubber ground they'd installed to keep him safe. "Good morning, Detective."

"Please, call me Ellen. Do you mind if I sit?" She flicked her wrist toward the empty chair to Vivian's side.

"Of course." Vivian might not like the tactic the other woman used the night before, but she couldn't let that get in the way of having a conversation with her. She was the one in charge of finding Tabitha. "Ellen."

Ellen sat sideways on the chair, facing Vivian. "How are you holding up?" Kindness coated the question, lowering Vivian's guard.

She sighed. "Lost in a nightmare. Scared to close my eyes because of the horrible images waiting to greet me. Afraid to be awake because at any minute, bad news could bring me to my knees."

"I understand."

Vivian ripped her gaze from her son and stared at the detective—at Ellen. Pity shone from her hazel eyes, even if the rest of her round face hid any hint of emotion. "I get your job puts you in contact with a lot of families in this situation, but you couldn't possibly understand. No one could."

Except maybe her mother-in-law, but Lilith had made it clear that just because the two of them shared a horrifying experience, it would do nothing to bring them closer. Hell, Lilith refused to even soften her tough-as-nails exterior enough to comfort Vivian. Despite the loss of her own daughter.

"That's where you're wrong." Ellen's soft voice broke into Vivian's thoughts.

She squinted. "Excuse me?"

"My daughter, Sara, went missing two years ago. So when I stand for you and your family, I stand for her as well. When I tell you I'll do everything I can to bring your daughter home, I mean it. Because I know how much it hurts to lose a child."

Vivian's heart lurched. "I'm so sorry."

Ellen pressed her lips together and gave a brief nod. "But that's not what I'm here to talk about."

Exhaustion pressed Vivian against the chair, and a dull thud pulsed inside her skull. "I don't know what else I can tell you. I swear."

Ellen waved away her objection. "I don't have more questions for you. At least not right now."

Vivian dipped her brows. "What about Sylvie and the rest of the staff? Aren't they being interviewed?"

"Yes," Ellen said. "We want to talk with anyone who is close to you or the family. Anyone the children are familiar with. Your son might not be able to talk, but from your own statement, it didn't appear as though he was too upset when Tabitha went missing."

Heat infused Vivian's cheeks. "He just turned three He doesn't understand."

"I didn't mean any insult. I meant he wasn't alarmed by a stranger being near. His reaction leads me to believe he was familiar with whoever took Tabitha. At least enough to not be frightened that they were near. I'd like for you to write down a list of people James is in contact with on a semi-regular basis. People outside of the home."

Vivian pressed a hand to her chest, and the picture she still clutched rubbed against the exposed skin at her collar.

Ellen leaned forward. "What's that?"

Vivian frowned, unsure of how to answer. Was a picture of an unknown woman locked in her husband's office something she needed to confide to the detective in charge of finding her missing daughter? Part of her—the part who'd been a Walker for the last seven years and groomed to be the perfect politician's wife—screamed no. The other part—the mother who'd do anything to bring her baby home—had a different answer.

If the hollow sensation in her gut was right, her husband was involved in an affair. Who knew what that relationship was like? How Will treated this woman? This piece of information could be useful so she had to come clean.

Licking her dry lips, Vivian steeled her resolve, consequences be damned. Will would be furious, but his anger was worth it. She'd withstood it before, and she'd do so again in a heartbeat. Especially if it helped find Tabby. "I found this picture today." She thrust it forward.

Ellen screw up her face, taking the photo between careful fingers. "Who is this?"

Vivian shrugged. "I wish I knew."

Confusion as clear as the blue sky skittered across Ellen's face. "What do you mean?"

Betrayal constricted her veins. "I found the picture locked in Will's desk." Realization struck her quicker than a bolt of lightning, and she shot to her feet. "Oh no. No. No. No." She pressed a closed fist to her mouth.

Ellen rose, glancing around as if searching for the source of Vivian's sudden angst. "What's wrong? What happened?"

"I left the key in the drawer." She flung her hand toward the picture in Ellen's grip. "I took this stupid photo. I was so caught

up, so surprised, I didn't even stop to think about putting everything back the way I'd found it. He's going to be so mad." No
excuse, no well-thought-out-plan would appease Will. She was
screwed.

Ellen laid a calm hand on her shoulder, catching her gaze.
"You took the picture from your husband's locked desk and
now you're scared because he'll find out? Because of the key in
the drawer and missing picture?"

Vivian nodded, her words trapped in her tight throat.

"Will he hurt you? If he knows you were searching his
desk?"

Vivian dropped her gaze. Confessing her husband might be
harboring feelings for another woman was one thing. Peeling
back the curtain on her and Will's relationship was another.
She wrapped her arms around her middle. "He'd just be upset."

"Okay." Ellen drew out the syllables an extra beat. "Officer
Daniels and I are conducting interviews with the staff in the
study. I noticed Mr. Walker isn't in his office this morning. Is he
elsewhere in the home?"

"He left earlier. Went to work." She shifted her stance to
face James. He'd moved on to the swing. Throwing his belly
onto the yellow strip of plastic and letting himself fly, squealing
in delight with the motion. Oblivious to the tension
around him.

She cringed. A memory crashing into her thoughts of
another morning. Another accident. With James huddled on
the ground, blood splattered around him.

Ellen blinked and reared back. "I'm sure he had things to
get done, but that's good news. At least for the moment. I can go
in the office and replace the photo and key. If you tell me where
to put it."

Shaking her head, she pushed away the memory and bit
into her plump bottom lip. She needed to stay focused on what
needed done now, not what she couldn't prevent in the past.

What Ellen suggested was the only way to undo what she'd done before Will found out. But should she divulge where she'd found the key? Compromise Will's privacy? If Detective Olsen knew where Will kept his key, nothing would keep her from using it for her own snooping purposes.

"Vivian. Do you trust me?"

She wanted to say yes. Wanted to believe this woman had her best interest at heart. Had the best interest of her family and her baby at the forefront of her mind. But a tiny ball of dread sat in her gut like a boulder. After their conversation the night before, she wasn't sure what Detective Ellen Olsen's motives were. She might fight to find Tabby, but who did she want to bring down in the process?

Did it matter as long as Tabby was found and brought home safely?

Vivian stared Ellen in the eyes. "I trust you to do your job. I don't know beyond that."

Ellen quirked up one brow. "I appreciate your honesty."

"And I'd appreciate your discretion in this matter." Vivian handed her the picture.

Ellen held it up, studying the glossy paper. "You really have no idea who the picture is of?"

Vivian shook her head. "None. The scenery looks familiar though. The view. The hill. It's like a memory is sitting at the back of my mind, but no matter how hard I try, I can't pull it forward. Can't bring it into focus."

"Is that what happens with all your lost memories? The ones when you're having a seizure?"

How many times had she been asked this question? How many times had she left the conversation feeling less understood and more frustrated? She ran her hand through her hair, the wind taking hold of her silky, black strands and whipping them around her face. She tucked them behind her ear. "Right after a seizure, I have no memory of what happened while I was out. It's like a complete chunk of my life is gone or never happened at all."

"That would be scary."

She snorted. "That's an understatement. The worst part is in the days to come, bits and pieces start flitting through my brain. A flash of this, an image of that. Nothing clear or concrete. And the more I try to see it, to put those pieces together into even one snapshot of time, the more those bits slip away. Or morph into another memory altogether."

Ellen stood still, eyes narrowed and mouth pressed in a firm line.

Vivian fought not to fidget with the hem of her shirt.

"I'm sorry you have to experience that. It must be awful."

Vivian's jaw dropped. Out of all the responses she'd expected, compassion wasn't one of them. Tears misted in her eyes. Staying strong was easier when her guard was high to protect her battered heart and constantly trampled pride. Keeping her walls up and emotions at bay in the face of empathy was nearly impossible. Particularly in a moment when comfort and sympathy were all she yearned for.

Words failing her, she nodded.

"Have you ever tried therapy?" Ellen asked.

Vivian wrinkled her nose and swallowed a harsh laugh. "The Walker's don't believe in therapy. That would prove things aren't perfect. People don't vote for politicians who have problems."

Ellen rolled her eyes, making Vivian like her even more. "Therapy helped me work through a lot of my grief when Sara disappeared. The brain is a crazy thing, and there's no telling what speaking to a professional could do for you. Now, especially."

The idea was appealing, but she wasn't sure Will or Lilith would approve. "I don't know."

"Even if talking to someone can't help with your memories,

it can help you process what's going on right now. It's important you take care of you, too. Your children need a happy, healthy mother."

Vivian sucked back the growing tears. She didn't want to fall apart in front of her son. Not today. Even though Ellen's words stuck a chord in her heart that longed to be touched. She'd surrendered her entire life to the care of other people. People who thought they knew what was best for her. Who insisted she wasn't capable of taking care of herself because of her disorder.

Therapy could give her the tools she needed to handle the plethora of emotions raining down on her, drowning her from the inside, sucking her into a vortex so strong some days she didn't even want to climb out. And if someone could help her regain her memories, she could bring Tabby home where she belonged.

Before anything worse happened. Something Vivian could never come back from.

"I think you might be right," she said. "Thank you."

Ellen smiled. "I better get in there and put this back. Where does the key go?"

"A portrait of Will's father is hanging on the wall. The key was placed on the edge of the frame."

"We'll talk soon." Ellen jogged up the steps, taking the photo with her.

A tiny shred of hope took hold of Vivian. She might be in a sea of turmoil, barely keeping her head above the crashing waves, but she may have just found an ally. One she hadn't even realized she needed.

8

T he mysterious picture Vivian entrusted Ellen with sat heavy inside her suit jacket. She kept her pace at a quick clip as she hurried down the hall toward the study. The thick rug along the wide corridor muffled her booted steps. A housekeeper dusted a sconce outside the double French doors leading into the study. Ellen nodded a greeting before entering the room.

Officer Daniels glanced up from his position on the wing-backed chair to the side of the large, stone hearth. The nanny sat in front of him on a two-person sofa with her hands clasped securely in her lap and concern contorting the smooth lines of her young face.

Ellen held up a finger and crossed the room to the office Mr. Walker had occupied the day before. Not wanting to draw unwanted attention to her mission, she entered the shadowed room and refrained from flipping on a light. Enough sunshine filtered through the window to illuminate the space.

She rounded the massive desk and tried not think about the man who used it. When Vivian mentioned her husband had gone into work this morning, it'd taken every ounce of self-restraint not to scoff. Ellen's ex was an ass, but he'd grieved the loss of their child as much as she did. But maybe William Walker chose to grieve with someone else—a woman who wasn't his wife.

Pulling out the picture, Ellen used the camera on her phone to capture her own copy of the image to study later. This woman meant something for a man like William to keep a hard copy of her photo in his desk. She needed to figure out exactly what that was, even if it meant hurting the sad Mrs. Walker even more.

Not wanting to waste another second, she slid out the middle drawer Vivian described and shoved the photo under the random debris inside. She closed and locked the drawer, then studied the framed art lining the far wall. The portrait of William's father stuck out, but it was the landscape painting beside it that caught her attention. She put the key on the ledge where it belonged then sidestepped to the right, studying the bright beams of sun streaming down on the green expanse of forest. Hills peaked and valleys dipped, and something familiar tugged at her brain.

Grabbing her phone, she brought up the picture she'd just snapped and compared it with the thick brush strokes of earth-toned paints on the framed canvas. Were the scenes from the same place? She scanned the other paintings hanging on the walls. They all appeared similar. She'd have to ask about the locations. Maybe it would help her find the mystery woman. She'd rather uncover the identity of the woman before she spoke to Mr. Walker about her. Better to have him wonder at her ability to dig up dirt.

A soft rap against the doorframe turned her head. Officer Daniels stood with his arms crossed over his chest and a frown tugged his lips. "I'm done questioning the nanny. Did you have anything you wanted to ask her while she's here?"

She waved away the question. "Let her get back to the boy.

You can tell me what you found out before I speak with her."

She gave the paintings one last glance, secured her phone in her pocket, and left the office. Her presence in the house was already unwelcome. No need to piss anyone off more.

The fresh-faced nanny perched on the edge of the sofa with red-rimmed eyes, hands still in her lap. Ellen offered her a small smile. "We're done here for now, but I may have more questions for you later."

Sylvie bit into her quivering lip and rose to her feet. "Anything you need. Anything at all. I'll help however I can. That poor baby." She covered her mouth with her hand, but couldn't hide the muffled sob.

"I appreciate that," Ellen said.

Sylvie fled toward the door then slowed when Lilith Walker appeared. Her small frame somehow managed to dominate the archway. The older woman raised her thin brows, upturned her nose slightly and shifted her head back, as if telling the nanny where to go without uttering a single word. When Sylvie was gone, Lilith's narrowed eyes turned toward Ellen. "Are you done speaking with the staff?"

Ellen shifted her weight, considering how she wanted to play this conversation. "Mostly. We still need to speak to the driver who was with Mrs. Walker when the baby went missing."

"Patrick drove my son to the office today. I'm afraid he won't be home until this evening."

"I'm surprised Mr. Walker made it in to work today—with everything going on." She bit back the rest of her opinion of William Walker leaving his wife and son to deal with the stress of their missing daughter on their own. Even if Vivian now suspected her husband was involved in an affair, she still needed him by her side today.

Lilith's perfect posture straightened impossibly further. "It's an important time in my son's career. He can't afford to linger around the house all day. No matter how tragic the circumstances."

Ellen took note of the woman's language. *Tragic.* Yes, the disappearance of a child was a horrible thing, but most people wouldn't refer to it as tragic until the horrible thing took a turn for the worse. Until they knew the child would never come home. "I understand this isn't the first time you and your son have dealt with this type of situation. He must have learned a few coping mechanisms to be able to put his missing daughter in the back of his mind and focus on his job. Or is he more concerned with damage control? Can't have the voting public thinking something's amiss with the depressed wife up at the big house."

Lilith tightened her jaw, and a tiny twitch pulsed against her cheekbone. A diamond pendant hung from her neck, and she rubbed it between her thumb and forefinger.

Ellen smoothed the lines of her face, determined not to give any indication of her intentions or emotions.

Lilith took one step into the office, her mouth pinched. "My son is a very important man. Things don't simply stop because of misfortune—that much we did learn all those years ago."

"Very true, but I must admit, I find it unusual that two crimes have been committed against the little girls in this family. It raises a few red flags. Both children being taken without a ransom request or any witnesses." Ellen pivoted to study a picture of what she assumed was William as a boy. "I guess that's not completely true. William saw a man grab his sister, correct?" She hadn't had time to study all the details of the disappearance of Daphne Walker, but a quick glance at the file told her William was the only one who saw his sister taken —a game of hide and seek turned into a nightmare.

"I don't understand how what happened to my daughter

has any bearing on finding Tabitha. Now, if you have spoken with all the staff, I'd prefer if you'd leave." Lilith lifted her chin. "I'm sure you have plenty of work to do elsewhere. Work that involves figuring out what happened to my granddaughter."

Ellen cut her gaze to Daniels. He gave a tiny shake of his head. Dammit, he was right. They had enough to wade through with the staff interviews. Now wasn't the time to go head-to-head with the puppet master behind this powerful family. No matter how much she wanted to put the older woman in her place. A place that proved money and influence didn't mean shit. Not in her world.

She returned her attention to the framed picture of the light-haired little boy with a wide grin and fishing pole in hand. She needed to do a full-press attack with as much information as she could get if she was going to shake anything loose, but one more question lingered in her mind. "All the artwork in the house is amazing, as well as the pictures of the family."

Lilith scowled, as if the sudden change of topic was unsettling. "Thank you. We take great pride in what we display in our home."

Ellen nodded toward the office. "What about the landscape portraits in there? Are they of some place in particular?"

"I wouldn't know. William selected those."

Ellen rocked back on her heels, not sure if she believed the elder Mrs. Walker. Chances were not much happened under this roof she wasn't aware of. "I'll have to ask him about it."

"Please do. Now, if you'll follow me." Lilith swept a hand to her side.

Ellen followed Daniels out of the room and down the hall, Lilith at her back. She stopped in front of the massive double doors that spilled out onto a brick courtyard like she'd only ever seen in movies. "Vivian gave me some clothes that belong to Tabitha. We will have trained search dogs scouring the property."

Shock widened Lilith's eyes. "You think Tabitha could be here, right under our noses? Who in the world would do that?"

"We need to cover all bases," Officer Daniels said.

What he didn't say was that with no ransom, no motive, and no real clues present, the possibility of someone close to the family taking the child rose higher and higher. Ellen hadn't spoken yet with Daniels regarding what the staff disclosed, but if he'd learned something urgent, he'd have told her by now.

"Our property is extensive. Over fifty acres of mostly woods. There'd be no way to house a child back there." Lilith lifted her hands to rub at the diamond pendant again.

Ellen took a minute to study the motion, wondering at its meaning. Lilith hadn't shown any emotion or even concern, but twice now had moved the jewelry between her fingers. Either this was a tiny glimpse of the fear she tucked inside, or maybe it was nerves. "We're aware of the size and scope of the property. What can't be covered today will be done tomorrow."

A slight tremor shook Lilith's wrinkled hand, and she dropped it to her side. "You don't think she'd be alive if you found her close by."

Officer Daniels shoved his hands in his pockets. "We don't know what we'll find, ma'am. That's why we need to look."

Lilith gave one nod. "Very well."

"We also still need to speak with you and your son. You mentioned yesterday wanting a lawyer present for all conversations." Ellen rose her brows, making her opinion of this clear as the blue sky overhead. "Please make yourself available. We'll be in touch to nail down a time."

She made her way down the stairs rivaling Versailles and almost laughed at how ridiculous her beat-up four-door sedan looked parked on the spotless brick. She didn't say a word to Daniels until they were both tucked in the vehicle and through the front gate. "Anything interesting come up while I was outside?"

Daniels rubbed small circles against his temples. "The nanny was a mess. Hard to get much out of her. But there was some inconsistencies regarding how she came to work with the Walkers."

Ellen raised her brows. "Such as?"

"She claims to have been hired through an agency with no knowledge of the family before being hired. She failed to mention that her aunt runs the agency and had worked with the Walkers as a teenager. A connection like that could mean something."

Agreeing, Ellen nodded. "We need to speak with the aunt. Anything else?"

"She confirmed what the rest of the staff said about the Walkers. The mom is barely holding it together since the baby was born. The father is rarely ever home. He seems to adore the boy when he is around but doesn't show much affection for the little girl. Grandma is always around, but not an ill word was uttered against her."

Ellen snorted. "That's hard to believe."

"I got the feeling it was more from fear of being overheard than of anyone actually liking the woman."

"That I believe." She took the next turn toward town, the need to pour over their notes at the station making her press a little harder on the gas.

Daniels stopped rubbing his temples and stared out the window. "Do you think the dogs will find the baby behind the house?"

"No, but we need them to look anyway."

"How can you be so sure?"

A lump formed in her throat. "I'm not. I just need to believe she's not there."

"Why?"

"Because the only way that baby will be found on the family's property is if she's already dead." Saying the words out loud sucked the air from her lungs. She didn't want the dogs to find the little girl, but she knew better than most that in some cases, you didn't get what you wanted.

She still had nightmares to prove it.

9

James' squeals of laughter from the bubble bath lifted Vivian's heart. Well, lifted her heart as much as possible when it was shattered into a million pieces. Another day was almost gone and there were still no leads on who took Tabitha. Pain fisted her lungs and refused to let go, making it hard to breathe.

She tucked her feet beneath her in the chair she'd dragged into the bathroom. Sylvie might be scrubbing the dirt behind her son's ears, but Vivian wanted to remain close. Needed to know he was safe.

With one ear trained on the giggles, she focused on the pad of paper on her lap. She'd written as many names as she could think of as Detective Olsen had requested. She didn't often leave the house, so the list of people her children were accustomed to seeing was rather pathetic. A few moms at the music class they visited, the librarian in the children's department, the server at the diner downtown who took her order on the few occasions she popped in for breakfast with the kids—especially before Tabitha was born.

Slumping against the chair, she stared at the short list.

None of these people stood out as anyone who would have taken Tabitha. Why would they? She added the few relatives she still had back in Ohio but didn't really think her eighty-year-old great aunt or handful of distant cousins were even aware of where she lived, let alone would take the risk to stalk her and steal her child.

"Hello, hello!" The high pitch to Harper's voice called out the bluff in her cheerful tone. Not even her usual skillful hand with makeup could hide the heavy bags under her eyes.

James squealed and clapped under the bubbles coating his chin.

Harper crossed the bathroom and pressed a kiss to his brow then smiled down at Sylvie before turning her attention to Vivian. "Can I steal you for a minute? I'm sure Sylvie has bath time under control."

The sad smile that barely lifted Harper's lips almost brought on a fresh bout of tears. She'd been so lost in her own misery, she hadn't thought to ask her friend over. But Harper needed no invitation. She'd move hell and high water to get to Vivian—or push past Lilith and Will. Vivian nodded and rose, keeping her notepad clutched to her chest. "Mommy will be in her office, honey. I won't be long."

James puckered his lips in an exaggerated kissing motion then grabbed a toy boat and motored it over the water.

Vivian blew him a kiss before stepping out of the bathroom.

Harper looped an arm through her elbow, hugging Vivian close to her side. Her big, black tote hung from her other shoulder.

A bit of tension loosened from Vivian's shoulders. Having her friend near gave her strength. She wished she could move Harper into the house until this nightmare was over, but Will would never allow it. He'd never warmed to the only friend she'd made since moving to Connecticut, preferring to keep Vivian isolated. For years she'd told herself he just wanted to keep her safe, but now she knew better. He wanted to control her just like he controlled everything else in their lives.

A fresh wave of anger swept in and brought back all the tension that had briefly unwound. Did he control whoever the hell the woman from the picture was in his desk? Did he keep her under lock and key in a big house the same way he hid her picture, only willing to let her out when she was watched over by staff or, God forbid, her mother-in-law?

Harper yanked against her arm. "What's with the death grip? I know this is a stupid question given the circumstances, but is everything all right?"

Vivian glanced over her shoulder, wanting to make sure no prying eyes or ears followed them down the hall. "We'll talk when we get to my office. I don't want anyone to hear what I have to tell you."

She ushered Harper inside then quickly closed the door behind them. She tossed the notepad on her desk then clasped Harper's hands, staring intently into her wide eyes. "Everything is falling apart. Tabitha's still gone. No one has told me a damn thing about where they think she might be or what could have happened. I'm losing my mind."

Harper tightened her grip. "I don't know how you're keeping it together. I'm sure the police will find her. They have to."

Vivian shook her head, strands of unkept hair swirling around her face. She couldn't even remember if she'd brushed it this morning. Not like it mattered if she looked as crazy as she felt. Anxiety rose about a hundred notches in her stomach. "That's not all. I think Will is having an affair."

Harper reared back her head, eyes wide. "What? Why would you think that?"

Scoffing, Vivian pulled away and shoved a hand through her rat's nest of hair, wincing as she worked her fingers through the tangles. "Would it really shock you? He's never home.

Doesn't spend any time with me or the kids." Her voice caught on the word—the reminder of her *two* children. One healthy and happy and clean in the bathtub down the hall. The other possibly cold and scared and hungry wondering where her mother was—or worse. Bile slid up her throat, stomach muscles clenching.

She shook her head, needing to focus on one horrible event in her life at a time. "I found a picture locked in his desk today. I was looking for something else when I found it."

Harper's jaw dropped. "I can't believe Will keeps a picture of a woman locked in his desk! Were you searching for proof of an affair?"

Vivian squeezed her eyes shut for a moment, needing a second to wrap her mind around all the information whirling inside her head before it made her explode. "The detective in charge of finding Tabitha told me last night Will had a sister. She went missing when she was a child. I wanted to talk to him this morning, but he rushed off to work—"

"He what? That asshole left you alone all day, scared and helpless, while he went to work?"

The pang of disappointment from earlier rang hollow. Now she wondered if her husband was as calloused as he appeared when he left her without a second glance, or if he'd left to seek solace in the arms of another woman. She drew in a deep breath then crossed the room and dropped into the same chair she'd occupied the night before when the detective dropped the bomb that had gotten this whole ball rolling.

Harper let her bag fall from her shoulder, carrying it low to the ground as she lowered herself in the seat beside Vivian.

"Him leaving this morning is just the tip of the iceberg."

Harper widened her eyes. "Good thing I brought wine." She pulled a bottle of white wine from her bag and set it on the small circular table nested between them. "Do you have glasses up here?"

Vivian rose to her feet and hurried to the antique sideboard along the back wall. She hadn't had a drop of alcohol since before getting pregnant with Tabitha, but the gentle buzz of the wine could calm her frayed nerves. She secured a pair of crystal glasses and placed them beside the now open bottle of wine.

"Sit and tell me everything. I'll try to keep my outbursts to a minimum." Harper poured both glasses half full and handed one to Vivian. "So, where do you want to start? The mysterious missing sister or the suspected affair?" She picked up her wine and took a large drink.

Vivian sipped her wine. The Pinot Grigio coated her tongue and slid down her throat. She wanted to tip the glass and down the contents, but she needed to take her time or she'd be flat on her back in fifteen minutes. "I'll start with the sister. Detective Olsen told me last night, and I wanted to discuss it with Will. It's weird he never told me this, right?"

Harper raised her brows. "A lot of things are weird about that man."

Vivian rolled her eyes. Harper always made her opinion of Will well known, and Vivian couldn't blame her for her disdain. He treated Harper the same as the people he kept on his payroll—which wasn't very well.

"Sorry. Yes, it's strange your husband wouldn't confide in you about a sister who went missing. But maybe it's hard for him to talk about. He could have been too young to remember what happened. There could be a lot of reasons he chose to keep this to himself."

Vivian twisted her lips to the side. "All good points, which is why I wanted to talk to him. I mean, what are the chances his sister *and* his daughter are both abducted?"

Harper winced. "Not very likely. Are you sure that's what happened to his sister?"

Vivian nodded and took another sip. "I did a little digging

this morning. Her name was Daphne and she was four years old. Will was eight. He witnessed a man in a van grab her and drive away. No one ever found the man, the van, or the little girl."

An elaborate shudder shook Harper's shoulders. "That's horrible. The whole thing might be too traumatic for him to talk about."

"Maybe." Vivian shrugged. "That's what Lilith said when I brought it up to her."

Harper wrinkled her nose. "You asked her about it?"

"She walked in on me in Will's office. I didn't want her to know what I found. And I thought...I don't know." Unshed tears burned her eyes. All she ever wanted was for this damn family to love and accept her. She'd tried so hard to win her mother-in-law's approval in the beginning of her marriage. She stopped trying once she realized all her efforts were pointless. Lilith's whole world was Will, and Vivian was just in the way. "It doesn't matter. It's stupid."

Harper leaned forward and rested a hand on Vivian's arm. "You thought she might show you compassion and understanding since she's been in your shoes."

"No surprise, that didn't happen." Vivian couldn't help the bite of sarcasm. She stared into the golden liquid as Lilith's words came back to her. "She said it was better to keep things in the past. Remembering horrible events doesn't make them easier to live with."

Harper settled back in her chair and placed a hand on her stomach. "I can't imagine not wanting to remember a child I bore and loved for four years, but I understand not being able to live with the pain of loss. Maybe it was the only way they could all move forward."

A twinge of guilt pinched Vivian's side. Harper may never have birthed a child, but she'd lost one—more than one— without ever being given the chance to hold the baby in her arms. "I still want to speak with Will. Something about what happened back then could be connected to Tabitha."

"Is that what you were looking for in his office? What did you think you could find that would help you?"

Vivian shrugged. "I had no plan—no expectations. Honestly, thinking back on it, searching his office was a stupid idea. But I'm going crazy sitting around and waiting. I wanted to do something, anything, to get some answers. Even if it was finding a simple photo of the little girl. Something could have sparked my motherly intuition." Anger burned her cheeks. "Instead I found a picture locked in his drawer. A smiling blonde radiating fucking happiness." The harsh word sounded strange from her mouth. She never raised her voice or swore, but she wanted to hold on to her anger as long as possible. The anger was better than the searing pain of missing Tabby.

Harper set her barely touched wine on the table and leaned forward. "Did you recognize her?"

Vivian shook her head. "No, but that won't stop me from figuring out who she is."

Harper sucked in her bottom lip, hesitation heavy in her hazel irises. "Why do you want to know? What good will it do?"

"What if she has my baby?" Vivian ran the pad of her thumb around the rim of her glass, voicing the concern that had been eating her away all day. "I'm not stupid. The chances of some random person happening upon me and the kids along the bluff are low. Especially since nothing has been found in the area and no harm came to James. Someone who knew I'd be there had to have taken her. What if Will told this woman where I'd be, and she snatched Tabitha?"

"But why would she do that? Wouldn't Will turn her in and just bring Tabby home?"

Setting down her wine, Vivian jumped to her feet and rubbed her closed eyes. Hysteria built in her chest until she was afraid she'd burst. "I sound crazy. I can't help it. I have to figure this out. Have to know where Tabby is, and if she's with this woman, maybe then she's safe." A sob caught in her throat, muffling her words as they rose in pitch and panic. "I have to believe she's safe."

Harper rose and wrapped her arms around her. She smoothed a hand up and down her back as her body shook from the force of the emotion pouring through her. "Tabby is safe. I can feel it in my bones. Everything will be okay. I'm here for you."

The words were like a balm over Vivian's broken soul. She sniffed, pulling herself together, then wiped the moisture from her face. "Thank you. I need to hear that. Often."

"Any time. Day or night." Harper tucked a strand of hair behind Vivian's ear. "Be strong."

Vivian nodded. "I'm trying, and there's something you can do to help."

"Anything."

Hurrying over to her desk, Vivian dropped into the chair and clicked the mouse to turn on her computer screen. She dipped her head toward the monitor.

Harper narrowed her gaze. "Did you already track down the hussy's address? You need me to take her down?"

A hoarse laugh grated against her throat. "Not yet. I made an appointment to see a therapist. Is there any way you can take me?"

Harper blinked, as if the idea of Vivian speaking with a counselor was the last thing she expected. Not that Vivian could blame her. She'd never considered such a thing until Detective Olsen recommended it. "Okay," Harper drew out the syllables. "You know I can take you wherever you need, but why do you want to talk to a therapist? Especially now?"

"I keep trying to remember what happened at the bluff. But whenever I bring that missing time into focus, everything blurs together—a kaleidoscope of sights and sounds—until I feel like

I might have another seizure. Maybe if I see a professional, I could learn some kind of trick to pull forward what is trapped in my mind." Her pulse raced at the idea of being able to remember anything that could help bring Tabby home.

Harper rounded the edge of the desk and stared at the screen. "Does it really work that way? Could someone help you?"

Vivian sucked in a deep breath, the possibility of retrieving her lost memories calming her nerves way more than the wine. "I have no idea. But it could be the only chance I have to find my daughter."

_____

10

Rain splattered onto the black pavement of the parking lot, creating a haze around the white Victorian house turned therapist's office. Another sleepless night had passed, leaving Vivian with more questions and no answers. But now was the time to find some answers of her own. Ones that could help lead the police to Tabitha. She clutched the strap of her purse and stared out the passenger side window, willing herself to move. Years of stifling every thought or emotion that could upset those around her turned her muscles to lead.

A light touch on her shoulder turned her head toward Harper. Empathy poured from her rounded eyes. "You don't have to do this."

Appreciation squeezed her chest. Harper was wrong. She *did* have to step out of the car and march up those stairs to the office, but knowing Harper had her back no matter what strengthened her resolve. "Thanks for bringing me. Patrick would have driven if I'd asked, but I don't want word to get back to Will or his mother. They'd be so upset if they found out I spoke to a therapist about anything—even if I only want to retrieve my own memories."

Harper scowled. "You should be able to do whatever you want without fear of your husband finding out. Speaking to a professional isn't something you should hide. It's a big step for you. One you only have to take when you're absolutely ready. There's no shame if that time isn't this morning. You've been through the ringer the last few days. You could put this off."

Vivian hugged her friend close, inhaling her familiar lavender perfume. "Thank you. For everything. But I can't wait. Not when my baby's life could depend on it." She pulled back and opened the door before she lost her nerve. A gust of wind slanted drops of water into the car, spraying her face as she stepped outside.

"I'll be right here waiting when you're done," Harper called.

Flipping the hood of her jacket over her head, Vivian nodded then dashed toward the house. She leapt up the stairs to the wraparound porch and swung open the door—Dr. Kudrin's name etched in the clear glass the only outward indication the home was no longer used for residential purposes. A tiny bell chimed, announcing her arrival.

Vivian dipped her chin and made a beeline for the welcome desk. No one occupied the limited seating lined against the far wall, but she still didn't want to catch anyone's eye if they happened to come in. She wasn't as recognizable as Will to many people in the area, but she needed to be as careful as possible. Even if she'd made sure to pick a therapist thirty minutes from Hollow Cove.

"Good morning," the receptionist chirped. Red curls swept the top of her shoulders and sea green eyes sparkled. Her warm smile—made impossibly sweeter by deep dimples—was welcoming, and the nameplate on her desk identified her as Suzy. "Can I help you?"

"Hi, I have an appointment with Dr. Kudrin." Vivian fiddled

with the thin purse strap across her chest. The lightness of the small purse an agonizing reminder she had no need to carry her diaper bag, stuffed to the brim with burp cloths and baby wipes. She tried to lift her lips but the pain in her chest was so intense she was satisfied her knees didn't buckle.

"Of course." Suzy grabbed a clipboard and pen and lifted them over the counter. "We need you to fill out some paperwork before going back to see the doctor. You can take the completed forms with you when Dr. Kudrin calls you back to his office."

Vivian accepted the plastic clipboard and settled into a chair in the corner. A chill settled in her bones, the air in the room not yet heated even though cold fall weather had swept into the area the week before.

Cold, wet, and miserable. A baby could never survive these elements. Not if the person who'd taken her was unprepared and running from the law.

She gritted her teeth and focused on the words on the page. Last night she'd imagined every horrible scenario Tabby could be in, each one worse than the last. Her eyes burned and a familiar fatigue pulled down her muscles, but she couldn't fall apart. Not now.

Scribbling her name and address at the top of the sheet on her lap, Vivian dropped her gaze to the rest of the questions. Family history was easy enough to provide, as was the information the doctor requested about her physical health. She'd lost count of the amount of times she'd had to describe her epilepsy or the medications she'd taken in the past.

But the questions prying into her emotional well-being had her hovering her hand in the air, pen poised and hesitant to confess her internal struggles. Depression, amount of sleep per night, how happy she was on a ridiculous number scale—all questions that couldn't be answered with a simple yes or no. All questions that would have had a different answer days ago.

Or would they? Her days held glimmers of joy and bright, hot flashes of happiness. But was that enough to sustain a person? To keep her in a loveless marriage—a marriage that made her feel small and insignificant? With a smiling little boy and a baby who cried more than slept. Had she truly been happy?

A wave of guilt slammed against her. Tabby was difficult, but Vivian still loved her with her whole heart. Life would never be the same if her precious baby didn't make it home. Even if her constant screams and demands for attention grated on Vivian's nerves and made her question her ability to take care of her own children.

"Mrs. Walker?" A deep, gravelly voice broke into her spiraling thoughts.

Vivian shot up her gaze. A man stared at her from the narrow hallway. The little bit of white sprinkled into his dark hair and thick black-framed glasses matched the picture that was plastered on the website she'd found when searching for a specialist in memory retrieval. Clutching the unfinished paperwork in her hand, she rose and offered him a weak smile. "Hello."

Kindness radiated from Dr. Kudrin's round face, and he eliminated the distance between them with an outstretched hand.

She rested her palm in his.

He placed his other hand on top of hers, a gesture that oozed compassion and chivalry. "I'm Dr. Kudrin." He released his grip and waved toward the well-lit hall. "You're more than welcome to call me Samuel, though. Whichever you prefer. Why don't you follow me back to my office so we can chat?"

The casualness of his well-worn jeans and soothing words instantly set her at ease. She followed him with her eyes downcast on the worn burgundy carpet.

He stopped in front of the entrance to another room,

allowing her access before closing the door behind them. "Take a seat wherever you like."

She scanned the large room. This must have been a family room before the place was converted for the doctor's use. The question of how the beautiful place had come to be transformed into something completely different sat on the tip of her tongue, but she bit it back.

Where she imagined family pictures must have once hung, now thick frames boasted prestigious certificates announcing Dr. Kudrin's credentials. She'd once planned to hang her own graduation certificate in her office, hopefully one day surround it with covers of her books or framed articles. But Will thought her idea to pursue her writing was silly, as well as displaying a frivolous degree which he deemed a good waste of money. Even if it had come from Yale University.

A roaring fire on the opposite end of the room caught her attention. The stone fireplace was small, a whitewashed wooden beam resting above it. She crossed the room, drawn in by the dancing flames. Wanting the warmth to chase off the chill that still clung to her bones. The simple beauty of the room—the leather chairs in dark tones, the cheerful vase of flowers on the credenza in the corner, the knickknacks and decorations scattered around the mismatched furniture—spoke of the piece of her she'd long ago suppressed.

More like the simple Ohio roots Will had stomped from her soul. He'd made it clear from the start he expected a certain kind of wife. A wife a politician could be proud to have by his side. She hadn't understood what that meant until it was too late to fight against it.

"What's going on in that head of yours? The emotions on your face seem to have one hell of a story to tell." Dr. Kudrin spoke from behind her, still rooted in the same spot.

Smoothing the lines of her face, she forced herself to turn away from the fire. "Just wondering about the house before you bought it. It's a beautiful home. One I would have liked to live in."

Smiling, Dr. Kudrin made his way to the high-backed leather chair and sat. "I lived here as a boy. Still do, actually. Once I inherited the place, I converted the downstairs into my office, but live upstairs." Steam billowed from the top of a giant mug on a wooden serving tray beside the chair. Leaning back, he crossed an ankle over his knee and cupped the mug in his hands. "Would you like anything to drink?"

She shook her head and sank onto the worn sofa across from the doctor. "No, thank you."

He nodded, took a long sip, then placed the mug back on the tray. "May I see the paperwork you filled out?"

The blank spaces she had yet to answer stared up at her, mocking her. She gulped, already aware of what a disappointment she was. A pit opened in her stomach, enveloping all the hope and even the tiny bit of excitement she'd summoned for this meeting. Who did she think she was kidding? She'd never be able to help the police. She couldn't even drive herself to her own appointment.

Dr. Kudrin grabbed the papers but kept his gaze fixed on her face. "There it is again. That look. Don't tell me you're still wondering about the house. I agree, it's beautiful, but not really all that interesting."

Stupid tears stung her eyes, and she shrugged, at a loss for words.

"Mrs. Walker, I just want to take a few minutes to get to know you. Who you are. Why you chose to see me. I promise, nothing too painful. We can take each session as slowly or quickly as you want."

Her sinus cavities throbbed, and she sniffed.

Dr. Kudrin handed her a box of tissues.

She grabbed a tissue and dabbed her eyes. "Thank you. But I don't have the option to go slow."

"Why not?" Dr. Kudrin furrowed his brow. "Why are you here, Mrs. Walker?"

She filled her lungs with air and rolled the wadded tissue in her hands. "As you can see on the sheet I handed you, I have epilepsy. When I have a seizure, I black out and don't remember anything that happened during an episode."

He nodded along with her words. "Yes, that's common."

"I need to remember. I need to know what happened when I had my last seizure." The tears came faster, and she grabbed another tissue. "I have no time to take things slow."

Dr. Kudrin lowered his propped-up foot to the ground and leaned forward. "What happened during your last seizure?"

She dropped her gaze to her hands. "Someone took my baby. She's so tiny. So helpless. If I could remember what happened when I blacked out, I could help the police figure out who took her. I could bring her home where she belongs."

Silence overtook the room, the sound of the crackling fire the only noise. Finally, Dr. Kudrin cleared his throat. "I'm so sorry about your child, but I can't promise I can help you retrieve your memories."

She clenched her jaw, refusing to believe she was at a dead end. "But your website said you specialized in memory retrieval. You're the only one who can help."

He frowned, and his glasses slid down the bridge of his nose. "I mainly work with people who've lost memories due to head injuries or traumatic events from their past. What you're talking about, that's a whole other part of the brain that I haven't explored much. At least not recently. I'm not sure if anyone is qualified to do what you're asking."

She shook her head, refusing to take no for an answer. "Please. There has to be something we can try. Something I can do. Hypnosis, maybe. Or hook my brain up to some sort of machine. Anything."

Standing, Dr. Kudrin clasped his hands behind his back

and stared into the fire. "I'm willing to talk with you, work through your issues. We can discuss what happened before and after your seizure. Maybe something can trigger a memory. It's not something I've ever attempted before. But we can try."

"Yes. Please." She hated the frantic plea in her voice, but she couldn't help it. This could be her only chance to get Tabby back in her arms.

Tilting his head, he stared down at her. "Can you tell me what happened before you had your seizure that day?"

"I took my children for a walk up by Lighthouse Point. My son loves to look out at the ocean. We made it to the top of the bluff, right beside the lighthouse. Tabby—my daughter—was crying. I tried to calm her down, but nothing worked. I put her back in the stroller and then..." She lifted her hands as emotion clogged her throat. Such a simple story of spending some time with her kids. No way she could have ever anticipated what tragic turn of events would unfold.

"Close your eyes."

She let her eyelids slide down.

"What sounds did you hear when you were standing by the cliff with your children." He softened his voice to just above a whisper.

She leaned against the cushy sofa and let her mind wander backward. "Birds chirping in the sky. Wind blowing and waves crashing. Tabitha crying."

"What about smells."

She drew in a breath, drawing back on that morning. "Salty sea air. A hint of something floral...lilac perhaps. Honey from the cereal my son ate in the car." A smile tugged at her lips. She'd give anything to go back to that moment in the car—with James munching on Cheerios and Tabitha crying. Back when she thought she'd hit her lowest point because she couldn't calm her crying baby. Now, she'd cut off her right arm to hear those screams again.

"Good. Good. Now just relax. Let your mind float away. Empty all thoughts and emotions. Let the sights and sounds and smells of those moments fill your brain. Visualize the colors, imagine the sensations surrounding you."

James' smiling face came into view. The stroller with Tabitha sitting beside her. The bright green of the unturned leaves and the blue of the deep ocean collided, the colors swirling together. Snapshots of images tumbled round and round, mixing and blurring. Dizziness danced in her head. She swayed, clutching her purse strap, trying to anchor herself and stay in the moment—to focus on what happened next.

"Mrs. Walker...open your eyes."

She registered the calm voice but it was so far away, like a dream calling her forward. Her head spun. Nausea pitched in her stomach. The bright colors that sparked behind her closed lids muted, dimming into the shadows.

"Vivian!"

She jolted awake, eyes now wide. Her heart hammered against her breast plate. Her breath tore through her lungs. Placing a hand over heart, she rubbed small circles over her soft sweater, willing herself to calm down.

Concern dipped together Dr. Kudrin's overgrown brows. "Are you all right?"

She nodded, unable to voice any words.

He rubbed a hand over the beard that covered his jaw. "I'm sorry. I think I pushed you too far."

She swallowed hard and stopped the motion of her hand, leaving her palm flat on her chest. "That's what happens every time I try to remember. It's like the harder I try to bring that part of my brain into focus, the more my brain rebels and attempts to spin me into another seizure."

Screwing his lips to the side, he grumbled under his breath. "If you're willing to work with me, I'm willing to do some research and see if I can find a way to help."

Hope blossomed to life for the first time since Tabitha went missing. "I'll do whatever you ask of me. Whenever."

He held up a hand. "Let's not get too excited yet. I make no promises. But now that I know what we're working with, I can try to uncover the best way to help."

She bobbed her head up and down.

"I'll be in touch. We can set up another appointment as soon as I have something useful. I promise, I will give this my utmost attention this evening."

She stood, gratitude showering over her. "Is there anything I can do? I can research on the internet. Maybe find a method we could use."

"I have something else I'd like you to try."

"Anything."

"I'm not certain it will help, but I suggest keeping a journal to most people I see. Usually, I recommend starting out small with writing down your daily tasks and any emotions you wish to examine. But I want you to do something a bit different. Write down how you felt before you blacked out from your seizure. It's obvious that just remembering that event isn't a good idea. But if you could write it down, it might trigger something new."

The idea that writing could help her brought a tiny burst of delight in her soul. Writing had always been her escape—a way to create her ideal world where everything was perfect and she didn't have something wrong with her that made her so damn different. The day she stopped writing, she'd quit on her dream. Quit on herself.

But now, maybe the one thing that had always been her saving grace could be the one thing that could save her daughter.

11

Thick mud clung to the bottom of Ellen's boots as she trudged through the hilly acres of dense woods behind the Walkers' estate. The rain had slowed, but the mess the torrential downpour created stayed behind, rendering the K-9 unit they'd brought out useless. Any lingering scents from the day of the crime would be washed away by now.

Conflicting emotions warred in the pit of her stomach. She'd meant what she'd told Daniels yesterday. She didn't want to find Tabitha Walker in the woods behind the Walkers' home. Not finding her amongst the trees and upturned roots of the forest floor meant there was still hope of finding her alive.

But where? Innumerable questions had nagged her during the few hours of shut-eye she'd attempted the night before. After spending hours combing the front half of the property and coming up empty handed, she'd fallen into bed with achy muscles and a sour mood. Neither had improved much this morning.

A K-9 officer—Officer Lopez—hiked a few paces ahead of

her. His large German Shepherd kept his nose to the sodden ground and ears on alert. But nothing had caught the dog's attention in the hours they'd searched the property.

A bead of sweat slid into Ellen's eye. She stopped and mopped her brow with the back of her long-sleeved shirt. Her thighs burned, but she had to keep pushing. Grabbing a bottle of water from the heavy pack on her back, she chugged the tepid liquid and swept her gaze between the thick tree trunks, as if she'd spot something—anything—that would give them a leg up in the investigation.

Lopez paused and swiveled toward her. "You okay back there?" He lifted a palm and the dog halted.

She shoved the bottle back in her bag and tilted her face up to the thick canopy of leaves overhead. The deep green shades were transforming to golds and reds, creating a tapestry of woven colors. Drops of water dripped off the outstretched branches. "I'm fine. Just needed a second."

Catching her breath, she tipped her chin back down and locked her gaze on Officer Lopez. Dark hair curled around the nape of his neck and rich, chocolate eyes studied her. Young, muscled, and full of youthful charm, he was exactly the kind of man she was attracted to before her disastrous marriage turned her off men.

Now she didn't have room in her life for complications. Her job, her grief, and her fierce desire to reunite missing children with their families was all she'd had the energy for since the day she got the devastating news her little girl would never make it home. Every day carefully orchestrated to keep her mind engaged and her heart locked up tight. Only the delicate balance she maintained in her life got her out of bed every morning.

Lopez rolled in his lips and ran his hand over his trusty companion's furry head. "I want to make it to the top of this hill.

I doubt Thunder will catch a scent, but I want to see the view from the top. Check out the lay of the land. We're pretty close to the back of the property. Getting a bird's eye view could show us something we're missing, even if Thunder can't point it out."

She nodded and made her way to his side. Thunder, as well as the other K-9s fanned out around the property, had all worked tirelessly but without success. Time was near to call it quits and dry off. She'd get ahold of Daniels, who'd stayed at the station to make some calls, and start pulling at a new string. Because this one wasn't getting them anywhere.

The wind chapped her cheeks as she pressed forward, the steep incline making her legs scream. Sunlight couldn't filter through the thick, gray clouds promising more rain soon, but a clearing came into view at the top of the hill. Wanting this torturous leg of the journey to be over before backtracking to the house, she quickened her pace. Once on top, she'd allow herself a few minutes to take a seat and eat a protein bar before turning around.

Lopez hustled beside her, letting out a low whistle when they reached the clearing. The trees gave way to a grassy spot of land, but it was the view of the surrounding area that was worth appreciating. Ellen turned in a circle. Something about this place was familiar, but she couldn't place her finger on it.

A large tree with a boulder resting against its base had her grabbing her phone and searching though her camera roll. Excitement kicked up her already laboring pulse. She showed the screen to Lopez. "Is this the same tree?"

Lopez finished pouring water into an inflatable bowl for Thunder and stood, taking the phone. He studied the screen, then flicked his narrowed gaze to the tree. "Looks like it. Weird place for a rock that size to be."

Ellen pocketed her phone. This was the place Will had taken a picture of the mystery woman. Why had he brought her all the way back here? The man sure had some balls to bring his mistress to his home, even if it was for a hike, acres deep into his wooded property. What was so special about this spot that it was worth hours to get there? Sure, the view was beautiful. But so were tons of other vistas on hiking trails in this area. Why risk bringing another woman so close to his wife and family? Not to mention having this exact scene depicted in a painting for his office.

She ran a hand over her sweat-soaked ponytail. The woman in the picture didn't have a lock of hair out of place or any hint of fighting through an hours-long hike. How had they accessed this spot? No way could someone look so flawless if she'd come from the main house.

Picking up the thread from his last comment, she muttered, "I thought so, too." She roamed a palm over the moss and dirt covered rock that came up to her knees. She scanned the area. No other rocks or boulders scattered along the tree line, making the presence of the rock even more intriguing.

"We could move it. See if there's anything behind it," Lopez said.

Weighing her options, Ellen crossed her arms over her chest. The idea of finding spiders and worms and God knew what else had her scrunching her nose. And really, what would moving an old rock prove? But curiosity and a growing sense of urgency tingled her nerve endings. "Might as well."

"I got it." Squatting, he secured his hands behind the rock and pushed it away from the tree. Years of mud and moss kept it from rolling smoothly away. The bottom scraped against the wet earth, making a tiny trail of muddy water.

She stepped closer, her boots sinking into the newly exposed earth. The bark that was hidden behind the large stone had turned black, the decay from the lack of sunlight pungent. A hollowed-out space—obviously manmade—was dug into the base of the tree. Ellen dropped to her knees and sifted through the layers of mud and dead weeds.

A thin sliver of fabric appeared. "What's this?" She swept away the remaining debris until a long length of soiled material was exposed. "A ribbon?" A lump wedged in her throat. She picked up the scrap of fabric and laid it flat across her palm. She used to put a simple ribbon in Sara's hair. Always matching the color to her outfit for the day.

"Looks like it's been buried under the tree for quite some time." Lopez stood over her, the nearness of his body making her feel suffocated.

Heaviness pressed on her chest. She tightened her jaw. This was not her daughter's ribbon. It was a random piece of fabric found in the woods. She couldn't get sucked into the past —not now.

She rose to her feet, the material still in her hand. Frayed threads lined the length of the ribbon, the original color unrecognizable under the dirt and stains of time. No. This wasn't a random piece of fabric. And she was going to prove it.

Dropping her backpack to the side, she retrieved an evidence bag and sealed the ribbon inside. "Good work, Lopez. We might not have found what we were looking for, but we might have come across something just as valuable to the investigation."

Confusion knit together Lopez's brow, but he didn't ask any questions as he packed up Thunder's water dish and prepared for the long hike back to the house.

Ellen appreciated his silence as she trekked back through the muck and sludge. So many questions lingered in her mind. She used the time—and the silence—to organize her thoughts. She needed to get the ribbon to the lab, and she wanted a description of the missing Walker girl the day she was taken.

Not Tabitha. Daphne.

She wasn't sure how the two were tied together, but something told her that solving one case would help her solve the other. She just hoped it wouldn't be too late to find Tabitha Walker alive.

The thicket of trees thinned and the outline of the estate came into view. Relief loosened her neck muscles, but only for a second. She had to meet with Mr. Walker, his mother, and their attorney before she could go home and warm up under a hot shower.

Ellen's phone chirped. She checked the screen then answered. "Hey, Daniels. Lopez and I found something of interest deep in the woods."

"Something related to who took the baby?" Anticipation made the words come out quick.

"Not yet, but it could lead us that way. I'll go over my thoughts with you when I get back. Are you still at the station?" The low branches parted and a sigh of relief slipped through her lips when she stepped onto the smooth grass at the edge of the Walkers' backyard. Her clothes were drenched, the smell of sweat rolled off her in waves, and she had one hell of a hunch she was dying to dive into.

"You may need to put whatever you found on hold if it's not a priority."

The hard edge in his tone had her feet stopping. "What'd you find?"

"An anonymous call came into the station today. William Walker wasn't in his office like he claimed the morning Tabitha went missing."

All the air left her lungs. "What? How can that be? We questioned the staff and they all confirmed his location."

"The staff must be more afraid of pissing off their boss than telling the police the truth about his whereabouts. Discretion is more precious than gold with these people."

Ellen needed to sort out this new information in her mind before confronting William, but she couldn't just leave. She rubbed her temples and stared with heated blood at the giant house looming in front of her. The implication of what Daniels found opened up a whole new angle. "You know what that means. William Walker doesn't have an alibi for the time his daughter was kidnapped."

12

Fatigue rubbed like grains of sand against Vivian's eyeballs. Exhaustion like she'd never experienced before made her body heavy, her mind slow. Each step toward the front door took agonizing effort. The combination of a rollercoaster of emotions, lack of sleep, and a constant state of fear had slammed into her after leaving Dr. Kudrin's office, nearly sucking her into a vortex of oblivion. She needed a few hours to bury herself under a mountain of blankets and get a tiny bit of relief from the hell that was now her reality.

Pushing open the door, she stepped into the house and let her purse fall to the floor. A gust of cold wind blew in behind her, reminding her she still needed to close the giant monstrosity. The thing weighed a ton, as if her husband's ancestors thought barricading the house would keep out anything that ventured near. She shoved it closed and glanced up the long length of the winding staircase that spilled out onto the marble floor. A feature she once found beautiful was now just another barrier keeping her from where she wanted to go—another spot filled with bad memories.

Heavy footsteps barreled toward her, and Vivian braced

herself for whatever intrusion approached. Will rounded the corner from the study, a seemingly permanent scowl etched on his handsome face. His fisted hands swung from his sides, his arms pumping back in forth at the same speed as his long legs.

She tensed her muscles. Whatever news he brought had to be bad or else he wouldn't have bothered to return home in the middle of a work day.

If work really was where he escaped to all the time.

Will didn't slow his pace until the tips of his leather loafers almost collided with her rainboots. His tightened jaw show-cased his irritation. Securing a tight grasp around her bicep, he yanked her close. The familiar scent of his sandalwood cologne made her heart lurch. She used to crave that smell—would wrap an old sweatshirt around her until surrounded by the comfort he once brought. But now she detected another scent lingering, one that made her stomach roll. Was her mind playing tricks on her, or were his skin and clothes now marked with the scent of another woman?

"Where the hell have you been?" He tugged her in the direction he'd just come. "Detective Olsen is here to speak with me and Mother. You should be in there with us—a united front."

She stumbled along beside him, relieved he hadn't demanded she answer any questions. Lying wasn't easy for her, and the truth would send him into a tailspin. Better to do as he said. Stay quiet and not let him know what she'd been up to.

Lilith and the family lawyer—Mr. Derby—sat in the study, the room thick with tension. Detective Olsen stood in the corner, her clothes caked in mud and dirt smeared across one cheek.

Vivian halted in the doorway, her breath caught in her throat, despite Will's remaining pressure on her arm. The detective had scoured the property this morning. Had she found something? Was that why she hadn't taken the time to clean herself before circling back to the house?

"Keep. Moving." Will all but growled the command in her ear.

Three pairs of eyes settled on her. Lilith—cold and calculating. Mr. Derby—detached but with an almost invisible layer of nerves. And Detective Olsen—questioning eyes with a hint of compassion.

Licking her dry lips, she dropped her gaze to her plaid boots and forced her feet to continue forward until she lowered her now-numb body onto the couch next to Lilith.

"Nice of you to join us." Lilith hooked a brow, mouth pinched.

Vivian bit her tongue, refusing to apologize. No one had told her she was supposed to be around today. No one imagined she could have her own plans, her own way of dealing with the nightmare she'd landed in. No one cared enough to ask.

But that was the only reason she was able to escape her beautiful cage and meet a therapist she would have been forbidden to see.

"Now that we're all here, let's get this started," Mr. Derby said. Shadows from the flames in the fireplace flickered on top of his bald head.

"Yes, lets." Detective Olsen scrunched her face, her annoyance aimed at the lawyer. "Even though there was no reason to wait. I need to speak with the elder Mrs. Walker and Mr. Walker at this time. We could have been done by now."

A little bit of terror faded. If she wasn't waiting for Vivian, she didn't have any news about what was discovered in the woods.

Which also meant the police still didn't know who had Tabitha.

Will thundered over to the sideboard and poured himself a

glass of scotch. "I still don't understand why you insist on speaking with my mother and me again when you should be looking for my child." He flung out his hand, gesturing toward the window. The amber-colored liquid sloshed with the motion. "If you're not going to do your damn job, I'll hire someone else who doesn't waste time traipsing through the forest and asking useless questions."

Vivian winced and peered over at the detective. Will's harsh words didn't even cause a single ripple of reaction to form on her face.

Detective Olsen tilted her head to the side. "Traipsing? Interesting description of hiking up and down barely established trails for miles on end. Do you like to hike? Like to traipse through your property much?"

Will snorted and downed the half-filled glass before pouring more. "Seriously? This is what I'm wasting my time on? Where's my child, Detective? Any clues on who took her?"

"We have a few leads. And if you would focus on answering my questions instead of asking your own, you can get back to your day."

Will slammed his glass onto the smooth top of the sideboard, the alcohol splashing onto the varnished grains of wood. "I demand to know what you've uncovered so far."

Vivian cringed, her shoulders bunching up to her ears on instinct.

"William." Lilith raised her brows toward her son then faced off with Detective Olsen. "Please, Detective. We are all busy and would like to assist with your investigation. Continue. We will answer whatever questions you have."

"Fine." Will pivoted and flashed his most charming smile— his politician smile. "No, I do not like to wade through the thick trees and dirt behind my house. Is that what you wanted to hear? Does that give you the one answer you need to uncover the truth?"

Detective Olsen shrugged. "I never know where the truth will pop up from, so thank you for your honesty. Now, can you tell me a little about the morning Tabitha was taken? Where you were? What you did before getting the call from your wife?"

Vivian bit the inside of her mouth to keep from rolling her eyes. He didn't take the call from his wife in the worst moment of her life. He'd ignored the call, waiting instead to hear the devastating news from his mother. Bitterness smothered her heart.

Mr. Derby rose to his feet and straightened his tie. "It's my understanding that my client has already answered this question. As our time is limited, I suggest you keep your questions to ones that haven't been asked yet."

Detective Olsen flicked her gaze to the paunchy lawyer, lips pressed in a straight line.

"Sit down, Derby." Will pinched the bridge of his nose, eyes closed. "As has been pointed out, I've already told you. I left the house around 7:00 a.m. I drove myself into work, where I stayed until I heard about Tabitha. At that point I hurried to Lighthouse Point to be with my wife and son."

"How many staff members were in the office with you?"

Will opened his eyes and worked his jaw back and forth. "A handful. I'm not sure of the exact number off the top of my head, but I could find out."

"Please do. And did anyone from either your law practice or members of your political campaign know where your wife would be that morning?" Detective Olsen asked.

Vivian shifted in her seat. She'd searched her brain for anyone in her own life who could have wanted to take her baby. She'd never imagined someone who worked for Will would have any reason to hurt them.

Will squinted, head turning slightly to the side as if trying to process the question. "Why would anyone I work with know my wife's daily agenda?"

Detective Olsen shrugged.

A frustrated breath blew from Will's nose and he crossed over to stand behind Vivian, latching his grip onto the back of the couch. "My campaign manager knew Vivian was taking the kids on a walk."

"What?" Vivian couldn't hold back any longer. She twisted in her seat to stare up at her husband. "Why in the world did Jim Ballinger know what I was doing that morning?"

Will tightened his grip on the couch until his knuckles turned white. "Jim knows everything, dear."

"Sounds like I need to have another conversation with your campaign manager then," Detective Olsen cut in. "I wasn't aware he was such a wealth of information."

Lilith sighed. "Didn't you already speak with everyone William works with? Really, Detective, this feels like a complete waste of time." She made a show of checking the time on the delicate watch on her wrist.

"I'm sorry you feel that way," Detective Olsen said, turning her attention to Lilith. "What about you? What was your routine like that morning? I don't believe you and I have spoken much about where you were when Tabitha was taken."

"There's not much to tell. I was home all morning. I seldom go out, especially when Patrick isn't around to drive me." She circled her hand around her diamond necklace dangling from a delicate silver chain.

"Is it common for Patrick to drive Vivian, leaving you to fend for yourself?"

Lilith lifted a slender shoulder. "Vivian doesn't leave the house much, so splitting his time between us is never an issue."

"And how long as he been employed by the family?"

"Since before William was born," Lilith said with a wave of her hand.

"And are you aware of the financial stress he and his wife have endured over the years? Seems they've found themselves in a mountain of debt with no way out. Must be hard on him, with a daughter still paying off her own student loans and his house close to going into foreclosure." Ellen flicked her gaze among them.

Vivian stiffened. Patrick was the one person who worked for them she actually liked and trusted. If she'd known about his problems, she'd have offered whatever assistance he needed. She studied Lilith's face, but the stony expression gave nothing away.

"Patrick's finances aren't something he's ever discussed with me, and I don't see why they should be important." The terse manner of Lilith's words belied her statement.

Vivian's stomach twisted at the detective's insinuation. She bit her bottom lip to keep from asking more about Detective Olsen's suspicions of her driver.

Detective Olsen narrowed her eyes, then nodded, before returning her focus to Will—dismissing Lilith's words with no more than an annoyed expression.

"Mr. Ballinger never indicated he was aware of your wife's schedule. He hardly said anything when Officer Daniels talked to him. Would he have any reason to be upset with you, Mr. Walker? Does he interact with any questionable characters who would want to strike out at you?"

"Do you think I would have hired him if I knew he interacted with questionable characters?" Will asked.

"You tell me." Detective Olsen held Will's gaze, tensions mounting.

"Enough." The hard edge of Lilith's voice could have cut through steel. "Detective, you have a list of names. We made sure of that. If you have questions regarding their character or activities, I suggest you speak to them. Now, unless the next words out of your mouth are the location of my granddaughter, I think we're done here."

Vivian wrung her hands in her lap. Lilith was used to barking out orders, but her harsh tone could have a direct impact on how the police chose to approach finding Tabby. Her last encounter with the detective left her feeling like she had someone who'd fight for the truth—someone to finally be in her corner. She couldn't risk alienating the one person she could trust to find her daughter and bring her home. "I made my list."

Will's hand slid onto her shoulder and clamped down, hard fingers biting into her flesh. "What list?"

She fought not to react to the discomfort, her gaze locked on Detective Olsen. "Of the people I could think of who James has spent time with. Anyone who James wouldn't be frightened of. I completed the list last night. It's upstairs. In my office."

"Let's head up and grab it, shall we?" Detective Olsen took a step in her direction.

"You? Walking through the house covered in mud? I hardly think so." Lilith clicked her tongue. "Vivian can run up and grab it and bring it down for you."

The idea of making her way all the way upstairs and back down made her limbs even heavier. Not to mention she wanted a few minutes to speak with Detective Olsen alone. Will would never give them the space to speak if he lingered in the room.

Raising to her feet, she aimed a well-crafted smile at Lilith. "I'm sure she'll be careful, and I'd much rather hand her the paper and lie down. I'm not feeling well."

Lilith widened her eyes a bit, but held her tongue.

"Besides, I'm sure Will and Mr. Derby both need to get on with their days, and you have things to do. I can get the information to the detective and she can be on her way."

"Yes, I have a lot to see to," Detective Olsen said. "I'll grab the names and get out of your hair."

Vivian hurried toward the door before Lilith or Will could protest. At the doorway, she braced a hand on the mahogany casing and glanced behind her to make sure Detective Olsen followed. Her gaze locked with Will and a flash of anger pulsed across his face, making the vein along his right temple bulge. He balled his hands into fists at his sides, his clenched jaw moving back and forth.

She hurried forward, the detective on her heels as she used all her remaining energy to climb the mountain of stairs to the second floor. She'd be safe from Will's wrath while her new ally was inside, but there was no telling when he'd punish her for stepping out of line.

But for the first time in years, she didn't care. Nothing could hurt more than the constant state of pain devouring her since Tabitha was taken. Not even the psychological warfare Will relished in waging—closing in for the proverbial kill only when he sensed she was at her weakest.

He could try his best. She was living at her lowest point, and nothing he could do would bring her any lower.

13

The cozy familiarity of Vivian's office helped ease the mental burden beating her down. Funny how she'd avoided this room after her writing slid to the bottom of her priority list—the sheer thought of attempting to create anything when her sanity was on the brink of collapse was laughable. Now, the room she'd painstakingly assembled in the early years of her marriage welcomed her inside with its soft furniture and delicate fabrics.

Detective Olsen stood at the threshold, a dirty boot print staining the cream-colored carpet. "This is everyone?" She glanced up from the piece of paper Vivian had handed her moments before.

The simple question was a punch in the gut. Vivian didn't explain her lack of a social life or activities with her kids. There was no need—the proof was on the page. "Yes."

"What about Sylvie? Does she take the kids on outings? Any regular classes with James?"

"Sylvie takes them on outings, but never without me." Resentment squeezed her throat, making her words come out tight. Sylvie was great with the kids, and Vivian *did* appreciate how much the nanny cared, but needing another woman to help take care of James and Tabitha was a pill she'd never swallow.

Detective Olsen shifted her stance, cringing when another boot mark marred the carpet. "Thank you for being so detailed. Placing your connection to each person, as well as how I can locate them, will help cut down on time."

Vivian shrugged and propped an elbow on her desk, resting her head in her palm. "I wish I could do more."

"Is your friend on here? The one who was here the night Tabitha went missing—when I found you in the baby's nursery." The detective lifted her gaze from the sheet and settled it on Vivian.

A slow smile took over Vivian's mouth. "Harper? She's like the sister I never had. The only friend I've made since moving here. She's not on there, Detective. She's family."

"I told you before, please call me Ellen." She offered a flash of warmth before continuing. "What's Harper's last name?"

Vivian frowned. "Kellington. Why?"

"Family friend, or not, I need to talk to everyone. If you're close to Harper, she could offer some insight you may have overlooked. Your head and your heart are struggling to put one foot in front of the other right now. At least that's how I was when I was in your shoes."

Emotion the size of boulder sat heavy on her chest. Here was the compassion and empathy she'd searched for with Lilith. A woman who'd been unlucky enough to walk the same path of fear and worry and wanted to offer whatever support she could. "Thank you, Ellen."

Ellen dipped her chin. "I should go. I'll let you know if anything comes up."

"Wait. I wanted to thank you. I saw a therapist this morning."

Delight lifted the corners of Ellen's eyes. "Good for you. I hope it helps."

Vivian twisted her lips to the side. "Me too. He wants me to write in a journal. See if it sparks a memory."

"Keep me updated. Sometimes it's the tiniest detail that helps." Ellen shoved the single sheet of paper into her pocket.

"Mama!" James zipped around Ellen's legs and ran into the room, throwing himself on Vivian's lap.

"I'll see myself out."

Vivian gave a little wave then wrapped her arms around James' small body. Inhaling deeply, her muscles relaxed with the smell of play dough and his favorite cereal. The scent tugged at her memories—the same hint of honey she'd recalled earlier at the therapist's office. The need to act quickly, to write down her memories as instructed, had her reaching for a journal in the bottom drawer of her desk.

James squirmed in her lap, unwilling to release his death grip from around her neck.

Sylvie hustled into the room with a canvas bin on her hip. "There you are little man. I thought you were going to help me pick up the toys? And we need to fold up the blankets from the fort before bed tonight."

A soft whimper tugged at Vivian's heart. "Any chance I can just hold him for a while? I haven't seen him all day, and I really just need some snuggles. James and I can both help you in a little bit."

"How about I clean up while you two spend some much-needed time together?" Sylvie brushed a stand of hair from her forehead and turned to leave, but not before a glimmer of tears sparkled in her eyes.

James nuzzled his head closer.

She gave him one big squeeze then turned him to face forward, securing one arm across his waist. "Do you want to draw?"

He shook his head and popped his thumb in his mouth.

She fought not to grimace. At two, he was past the age of needing his thumb to fall asleep or self-soothe. She and Sylvie had put a lot of effort into breaking the horrible habit. She supposed it was normal for him to fall back on old ways. Even if he ran around with an easy smile and bubbling laughter, he still picked up on the fear and anxiety oozing from everyone in the house.

He still understood his baby sister wasn't where she was supposed to be.

She ran her hand over his soft, blond hair, the ends curling at the top of his neck. "That's okay. You sit with Mama. I'm just going to reach for this pen and write down a few things, okay?" She grabbed a ball point pen and flipped open the blank notebook that had sat empty for way too long.

With her pen poised above the blank sheet of paper, she scribbled down the same scents and sights she'd described to Dr. Kudrin. Below the list, she wrote down her emotions. How she'd felt as she'd watched the birds fly overhead, free to do as they pleased. The helplessness rooted deep in her soul as she recalled how the baby screamed. She yearned to spread her wings and stretch toward her own freedom. A freedom to leave, or to stay, or to make her own decisions without the fear of doubt. Knowing that the limited choices before her would only lead to more disappointment—for her and everyone else around her.

A fountain of emotions welled in her chest, threatening to cut off her oxygen. The distant sound of the crashing waves beating against the jagged rocks echoed in her ears. Thoughts she'd buried, questions she never wanted to examine, floated to the surface. She still didn't want to examine her fascination with what it'd be like to throw herself from the edge, down into the icy waters below. The urge to fly toward real freedom— away from the restraints tying her down.

She wrapped her arm tighter around James. These thoughts had been buried under terror and anxiety for the last few days. Her goal was to remember what happened while she'd been in the dark parts of her mind, not the feelings of despair and helplessness that made her contemplate the inconceivable just moments before her world crashed at her feet.

Closing her eyes, her body swayed, as if moving with the distant sound of the sea. James' fingers clutched her forearm. Tabitha's angry screams combined with the waves, growing louder and louder until the cries were all she heard. She saw her tiny face in the stroller. Her cheeks red. Pissed at the hand life had dealt her. At the shitty mom who couldn't even take care of her most basic needs.

Tabitha deserved better. Deserved more than Vivian would ever be able to give her.

A shadow emerged, crossing the puckered lips and tear-stained cheeks. Vivian strained harder to make out the shape. A hand? Fingers moving closer to the baby. Slender fingers. Dainty wrist. A thick strap circling the arm, just above the hand.

A watch?

Her pulse raced, and with eyes still closed, she unwound her arm from James and ran the pad of her fingers along the grooves of the gold watch she only took off when she slept. She needed to see more—to remember more. Had she grabbed Tabitha from her seat? Picked her up while her mind was blank and unable to fight against the demons clawing at her psyche every damn day? Trembling shook her body.

No! I love my baby. I didn't hurt my baby.

Another cry combined with screams. This one closer, more frantic. But Vivian couldn't open her eyes. Couldn't tear her mind away from the scene unfolding. Tabby's face grew distant, her cries muffled. The image of the sleek stroller whipped in circles, causing the thick black lines to fade into nothing more than wisps of smoke snaking into the sky.

Pain beat against her temples. Her body ached, and she tried to come back to the present. The muffled cries came closer. *James!* She struggled against herself, needing to fight against the swirling colors in her head. Stars burst behind her eyelids.

The weight in her lap evaporated. A sharp yelp of pain sounded at her feet. And Vivian fell into the black pit of unconsciousness.

AGONY BEAT a constant drum against Vivian's skull. Moaning, she struggled to turn to her side and open her eyes. Muted shadows came into view. She roamed a hand beside her. A soft down blanket spread out over her bed. Sitting, she held her head in her hand. How had she gotten here?

Nausea gurgled in her stomach. Exhaustion made her mind slow, even as she forced it to remember how she'd ended up in her bed.

"You're finally awake." Lilith's tense voice sounded from the corner of the room.

Facing off against her mother-in-law was the last thing she wanted to do but, like usual, she wasn't given a choice. Leaning to the side, Vivian switched on the lamp on the nightstand and winced. The light was low, the weak beams barely illuminating Lilith's petite form in the chair beside the window, but it was enough to make her recoil from the stabbing pain slamming into her retinas.

"What happened?" She should be more specific. She'd suffered another seizure, not like that surprised her. Her episodes always came in threes, and she'd been fighting against another for days. Add in her constant state of exhaustion and onslaught of emotions—she was surprised she hadn't suffered her second seizure sooner. What she really wondered was who had carried her to bed and what were the results of her seizure this time. But she couldn't put all those questions into words at the moment.

"After the detective left, I entered your office and found you on the floor. James beside you." Lilith rose, hands clasped in front of her, and crossed the room to stand at the foot of the bed.

Vivian gasped, the sound of James' frantic cries coming back to her. She hadn't been able to separate the memories of Tabitha screaming at the bluff and James crying on her lap in her office.

The image of the shadowy hand closing in on Tabitha swept in, and she circled her grip around the watch on her wrist. The metallic taste of fear coated her tongue.

Lilith crossed her arms over her chest. "Aren't you going to ask about James?"

She shot her gaze up to meet Lilith's icy stare. "Is he all right?" Her heart raced and dampness coated the back of her neck. Her son had been hurt before because of her seizures. She couldn't live with herself if something else had happened to James because of her.

"He'll be fine. He hit his head on the side of the desk."

Vivian brought her fingers to her temple, as though caressing her son's wound. "I should go see him. He gets so scared when I pass out."

"He's with Sylvie, though I'm not sure she's capable of looking after him. She should have known better than to leave him unattended." A hint of weariness slumped the older woman's shoulders.

Vivian gritted her teeth, fighting through the turmoil the

effects of her seizure heaped on her shoulders. "He wasn't unattended. He was with his mother."

"And what good did that do?" Lilith snapped. "He's lucky he didn't need a stitch or two. The poor boy has been through enough. This environment isn't good for him."

Her temper flared, but she stomped it down. "This environment isn't good for any of us. We're all on pins and needles, waiting for word on Tabby. But she'll come home and everything will get back to normal. Everything will be okay." Her voice cracked. Did she really believe her life would tumble right back to where it had been before Tabby went missing? Did she want it to?

"This doesn't have anything to do with Tabitha. It has to do with you. You can't even keep yourself safe, let alone a child. You've proven that on more than one occasion." Lilith grabbed the diamond around her neck with more force than necessary.

Vivian's fingers itched to grab the stupid necklace and rip it from Lilith's throat. "I love James with my whole being. I'd never purposely hurt him."

Lilith tilted her head to the side. "Until you're back on your medication, you can't be trusted to care for him."

Vivian bit into her trembling lip, trying like hell to keep her composure from slipping. "The medication isn't good for Tabitha. I can't contaminate my milk supply." Her heavy breasts ached at the reminder of needing to be emptied, her milk leaking onto her shirt. She'd pump again as soon as Lilith left the room and store her milk in the fridge where it'd wait for Tabby's return. "I need to be prepared for when she comes home."

"Are you so sure she will come home?"

Vivian sucked in a sharp breath. "How can you ask me that? Your daughter might have disappeared forever, but that won't be Tabby. I won't let it."

The wrinkles marking Lilith's years, despite her best efforts to keep them at bay, grew unexplainably more pronounced. "Haven't you already done enough?"

The question stalled Vivian's breath, stealing her ability to speak. To explain. To profess her undying love for her children. Not like her words would matter anyway. Did Lilith have the same suspicions that continually crept around the edges of her own mind, tormenting her day in and day out?

"I'm taking James to the house on Martha's Vineyard. Sylvie will come too, unless I decide I need someone a little more trustworthy to look after my grandson."

Vivian bolted out of bed, the sudden motion causing dizziness to swim in her head. "You can't do that. You can't take my son from me. He needs his mother."

Lilith pursed her lips. "He needs to be kept safe. That won't happen here until you figure out how to take care for yourself first." Lilith dipped her gaze up and down Vivian's body, judgement coming through every pore. "If that's even possible."

"Please. Lilith. Don't do this. I won't let you." She grabbed Lilith's hand. Her mind raced. She was James' mother. She could stand up to this woman. Put her foot down and demand she back off.

"He's already gone. I'm leaving now with Patrick to meet him and Sylvie."

Anger swelled inside her. "I won't let you do this. I'll call Will. Hell, I'll call the police. James is my son. You have no right to take him from me. From his mother."

The hard lines of Lilith's face softened, and she wrapped her hand around Vivian's. "I have to. I can't let you hurt him. Not again. Not like you might have hurt Tabitha."

The accusation hit her like an arrow to the heart, and all the fight in Vivian's system melted away. She let her hand fall to her side and stumbled back until her knees hit the mattress. She couldn't argue. Couldn't demand a damn thing. Lilith was right. She was the reason James was hurt. She might be the reason Tabitha wasn't sleeping in her crib. She wasn't fit to be anyone's mother.

Crawling under the covers, she closed her eyes and prayed the darkness would come back and carry her away.

14

E ven with all four windows rolled down in Ellen's car, the stench of her sweat and dried mud on her boots hung heavy in the small space. A shower would be heaven right now, but she didn't want to miss her chance to follow William from the house. She'd assumed he'd leave after he was sure she'd stepped foot off their property, but twenty minutes passed, and he still hadn't driven through the front gates of the estate.

Swiping her finger over her phone's screen, Ellen searched for the last number on Vivian's list she needed. Harper Kellington was the one person left to speak to. A number Vivian hadn't written down. A quick Google search listed Harper as the events coordinator at the local hospital.

She located the contact information, pressing the numbers to dial.

"Good afternoon, Hollow's Hope Foundation." A deep tenor boomed through the line.

The husky male voice made Ellen hesitate. "Hi, I'm looking For Harper Kellington."

The steel gates in front of the house swung open, and

William Walker emerged in his expensive, black sports car. Ellen pressed her foot on the brake and shifted into Drive.

"I'm sorry, but Harper isn't in today. I'm Jeff, Harper's temporary replacement."

Replacement? Why did Vivian's friend need to take a leave of absence from her job? Being around for Vivian was nice, but taking extended leave seemed like overkill. "Will Harper be in soon? I spoke with her a few months ago about sponsoring one of the fundraising events the hospital holds. I just wanted to touch base again before I make a final decision." She slid onto the street, making sure to keep a car between her and William.

"I'd be happy to speak with you about that. If you give me your name, I can pull up your file really quick." The sound of fingers hitting a keyboard floated through the speaker.

"I can call back tomorrow. I don't want to be a pain. And this can wait."

William turned in the opposite direction of his law office downtown. Curiosity piqued, she scanned the area. She drove parallel to the Walker's property. Trees lining both sides of the winding road.

"I'm afraid she won't be back for awhile. Really, it's no problem. That's what they pay me for." His jovial laugh echoed across the line.

Shaking her head, she hitched her lips in a grin. She couldn't help but be amused but the man's good nature. "Oh, no. I hope she's not sick. Seems like this is the time of the year people start going down with the flu." A sudden illness wouldn't lead Harper to ask for extended leave, resulting in a temporary replacement, but maybe Jeff would spill some more details if she pressed lightly.

"I'm not sure why she requested so much time off, but if you give me your information, I'd be glad to assist you."

A flash of the conversation she'd walked in on between Harper and Vivian came to her. Hadn't Harper's mother been sick or something? That would explain her absence and make it more difficult to contact her. Jeff might be an easy-going guy, but she'd push her luck if she asked for Harper's personal contact information. She'd look up Harper's information when she got back to the station. "Oh, you know what, someone just stepped in my office. I'll call you back in a minute."

She clicked off before Jeff responded. Dropping her gaze for a second, she found Daniels' number and pressed send. She slowed to let another car in front of her, keeping a sharp eye on the BMW. Her gut told her exactly where William was headed, but she needed to know for sure. Hopefully, he would lead her right to the other woman in the middle of this mystery.

Then she could bust him red-handed, using leverage to squeeze information from him that he thought he was smart enough to keep hidden. She could press him about where he was when Tabitha went missing, as well as ask about his sister. Things didn't add up, and she needed him willing to answer her questions with no chance of dishonesty. William Walker was the kind of man who'd lie with his dying breath. She'd steal any opportunity this man had to squirm away from the truth.

The ringing stopped, and Daniels clicked on the line. "You on your way? Thought you were headed back to the station after interviewing the Walkers."

"That was the plan, but I took a detour." She pressed the speaker button on her phone and placed the device on the little holder on her dashboard. She needed her hands on the wheel and her eyes trained on William's car.

"Anything interesting?" Daniels asked.

"Following William Walker. He's driving on a country road that wraps around his property. Pretty sure he's meeting his mistress."

Daniels whistled, vibrating her speaker. "Be careful. He won't like that."

She chuckled. "That's what I'm hoping for. If I can nail his ass about the affair, maybe I can use the threat of a scandal to get him to open up about whatever he's hiding."

"Isn't the affair what he's hiding?"

Ellen lifted her shoulders. "Maybe, but my gut tells me there's more and there's only one way to find out."

"When you're done with that, I pulled up pictures of Daphne Walker, as well as the description given of the girl the day she went missing. No mention of a ribbon."

Disappointment pressed her back against her upholstered seat. "Dammit. What about her hair? Did it say if it was up or down?"

"Umm, let me check." The sound of shuffling papers rustled in the background. "Let's see. Yellow gingham dress. White patent leather shoes with white lacy socks. Blonde hair in a ponytail."

She nodded along with the description. "Might have forgotten to mention the ribbon. But if it was pulled up, chances are higher the ribbon was hers than if her hair was down. Something to ask Lilith Walker about. A mother wouldn't forget that detail."

Her mind flashed to Sara's stubby brown ponytail, tied on top of her head with a bright blue ribbon to match her eyes. She rubbed the pain in her chest until her airways opened again.

Another thought dawned on her. "Weird thing for a little girl to wear for a game of hide and seek with her brother."

"I thought the same thing. I mean, rich people like to always look nice, I guess. But let kids be kids."

"See if you can find out what the weather was like the day she disappeared. She was taken in March. Hard to tell if it was nice or they were still fighting off a bitter winter. Either way, I'd think she'd have worn a jacket." William pulled into a tree-lined lane. "Shit."

"What's wrong?" Daniels asked.

"Looks like Walker is going down a private driveway. Surrounded by woods. No way for me to just follow him back there. I'd hoped to grab a house number, park, and poke around a bit. Can't do that here."

"Any space on the side of the road? Or even a small clearing off the road you can hide the car? Then you can hoof it through the woods. Better for you to remain unseen that way anyway."

She scrunched her nose. Her entire morning had been spent navigating the thick forest. The last thing she wanted was to head back into the dense patch of trees, with no idea how long she'd have to walk before reaching a house.

Slowing, she scanned either side of the deserted road. Luckily a thin strip of flat grass met the edge of the shoulder instead of a drainage ditch. A line of trees met the grass, leading into the forest William had disappeared inside. She'd be able to navigate her sedan off the street, it was just a matter of finding a place to wedge her car between the massive trunks keeping guard of the woods to keep her vehicle out of sight.

"Anything else I can do while you're gone?" Daniels cut into her concentration as she continued to search for a pull-off spot.

"Call Jim Ballinger."

"Walker's campaign manager?"

A sliver of open space caught her attention. Cutting the wheel, her car jostled as the tires left the smooth pavement and lumbered along on the soft grass. She crept forward, just enough to conceal her car. Branches scrapped the driver's side door, and leaves crowded her windshield. She winced. "I think this guy knows more than he's saying. William made it sound like he was privy to a lot of information regarding the family. Including his wife's schedule."

"That's odd."

"My thoughts exactly. I want to grill him at the station. Might make him open up a little more about what's happening below the surface." Putting the car in park, she squeezed through the thin space between the barely open door and the base of a towering maple.

"I'll set up an interview. Call me when you're done playing stalker. Good luck."

She chuckled and pocketed her phone. She jogged to the lane William had driven down moments before, making sure to stay hidden from anyone who might travel back down the path. A mailbox sat at the front of the drive. She texted the house number to Daniels, wanting to get as much information as possible about whoever lived here.

Sun filtered through a break in the trees ahead. She slowed her pace, making sure to stay concealed. Daniels was right, sneaking around this way was much easier. She just hoped no one saw her and took a shot, thinking she was an intruder.

A two-story stone cottage appeared. William's fancy-ass car sat in the driveway beside a mid-level luxury SUV. She crept forward, cringing at every snapping twig. No one would hear inside, but outside was a different story. And since she couldn't view the backyard from this angle, there was no telling where William and the resident of the cottage were.

The front door swung open, and Ellen darted behind a tree. Her heart leapt to her throat. She held her breath, straining her ears in an attempt to overhear any snippets of conversation.

A throaty laugh had the hair on her arms raising. A woman's laugh. She ached for Vivian. Even if William was a cold bastard, no woman deserved to be cheated on. Maybe having evidence of her husband's indiscretions would force her to end the marriage and move on to a healthier relationship.

Ellen's own husband hadn't cheated on her, but circumstances beyond her control were what shoved her from a home that had been broken long before her daughter was ripped away. She'd gladly return to her asshole of an ex if it meant having Sara back, but since that wasn't an option, Ellen would never regret her decision to walk away from a man who did nothing but bring her down.

Wanting to make sure she got what she needed to make William squeal, she brought up the camera on her phone. Placing her thumb on the screen, she crouched low to the ground and counted to three. On three, she pivoted to the side, staying as concealed as possible, and snapped several photos.

She moved back to her hiding spot at the base of the tree and studied the pictures. William had a petite woman pulled in close, her head nestled under his chin. He pressed his lips to the top of her head in a position that seemed way sweeter than she'd imagined him capable of.

Swiping to the next photo, her pulse picked up. There could be no misinterpreting this relationship. No question that the woman in the woods with her lips locked with William's was the same woman in the picture Vivian had found in William's office.

"Call me later. I love you." A cheery voice called followed by the sound of footsteps. A car door opened and closed, and the BMW made its way down the long driveaway.

Ellen said a quick prayer. If William spotted her car parked on the road, no way he'd just let it be. She'd wait a minute until she was sure William was well on his way to wherever the hell he planned to go next, then she'd go back through the forest for the last time today. A hot shower and even hotter meal waited for her.

A baby's cry sounded from the house. Not the scream of a toddler or even the wails of a child whose lungs were developed enough to deepen their cries. No, there was no mistaking the piercing cries of a young baby. No more than a few months old. Ellen sucked in a breath.

"I'm coming, little one."

The front door closed, and Ellen's blood turned cold.

15

The silence that filled Vivian's bedroom was deafening. The airwaves stirred with nothing but dust particles from the heating vents. Two days ago, she'd have given anything for just one minute of silence. Now, it was an agonizing reminder of everything she'd had ripped away.

Forty-eight hours. Wasn't that the magic number the police always spouted about missing children? If not found within that window, the chances drop drastically of returning the child where it belonged.

So she'd lay here in the dark, in the silence, and torment herself with memories of everything she'd wished she'd done with her children. One who was stolen from her stroller on a bright, sunny morning. The other taken by the hand and led out of the house without even a goodbye kiss.

Pain like a kick to the ribs stole her breath. She turned to her side, cradling her stomach. Tears leaked from the corners of her eyes. Weights pulled down her eyelids. She didn't want to check the time. She had nowhere to be—nothing to do. All she wanted was to lose herself in sleep, even though the bright rays of sun filtered through the partially opened drapes.

"What are you doing still in bed? I've been calling and texting you all morning." Harper's concerned voice drifted toward her. The mattress dipped, and a gentle palm rested between Vivian's shoulder blades. "Are you okay?"

The temptation to burrow under the warm covers had her curling her fingertips around the edges of her blanket. The need to keep what happened with James a secret sat heavy on her chest. Admitting her failures out loud made it too real. Even if it was to her best friend.

Harper smoothed away a lock of hair from her forehead. "Honey. Did you hear something about Tabitha?"

The fear twisting the lines of Harper's face had Vivian pulling herself to a sitting position—the amount of energy it took to move turned her cheeks warm. She couldn't let her friend think the worst about Tabby, which meant she needed to come clean about James. "No word on Tabby." Her daughter's name grated against her dry throat.

"Okay. That's not ideal, but the day's still young. Who knows what the detective will find today? She might be on her way to rescue her right now."

Vivian shook her head, the tears returning and falling down her cheeks in big, fat drops. "She'd call if she'd found her. And now James is gone, too."

Harper shot to her feet, eyes wide and full of terror. "What happened? What do you mean he's gone? How is that possible?"

"Lilith took him. Away to Martha's Vineyard. He's not safe here with me." She covered her face with her palms, and sobs wracked her body—all the turmoil and horror of the last few days spilling forward with no way to control it.

Harper's arms came quickly around her. "She can't do that. You're his mother. He needs you. You have to fight her. Stand up for yourself. Stop letting these people control you, honey."

She fell against Harper's shoulder, unable to keep herself

upright. "She's right. I can't take care of him. He fell last night and hit his head on the desk. He got hurt again because of me. Because I can't be a normal mother who can take care of her kids. James was taken away because of me. Tabby is gone because of me." Hysteria spiraled higher and higher, mounting pressure in her chest until she thought she'd explode.

Clutching her shoulders, Harper pulled away to face her. Wild wisps of hair spilled from her bun, and she hadn't even bothered with makeup this morning. "Listen to me. You are a great mother. You need to be with your son. Especially now. Call Lilith and tell her to get back here."

"I've called her. I've called Will. No one will answer. I don't know what to do." She leaned back, resting her head against her tufted headboard.

"Where's Will? Does he know what his mother did? I find it hard to believe he'd just let her take him away. He might have a lot of shitty qualities, but he adores that boy. He'd want him close."

Vivian shrugged and finally dropped her gaze to the red numbers screaming the time from her alarm clock. 10:30 a.m. She'd slept away most of the morning. Not like it mattered. She had no children needing her attention—nothing waited for her.

Harper swiveled toward the nightstand. "Where's your phone? Maybe he's called. Or that detective. You can't just hide away in your room."

Heaving a sigh, Vivian swiped her phone from the stand. The battery was low. Placing the device on the charger hadn't been high on her priority list the night before. Missed calls and texts from Harper dominated the screen, as well as one from the therapist's office. "Dr. Kudrin left a voicemail."

"Good. Maybe you can go in and see him today."

Indecision had her floating her finger above the button to dial her voicemail. She'd reached out to Dr. Kudrin to retrieve her memories, but what was the point? The more she tried, the worse her life became. She ran her knuckles over the thin band of her watch. She didn't want to remember what happened that day. Not anymore. She feared the truth would only make things worse.

Harper blew out a frustrated breath. "Call. Now. You can't just lie here and do nothing."

Vivian pushed the button and pressed the phone to her ear.

"Hi, Mrs. Walker. This is Dr. Kudrin. I wondered if we could schedule an appointment for this afternoon. I know it's last minute, but with your pressing situation, I thought you'd be able to squeeze this in. Please get back to me at your earliest convenience."

Straightening, Vivian stared at Harper. "He wants me to come in this afternoon."

Harper grabbed her hands and squeezed. "That's good, right? Maybe he's figured out a way to help you."

Vivian dropped her gaze and slid her hands from under Harper's. Did she really want the doctor to help her now? After the flash of a vision last night?

"What's wrong? Why aren't you calling him back?"

"What if I hurt her? What if while I couldn't control my actions, I picked up my daughter and did something so unthinkable, so horrible, that I could never live with myself? What if I'm the reason she isn't here?"

"You don't really think that's possible, do you?" Harper extended a hand, but Vivian flinched away.

She shook her head and lifted a palm to stop Harper's sympathetic gestures. She didn't deserve them. "It's possible. I mean, look at my history. I walked toward the stairs while pregnant and fell, losing the baby I carried. I shoved James too hard on the swing." A fist squeezed her throat, memories crashing into her brain of her little boy huddled on the ground, blood staining his clothes.

Harper twisted a silver band on her ring finger—the only reminder of a life she'd lost. A husband gone. A child never born. Her hazel eyes latched onto the motion of the ring. "Wouldn't it be better to know?"

A wave of anguish crashed over Vivian. Harper had always been her champion, her one source of support and friendship. A part of her hoped Harper would step in and tell her what a ridiculous thought it was. Demand she toss away the idea of being the one responsible for hurting Tabby.

Instead, Harper refused to meet her gaze as she told Vivian it was better to know for sure if Vivian had killed her own child than to sit around wondering.

Maybe she was right. At least the fear of the unknown would vanish. She could finally be punished for all her failures and know that James would forever be safe away from her. "Okay. I will go in and talk to him if he still has the time."

"It might be the only way to ever get any closure." Harper finally lifted her gaze, and a myriad of emotions sprung forth from her wide eyes.

Closure.

Vivian sucked in a deep breath and closed her eyes as the pain of the word zapped all her energy. Closure meant coming to terms with whatever had happened on that bluff. Closure meant that Tabitha would never make it home.

"Can you drive me?" Lilith might not be here anymore, but Will would still find out if Patrick drove her to some unknown destination. The sad state of her marriage was the last thing she was worried about, but she'd rather avoid a blow-up if possible.

Harper frowned and shook her head. "I'm so sorry. But I can't."

Vivian winced. "Is it your mom? I'm a horrible friend. I'm so sorry. I haven't even asked how she's feeling."

"Totally understandable." Harper frowned and ran a hand

over the comforter. "You've had so much going on, and I haven't wanted to burden you with anything else."

"Your mother's health and how you feel are never a burden to me. Especially now. When you're the only one holding me together." She forced a smile and hoped her friend couldn't see how much effort it took to ask after her mother. Harper deserved to have a friend who cared about her—cared about her family. Even though the weight of someone else's problems might crush her. That's why she hadn't commented on Harper's disheveled hair and deep lines that had suddenly appeared around the corners of her eyes before now. "Is everything okay? Did the surgery to repair her hip go well?"

Harper's shoulders rose and fell on a deep sigh. "The surgery went fine, and Mom's healing well. But she needs extensive therapy."

Vivian furrowed her brow. "Don't they offer physical therapy at the assisted living complex where she lives?" Even though she'd been friends with Harper for years, she'd never met her friend's mother. Harper had helped her mom move into an assisted living facility twenty miles away right after they'd met.

"I wish. That'd make everything so much easier. I have to get her into a long-term care facility, and my brother is raising hell about the whole thing. He wants her closer to him, which is a couple hours away from me. The whole thing just sucks."

Having to make decisions for parents was something beyond Vivian's scope of experience. Her parents had coddled her and tried to control her until the day they died in a car accident while she was in college. Hell, who was she kidding? Making decisions for herself was something she had limited experience with. "What does your mom want?"

"She's torn. Wants to make me happy because we've always been so close. But this could be a chance for her to get closer to my brother."

"What are you going to do?"

"I'm going to tour a bunch of places that take Mom's insurance by my brother over the next few days. She'll be discharged soon, and they need to know where she's going. I told her I'd do some leg work, then she can make an informed decision about where she'd be the most comfortable." She drew in a shuddering breath. "I want her to stay close, but I can't be selfish."

A rush of sympathy pooled in Vivian's core, and she smoothed a palm over Harper's arm. She'd been a shitty friend to not take a minute to check on Harper. Friendship was a two-way street, even when Vivian was barely keeping her head above water. "You're anything but selfish."

Harper shoved a hand through her hair and stood, shoulders drooping. "It doesn't feel that way. I want to stack the deck in my favor and only show her the good places close by. I can't imagine not having my mother near. She's been my rock my entire life. Without her—I don't even know what I'd do." Tears hovered over her lashes. She sniffed and pressed the tips of her fingers against the corners of her closed eyes. "And now here I am whining to you about my mom maybe moving when you're searching for one child and the other's been taken from under your nose."

Vivian cringed, the description of her heartbreaking state of affairs stealing the air from her lungs. She cleared her dry throat, wishing she'd set a glass of water on her nightstand before she'd fallen asleep. "The severity of my problems doesn't diminish the size of yours. You have every right to be upset about what's happening with your mom. I wish there was something I could do to help."

"Thanks, but I have to head out of town as soon as I leave here. That's why I stopped by when you didn't answer. I wanted to tell you what's going on and why I won't be around for a few days."

Vivian bit into her cheeks to keep from letting her emotions show on her face. Harper was like an extra limb—the only one left for her to lean on. And now she'd be torn away. Just like Tabby and James. "You've got to look out for your mom. I understand."

Harper fixed a sad smile on her face. "I'm only a phone call away. Day or night. And this shouldn't take more than two—three—days tops. I'll be back before you know it, and when I return, I'm sure Tabby will be here waiting. James, too."

"I hope you're right." But a sinking feeling in the pit of Vivian's stomach warned her not to be too hopeful. She might know the monster who took James, but Lilith's power and influence made her untouchable. Even to the mother of the child she'd swept away.

And Tabitha was still missing without an indication of who took her or where she'd gone. Dread spread out from Vivian's core, entangling her organs and reaching throughout her body. She'd go to see Dr. Kudrin. She owed it to Tabby to try and uncover the truth. Even if it meant discovering she was the real monster.

16

The fire crackled in the hearth, giving Vivian something to focus on beside Dr. Kudrin's owl-like eyes and her fried nerves. She sat on the same sofa as the day before, hands clasped in her lap and back straight. The heat blasting from the flames did nothing to warm her, but she doubted anything would ever chase away the icy grip of despair clinging to her bones.

"Would you like something to drink, Mrs. Walker?" Dr. Kudrin asked. "It's about time for my afternoon coffee. I always need that extra zip of caffeine to push me through the rest of the day." He faced her from his weathered chair, hands entwined in a sturdy grip as he leaned his forearms on his thighs.

Her stomach growled, reminding her she'd put nothing in it since the day before. The acidic coffee might not sit well, but tea might be okay. "Do you happen to have any hot tea?"

"I'm sure I can find some. Give me a second."

She watched him hurry out the door then returned her gaze to the flicking flames. She tapped her toe against the carpet, ticking the passing seconds off in her mind. Passing time the cab driver she'd been forced to call would rack up the meter as he waited in the parking lot. Of course Lilith had secured Patrick in her drive to Martha's Vineyard, and Vivian couldn't risk driving herself. Not when chances were high that a third seizure lurked around the corner, just waiting to strike.

"I managed to find some Earl Grey." Dr. Kudrin walked slowly with a mug in each hand, arms held outstretched probably so the scalding hot liquid wouldn't burn him if he spilled. "Sorry I don't have a proper teacup."

Vivian hurried to his side, grabbing the cup he offered. "Oh, that's not a problem. I appreciate the effort." She settled back into her seat and wished she could grab the blanket thrown over the couch, tuck her feet under her butt, and close her eyes. Instead, she took a sip of unflavored tea, letting the bitter liquid slide down her throat. The instant it hit her stomach, bile began to swirl. She forced a swallow and set her mug beside her on a little stand.

"How are you? Did you write in a journal like I recommended?" Dr. Kudrin mimicked her motion and discarded his coffee beside him after a long sip.

She chewed her lip, not wanting to get into the messy details of what transpired the previous night. But if this wasn't a safe space for spilling all her secrets, where was? "I did, but it's hard to know for sure if the images in my mind are forgotten memories resurfacing or my imagination conjuring up details."

He nodded, as if what she said made perfect sense. "Did you have a reaction to the writing?"

She shrugged. "I had another seizure, but once I started picturing details, I fell into a stupor while trying to pull forward more memories—more facts that could make sense of everything." She cupped her palm over her wrist and rubbed her thumb over her watch. She couldn't bring herself to tell him what she saw. It was too much. Too hard to utter the words out loud.

"Interesting. I wonder, would it help if you stuck with simply writing and not straining to remember if it would help."

"Maybe. Did you find anything last night while you were researching?"

He retrieved a notepad from the wooden trunk turned coffee table in front of him. "Nothing that pertains to this. Most of the research that's been done revolves around memory loss that occurs as a result of having epilepsy. Short-term memory loss. That kind of thing."

"Oh." The word was so little yet the only thing she could muster—the only sound to convey the devastating disappointment at the therapist not having any secret new tools to help her. She hadn't been sure before she'd arrived, but her reaction showed she wanted to know what happened that day after all—even if it painted her as the villain.

"I'm sorry. I know that's not what you wanted to hear."

"No. It's not. I thought you'd have found something if you asked to see me this afternoon."

"I touched base to see if the writing worked. Can you tell me what you wrote? What you might have remembered that had you straining so hard?"

She shifted in her seat and licked her dry lips. This was why she was here. She needed to dive in and get it over with. Keeping things from this man would accomplish nothing. "First I wrote down the same things we spoke about. Sights, sounds, smells from that morning. A flicker of a shadow appeared over my daughter's face. Something I'd never remembered before. I tried to picture it, to bring it into focus. That's when I seized."

He wrote something on his notepad. "And after the seizure?"

Clearing her throat, she concentrated on her lap, not wanting to see any judgement skitter across his face. "I woke up hours later. In my bed. I didn't try to remember any more because my son was hurt while I blacked out. He'd been on my lap and fell off, hitting his head."

"That's unfortunate," Dr. Kudrin said. "Did this seizure impact you any differently than previous ones? Is it normal for you to suffer seizures so close together, or is reaching for these memories really throwing you off balance?"

Vivian blinked and tilted her head to the side. "My son hurting himself because of me is just unfortunate?"

He lifted his gaze, bushy brows almost touching above his nose. "Why, yes. No one wants to see a child get hurt, but it's not like you purposely made him fall and hit his head. Accidents are always unfortunate."

Accident. She rolled the word around in her brain. No, what happened with James wasn't an accident. She was at fault for harming her child. "James would never have fallen if it wasn't for me. I'm the reason he was hurt."

The lines of Dr. Kudrin's face thinned. "Mrs. Walker, you are not at fault here. Your epilepsy does not transform you into someone who must take responsibility for actions outside of your control."

She shook her head, every fiber of her being refuting his statement. "I should have anticipated what would happen if I wasn't more careful."

"So you should never hold your son because you might have a seizure? Do you hear how ridiculous that sounds?"

"I...I mean...well." She couldn't find the words to make him understand why she should have predicted the outcome with James. Frustration pushed her to her feet and she paced along the thin strip of carpet in front of the sofa.

Stopping, she faced the doctor with one arm wrapped around her middle, her other hand covering her mouth. "I've hurt him before. I should know better by now. He's not safe with me. Neither of them are." Pressure expanded against her ribcage. Her breath hitched, the racing of her heart making her pulse race and palms sweat. The truth was right in front of her —had been all along—and she couldn't hide from the awfulness of it anymore.

Dr. Kudrin set down his pen and paper, his gaze fixed on her. "Do you love your children?"

"More than anything." Her voice caught—her arms ached to hold James and Tabitha.

"Have you ever hurt them while conscious and aware of your surroundings?"

She shook her head. "Never."

"Have you done everything you can think of to keep them safe and protected?"

"Yes."

"Then you're a good mother."

She closed her eyes and let the words wash over her and wear away a little of the doubt and self-loathing she'd worn draped across her weary shoulders for too long.

"I would like to take a minute and discuss your seizures," Dr. Kudrin said, breaking into her thoughts. "I asked a second ago, but you never answered me. Do you often have two seizures this close together?"

Sighing, she settled back in her spot. Wasting time talking about her seizures wasn't what she'd hoped to do here, but it had to be better than jumping into the deep end only to emerge wet, shaken, and with no more answers than before. "They always come in threes."

He scooped up his notes and scribbled something down. "That's common. For seizures to follow a pattern."

"Glad something about me is normal." Snorting, she propped her elbow on the arm of the sofa and rested her head in her hand.

He dipped his chin, his glasses sliding just a tiny fraction down his nose. "One thing I've learned over the years is that no one is normal."

She smiled. Something about the sincerity in his tone and twinkle in his eyes relaxed her muscles, almost made her forget she was speaking to a trained therapist and not chatting with an old friend. A friend who didn't pass any judgement on her shortcomings.

"Are there any other patterns or similarities with your seizures?" he asked, getting back on track.

"I've learned my triggers. Lack of sleep. High emotions. Stressed. I'm surprised I haven't had more since I had Tabitha. She isn't a good sleeper. I'm lucky to get three hours a night. Which in turn makes me emotional and stressed." She twirled her finger in the air. "A vicious circle."

He set his notepad on his lap, hands rested on top. "That must be tough. Especially with another child to care for."

The urge to cry had her biting her bottom lip. "It is. Some days I don't want to even get out of bed. Just want to pretend I don't hear the constant crying or refuse to tend to my son. It's like I'm treading water in the middle of the ocean while rain pelts me from above—obstacles at every angle and no chance of making it out alive." She let her elbow fall, dropping her chin to stare down at her lap. "That was a horrible thing to say. I'm sorry."

"Mrs. Walker. Please look at me."

She forced herself to do what he asked. His eyes didn't look so owlish now, but filled with concern and compassion. His lips dipped down, but not an ounce of pity showed on his full face. Her throat tightened, and she didn't even attempt to speak. What else could she say?

"Never apologize for how you feel. Being a mother is hard. Hell, sometimes just being a human being is hard. We're all trying to make it through life the best we can. The reason you were compelled to come and see me is truly horrendous, and I hope to help you find your daughter. But I'm glad you found your way to my door because you are worthy and you deserve your feelings to be heard and validated."

Her jaw dropped and she fought the urge to leap from the couch and throw her arms around this man who'd just said the kindest things she'd ever heard. Her entire life had been filled with people making excuses for her, apologizing for actions she couldn't control, or confirming her deep-rooted belief that she wasn't capable of even making her own decisions. Could they have all been wrong? Could she really be enough—enough of a woman and mother and wife to live her life without apology?

"I looked over the forms you filled out yesterday and noticed you aren't currently taking any medications. Is that correct?" He weaved his fingers through the handle on his mug and lifted it to his lips.

She nodded.

"May I ask why you aren't taking your seizure medication?"

Tensing, she mentally prepared herself for explaining her decision for the hundredth time. Everyone disagreed with her choice to not start her medication again after Tabby was born. A doctor would find her fear downright laughable. "I had a hard time seeing a pregnancy to term. After several miscarriages, I decided to not take the medications when I became pregnant with James. Even though I was told there was no correlation, I couldn't help but feel like the pills did something to cause my miscarriages."

"That's a natural assumption. No one can blame you for thinking the two could be connected." He leaned forward, taking his now-familiar position, forearms on knees. "But are you pregnant now?"

She frowned, not understanding the relevance of the question. "No. Why?"

He shrugged. "Then why not take the medication?"

"I'm breastfeeding. I don't want to contaminate my milk." She winced as her breasts grew heavy. It never failed, if she thought about her milk or heard a baby cry, her body took is as a cue to kick into gear.

"See," he said, pointing a pen toward her. "Good mother."

She couldn't help but smile.

"I'm sorry you experienced miscarriages. Were you taking medications with every pregnancy that was lost?"

An image of waking on the marble floor at the base of the stairs, blood soaked through her jeans, flashed in her mind. The deep pain of loss that never seemed to leave flooded her system. All the moisture in her mouth evaporated, and she reached for her tea. She took a sip, cringing as the tepid water hit her tongue. "No. I lost another baby because I fell down the stairs when I had a seizure."

He tented his brows. "I'm sorry. That had to be a very traumatic experience."

She nodded. "Yes. But I had to get away. I had to get down the stairs. Even with a blank mind and no control of my muscles, my body seemed to understand getting away was my only choice."

A memory of the scent of her blood floated into her nostrils, the sensation of waking to the crippling agony in her stomach overcame her. The overwhelming knowledge that another baby would never be born.

"Taking actual steps while you're experiencing an epileptic episode is very rare. Does that happen often?"

She shrugged. "I move my arms and legs, not like shaking uncontrollably and falling to the floor, but more sharp, jerky motions. Sometimes I just freeze and stare. I don't often end up in a different location, unless someone carries me to my bed after I pass out."

"Attempting to walk down the stairs isn't a usual occurrence?"

She stifled a sigh. She didn't want to think about the huge fight she'd had with Will right before the accident. She didn't want to examine the emotional pain of realizing her husband couldn't have cared less that the life she'd carried inside her was gone. She'd never forget waking to the sight of him standing over her, a smirk on his lips—morphing into concern only when footsteps padded toward them. Something she tried to tell herself she'd imagined...couldn't possibly be real. But there was no point in pretending now.

"Mrs. Walker?"

"I'm sorry. What?" She blinked, trying to remember his question.

"What were you just thinking about?"

She stared past him, details of that day filtering back. "That day was so horrible. After having James, I thought everything would be great. I was pregnant with our daughter and everything had progressed so well. I was so close to my due date, and savoring each moment. I'd told my husband we could stop trying for more kids—now that we'd have two."

"You only wanted two kids?"

"I dreamed of a houseful, but my husband didn't agree. I had to twist his arm to try for a second. He said he had the boy he always wanted. A son to carry on the family legacy. That's all he needed." Sadness tugged at her mouth. So many hopes and dreams dashed because of her husband's refusal to bend.

"You said that day was horrible. Was the day bad before you fell?"

Tilting her head, she tried to bring the rest of the day into focus. She blocked out the memories as often as possible, and whenever they slipped through the cracks of her mind, it always spotlighted the worst moments—the aftermath of it all. "My husband and I had a fight. Right before."

"Makes sense."

She scrunched her nose. "Why's that?"

"You mentioned emotion and stress are triggers. What were you fighting about?"

She'd never connected those dots. The fight—the constant strain of Will pressuring her—triggering her. Screwing her lips to the side, she struggled to remember the argument. The last couple years there were too many disagreements to remember which one was when. But at that time, James was almost a year. "We argued about our son's first birthday party. I wanted small and simple. Will wanted something big and splashy. Something he could use for publicity."

She'd hoped with the birth of their first child, Will would change. Want to spend more time together as a family. Instead, he wanted to use their child to win favor with the public. The first time she'd ever resisted his big plans was when he'd wanted to control James' birthday party. She'd snapped, he'd grabbed her wrist, and she slapped him.

A beat of anxiousness pulsed her heart. "I slapped him. He grabbed my hand and wouldn't let go. He was so surprised I fought back. Refused to just let him do what he wanted. His eyes got so big—so angry. He took a step toward me and I backed up...to the edge of the stairs. I needed to get away, so I turned to run down the stairs."

She gasped, the past coming back to her with full clarity. Not the forgotten moments that seemed lost forever, but the second before she passed out. She locked her gaze to Dr. Kudrin, her limbs trembling. Fear twisted her gut. "My husband shoved me in the back." She touched her head in the same spot that had throbbed for days after her tumble. "Will's the reason I lost my baby."

17

The florescent light above Ellen's desk at the precinct gave off a low buzz—constant and annoying as hell. After leaving the dreaded woods where William Walker's mistress lived, she'd rushed home and given herself enough time to get through a cold shower and stuff her face with a protein bar. Now, after a long day, she was irritated and hungry. Not a good combination.

A mess of papers cluttered her desk and even more information dominated her computer screen. She shoved a hand through her still-damp hair. Not wanting to waste time on her appearance, she'd opted to let her long strands air dry. It didn't matter if her mousy brown hair frizzed a little and didn't lay flat and shiny. No one gave two shits about that here. Especially her.

A knock on her open door lifted her head. Daniels lingered in the doorway, a file in hand. "Come in." She dipped her head toward the single chair in front of her desk.

He dropped down and tossed the file on top of the overflowing paperwork already demanding her attention. "Here's everything I could find on the woman from the cottage. Name is Jessica Stevens. Has lived at that address for the last ten years. Mortgage is in her name, but I did a little digging and the payments for the house aren't coming from her account."

Ellen leaned back in her chair. "Let me guess. William pays."

"Yep. Has the entire time she's lived there."

Ellen raised her brows. William paying for his lover's house payment wasn't surprising, but the duration of their affair was. "That was before he married Vivian."

"The two go back to childhood. Same schools. Same social circles. But her dad was involved in some sort of scandal when they were in high school. My guess? William was pressured to forget her since her family's actions could hurt his political aspirations." Daniels ran a palm over his face then through his receding hairline. Fatigue showed in the dark circles under his eyes and drooping posture.

"Good guess. Any idea what Jessica's dad was busted for?"

"Money laundering and fraud. He's still in prison. But even more interesting, his nephew is Jim Ballinger."

"No shit?" The strings kept overlapping, the secrets growing more interesting. "I wonder if Jim would cover for Jessica if she took Tabitha? The crying I heard coming from her house was from a little baby. No doubt about it."

Leaning forward, Daniels flipped open the file and slid out the first page. "You didn't hear Tabitha. At least, there's a chance it was a different baby you heard, even if Tabitha was in that cottage."

She grabbed the paper and studied the sheet. "A birth certificate?"

"Two actually." He swept out another sheet for her inspection. "Jessica has two children. A nine-year-old daughter and a two-month-old son."

She studied the information on the scanned documents. "No father is listed for either child."

"I noticed that, but I have a feeling I know who dear old dad is."

She locked eyes with Daniels over the paper. "Walker."

"That'd be my guess. A question for Ballinger." He swiveled toward the standard-issue round clock on the wall behind him. "He should be here any minute. You want to talk to him in here?"

She bit the inside of her cheek and considered her options. "I want you with me for the interview. It'd be too cramped in here. Let's use the conference room."

"I'll get it set up." Daniels pushed to his feet, a yawn stretching his mouth. "Sorry. Long day."

"We can call it quits after this. Not much else to do after we talk to Ballinger. Just more bullshit to wade through, and I can do most of that at home. After I eat a big juicy steak."

Daniels rubbed a hand over his stomach. "Don't mention food. The wife has dinner waiting for me."

She laughed and watched him go. Daniels might have a good ten years on her, but he hadn't once made comments or acted annoyed taking orders from her. Not to mention what a huge help he'd been digging up information and sorting out interviews. She'd make sure to mention to Captain Marther what an asset Daniels had been.

The phone on her desk rang. "Detective Olsen."

"Mr. Jim Ballinger just arrived. Said he has an appointment to speak with you."

"Thanks. I'll meet him in the lobby and walk him back." Standing, she hung up the phone and gathered the mess of papers from her desk. She straightened them into a somewhat neat stack, shoved them in a manilla file, and strolled out. She hadn't been a part of the interviews with William's staff, and she'd have to try damn hard not to let the information she'd just learned color her judgement.

The evening hour made the police station abnormally quiet

—at least to her. She usually put in her hours during the day at the station, when she wasn't running around trying to solve a case. Any later hours were spent in her home office with a giant cup of coffee and whatever junk food she had on hand. She could swing by the break room and fill a to-go cup and chance something from the vending machine, but the sludge at the bottom of the pot would probably eat through her stomach lining.

The lack of any uniforms sitting at their desks made her trip across the large room quick and uneventful. She opened the door to the lobby and came face-to-face with a medium-sized man with perfectly tousled black hair and at least a day's worth of stubble on his square jaw. A laptop bag hung over his shoulder, and he scrunched his face in such an irritated scowl she would have missed the nervous energy tapping from his loafered foot if she hadn't been looking for it.

She propped the door open with her hip and extended a hand. "Mr. Ballinger. Thanks for coming in."

He cupped his palm in hers, gave a sturdy shake and a nod. "Not sure what more we have to discuss, but whatever you need to help find Tabitha."

"Appreciate that. Follow me, please." She waited for him to take the edge of the door then skirted around the clutter of desks in the middle of the room to get to the conference room where Daniels waited. She halted at the doorway and waved Mr. Ballinger through before following behind and closing the door.

Daniels stood from the U-Shaped tables that dominated the small space and dipped his chin. "Nice to see you again. Take a seat."

Jim pinched together his mouth and took a seat across from where Daniels stood. "Officer. What can I do for you?"

Ellen strolled to an empty chair at the head of the room,

adjacent from Daniels, but remained on her feet. "We just have a few follow up questions for you."

Jim lifted the thick strap from his shoulder and let his bag fall at his feet. "Ask away."

She set down the file. She could dance around the truth and wait for the man to trip up, or she could just come straight at him with everything she knew. Throw him off balance with the truth—truth he no doubt thought was well hidden.

To hell with dancing, she had no time to waste and William's campaign manager was probably just as good a bull-shitter as his boss. If not better. Decision made, she wheeled out the chair and sat, swiveling to face Jim. "I want to know why you lied to Officer Daniels about where William Walker was on the morning his daughter was kidnapped."

The pinched-up face before her became even tighter, blue eyes narrowed as if considering his options.

She held up a hand. "Before you answer, remember that lying to an officer about an ongoing investigation is considered obstruction of justice. Not to mention if your lies are the reason I can't find a missing child, it just makes you look like an asshole."

Jim placed his clenched fists on top of the table, knuckles white. "I was told Mr. Walker was in the office that morning. As I wasn't in until after his daughter turned up missing, I had no reason to question what I'd been told by the staff."

She had to hand it to him—he was good. Quick on his feet. He'd have to be if he was in charge of getting William Walker elected to the senate. "Makes sense. Don't you think, Officer Daniels?"

He shrugged. "I suppose. Seems fishy to me, though. Also means someone in the office *did* lie to cover for the boss. Not to mention the fact Mr. Walker wasn't where he claimed to be when questioned by the police. Why would *he* lie? Especially when it's his daughter at risk."

"Mr. Walker has his reasons for everything he does. Doesn't mean he always confides in me. I run his campaign, not his personal life."

"But you are told about his wife's daily activities. Where she'll be and what she'll be doing." She wagged a finger in Jim's direction like a mother who caught a child in a fib. "And don't try to refute that claim because Mr. Walker told us that himself."

Red clashed against the dark whiskers on his face. "Mr. Walker doesn't want me to ever be caught off guard. If I don't have all the information, I can't be prepared for what could happen."

She lifted a shoulder. "Makes sense. Even though I don't understand what Vivian Walker could do that you'd need to be prepared for."

Jim snorted. "Then you don't know her as well as you think you do."

She narrowed her eyes. "Care to elaborate?"

He licked his lips, eyes shifting. "She needs to be cared for —looked after—or she can find herself in trouble."

"Because of the epilepsy?"

Jim nodded.

She waited for him to continue but was given nothing more on the subject. She made a mental note to find out more about Vivian Walker. Her first impression had raised red flags. Painted a picture of a woman who played victim and didn't let on how much she really knew. Over the past few days, Ellen had reconsidered and reevaluated Vivian. Maybe her sympathy over the affair and kinship over a shared heartbreak had clouded her judgement.

Flipping open the file folder, she opted for a different approach. "How long have you worked with William Walker?"

Jim lifted his eyes, as if seeking the answer above his head.

"Five years. He was diligent about setting the groundwork for his campaign years in advance."

She nodded. "Sounds like Mr. Walker is a good planner." She slipped out a sheet of paper and lifted the edges so Daniels could see where she was going.

"Absolutely. And good move on Walker's part to hire someone he's known for so long. From childhood, right?"

Jim sat straighter on his chair and bounced his gaze between them.

Ellen tapped the pad of her finger against the edge of the table. "No. That's not right. He met Jessica in elementary school. Jim wasn't introduced into the group until high school. Right? Or am I getting my dates crossed?"

"What do you know about Jessica?" Jim clenched his jaw.

"I know she's William Walker's mistress and has been for years. I know where she lives and that she has two children. Now, I'm not positive those kids are William's since his name wasn't on either of their birth certificates, but chances are high he's the father." She swished her lips to the side. "Is that all, Daniels? Or am I missing anything?"

He pointed a pencil toward her and shook the end. "You left out the part about Jessica Stevens' dad being a criminal. That's a pretty big issue for a wannabe senator."

She raised her brows and smirked. "Not as big as a secret family waiting in the wings. Hell, waiting right behind that grand estate he keeps his legitimate family in."

"What do you want from me?" Jim asked.

Ellen smiled. "I want to know all of William Walker's secrets. I want to confirm he was with Jessica the morning he claimed to be at work. I want to know all about that missing sister of his. And I want to know if you think he had anything to do with his daughter vanishing into thin air." She fanned out the rest of the pictures and damaging documents in front of Jim.

Jim blinked and reared back, as if each question was a slap in the face. "You think William would hurt his child?"

"I think he keeps a lot hidden. Maybe he wasn't the one who snatched Tabitha from her stroller, but I wouldn't be surprised if he knows who did. So tell me. What am I missing? What secrets are lingering in his closet that could be connected to my case?"

Daniels leaned forward, pressing his gut against the table. "Let's be real for a second. Politicians usually have to skirt the law a bit to get to a place of power. It's only natural. Is there anyone out there who'd want to hurt Mr. Walker? Who Mr. Walker owes or who he wronged in some way?"

Ellen liked the angle Daniels pressed. She hated to admit it, even to herself, but she'd been so focused on William as the bad guy that her mind hadn't ventured to William being involved in something shady. Something that would cause retaliation.

"William Walker is an honorable man who deserves to take his family's seat in the senate."

Ellen tapped on the photo she'd printed of William kissing a woman who wasn't his wife. "I don't think the voters will think he's too honorable if they see this. Spill."

Jim forced a swallow, his bobbing Adam's apple prominent. "William wanted to run for office this year but the current senator wasn't ready to step down."

"Isn't that what an election's for?" Daniels asked.

"Yes. When you have two nominees from opposite parties competing for the same seat. Not when you have two Democrats who both want the same position." Jim spoke slowly, as if explaining politics to two idiots.

Ellen might not have gone to school for political science, but she kept informed about what was going on. Especially in her own state. "I don't see how that's an issue. Senator Woods isn't running for reelection."

Jim released his tight fists and splayed his hands over the smooth wood. "Senator Woods has held the seat for the past eight years. She wasn't ready to let it go. William made sure she didn't have a choice."

"What does that mean?" Her blood pressure spiked and a million thoughts of how William could have played his cards to get his party's bid for senator played in her head.

Jim dropped his gaze, unwilling to meet either of their eyes. "We blackmailed Senator Woods. Threatened to release topless pictures of her with her chief of staff."

Ellen shook her head, disgust for the political system raising in her throat. "You mean to tell me William Walker is cheating on his wife but used another woman's infidelity to get her to step out of his way to the senate?"

Jim nodded.

"What a piece of shit." Ellen choked out a humorless laugh. William's secret mistress didn't take his child, but another secret might be the reason his daughter hadn't slept in her own crib for the last two nights. He might have finally pissed off the wrong person, and Tabitha Walker was caught in the crossfire.

18

Vivian sat at the island in the kitchen she never used and pushed around the eggs on her plate with her fork. She wasn't hungry, but the constant buzzing in her head and shaking in her hands told her that her body needed fuel. Even if the thought of filling her stomach with anything made her cringe.

The housekeeper—Mathilda—washed the egg pan and hurried out of the kitchen. Vivian didn't mind. She'd rather be alone with the rampant thoughts racing through her head. Ever since she'd left Dr. Kudrin's office the day before, she'd been jumping out of her skin. The spot on her back where she *knew* Will had pushed her tingled, and she went back and forth over what to do with this new revelation. A text to Harper had gone unreturned, leaving her tossing and turning all night.

She'd crawled out of bed before the sun had risen only to find the house empty. Even the staff had yet to greet the day when she'd staggered down the hall and came downstairs. For once, her husband's absence beside her in their bed didn't fill her with longing, but relief. Staring him in the face without throwing out accusations would be difficult, but she couldn't just make a claim he could easily refute. One he'd no doubt spin to make her look crazy.

Besides, if she tried to end her marriage or made Will mad, there was no telling what consequences would sweep in and make her life even worse. Better to bide her time. At least until Tabby and James were both home. Then she could examine what to do about Will. Even though her options were limited with no income and no family to support her. But that was a problem for another day.

The door cutting off the kitchen from the formal dining room swung open, and Will stormed in. His perfectly pressed suit and straight-as-a-pin tie appeared out of place with his blood-shot eyes and disheveled hair. "Where's Mother?"

A time once existed when his lack of greeting would have bothered her. Now, she was more surprised that he didn't know where Lilith was. The two of them had the kind of relationship she was once jealous of, but now understood was completely unhealthy and more than a little weird. "You haven't spoken with her?"

He crossed the gleaming tiled floors to the gourmet refrigerator and yanked it open, not even sparing her a glance. "Would I ask where she is if I had? I called and she didn't answer. I stopped by her quarters when I got in and she isn't there. It's important I speak with her. Now."

"Were you here at all yesterday?" The answer was obvious, but she didn't want to be the one to tell Will what his mother had done. He'd be livid, and despite what Harper said the day before, he wouldn't charge in and be her champion. He'd blame her for their son being taken away.

He waved a hand over his shoulder. "I've been busy. Things happened last night I had to see to, so I'm just now getting home. Nothing you need to concern yourself about. But I do need to speak with Mother." He poured a glass of orange juice then grabbed a bottle of vodka from the freezer and added a splash of alcohol to his drink.

She arched a brow. Curiosity gnawed at her, but she knew better than to ask more questions. She wouldn't get answers anyway, but something big must be happening for Will to be so off-center. "Your mother isn't here. She left the night before last."

He finally faced her, back against the marble counter and glass in hand. "Where the hell did she go?"

Vivian pierced a large clump of egg with her fork. "The house at Martha's Vineyard."

"Why? Especially now with Tabitha missing and shit exploding with the campaign. I need her here." He gulped down his breakfast cocktail and wiped the pulp from his top lip with the back of his hand.

She almost smiled—the motion so similar to James. His insistence on seeing Lilith for one small moment just a snapshot of a boy who wanted his mom. Hopefully James would want her around even when he was grown and with his own family to raise. Though she'd never overstep the boundaries Lilith often crossed. Taking the small bite of her barely-touched food, she mentally prepared herself for battle. "Your mom took James. She didn't want him here because she said it wasn't a safe environment."

Will tensed and his gaze turned hard and cold. "What did you do? What happened to James? Mother wouldn't have just left right now. She knows how I depend on her. Something must have happened to force her hand. *You* must have done something."

The silver prongs of the fork clattered against the plate, but she couldn't steady her shaking hand. "I...I had another seizure. James was on my lap and fell."

"Dammit." Will slapped the counter top.

Vivian jumped. "I didn't mean to hurt him."

"You never do. But Mother should have spoken with me before she high-tailed it out of here. Now isn't the time for more scandal. What will people think if they find out my son's been taken from my home?"

Vivian pushed aside her eggs, no longer interested in the pretense of eating. Her head throbbed, and she was so damn tired of tiptoeing around every single issue that popped up in her life. "Your mother had no right to take our son away, but I couldn't stop her. You know how she gets. She had him out of here before I had a chance to get over the effects of my seizure. I was still in bed when she ran off, without even giving me a chance to say goodbye."

Will swished his mouth back and forth then sighed. "You're right. She overstepped this time. I'm sorry."

Vivian blinked. "You are?"

Leaving the half-empty glass on the counter, he made his way to her side. From this close, she could see the imprint the last few days of strain had left on his face. Even his normally smooth jaw was covered with light whiskers—a few days' worth at least.

She longed to reach for him. Regardless of how rocky their marriage had been or the pain the revelations about Will over the last few days had caused, he was still her husband. And he was still hurting over the disappearance of their daughter.

Unsure of how to comfort him—how to let these new walls down around her—she sat still under his scrutiny. The warmth of his nearness had her leaning toward him, but she couldn't handle if he rebuffed her. Couldn't take more rejection from this man who she'd once loved so much.

Will opened his arms and engulfed her into a hug, pressing her tight against his muscled body. She tensed for a beat as memories flitted forward of all the tight grips on her arm and harsh words he'd uttered, but then she let herself relax. Let the tension coiling her muscles melt away like frigid ice in front of a welcoming fire.

Tears sprang to her eyes. Emotion pushed against the base of her throat. She buried her face against his shoulder and let herself accept this small gift of comfort.

Of love.

Will brushed his lips against her earlobe. "I'm so damn scared, Viv. Where is Tabitha? Who could have possibly taken our daughter? I keep thinking of any way I could have prevented this from happening. Any way I could have kept her safe. I failed her."

His words grabbed hold of her aching heart and squeezed. She fisted his suit jacket and held on tight. Shared heartache brought them together in this moment, and she didn't want it to end. Didn't want to go back to a life of loneliness and longing and trying so hard to make everyone happy only to come up short. In this moment, she was just a woman holding the man she loved. All the horrors of the past vanished from her mind.

"They'll find her," she whispered. "They have to."

"What if they don't? What it if it's my fault she never comes home?"

His words halted her breath and all the released tension from before seized her muscles again. She'd spent the past days agonizing over the possibility she had done the unthinkable. Other than the brief—yet crazy—idea Will's mystery woman had taken Tabby, she hadn't once considered that Will could be responsible. "What do you mean? How could someone taking Tabby be your fault?"

Will dropped his arms and moved away so fast she almost fell from her chair. He went back to his drink and downed the rest of the glass. "Nothing. I'm just being stupid. Spinning my wheels."

Narrowing her gaze, she studied the tight circle of his mouth and the way he refused to meet her gaze. She'd assumed his demeanor was because he was angry with her. Maybe his odd behavior had nothing to do with her at all. But if not her, then what?

"At least I can get one thing straightened out. I'll call Mother and tell her to get back here today. We'll hire another damn nanny if we have to. James should be home where he belongs. Regardless of what kind of mother he has."

And just like that, the spell was broken. Gone was the man who needed the love and support of his wife—who wanted to grieve together and share their fears over their daughter. Dejected, her shoulders slumped forward. But at least she would get James home. That's all that mattered.

Will jerked his phone from his pocket, pressed some numbers, and lifted the device to his ear. He tapped his foot against the floor, the cadence of his shoe hitting tile the only sound in the room besides the buzzing appliances. "Voicemail. Again." He waited a few seconds before continuing. "It's Will. Call me as soon as you get this. We need to talk. Now."

He huffed out an irritated breath and moved his fingers over the phone screen. "I don't know why she won't answer her phone. She always has it on her. I'll call Sylvie."

More buzzing from the fridge. More foot tapping.

"What the hell?" Will repeated the routine with his phone.

"Who are you calling now?" She asked. Anxiety rippled along her nerve endings. Something wasn't right. Lilith and Sylvie always answered when Will called.

"The Martha's Vineyard house. Someone has to be there. Maybe someone on the staff can get my freaking mother on the phone."

Vivian waited, her gaze never straying from Will.

"This is William Walker. I need to speak with my mother."

Vivian sighed, finally someone answered. Now Will could talk to Lilith and get this whole thing figured out.

Will straightened, his eyes going wide. "What do you mean

my mother isn't there? She left two nights ago and told my wife she was going to our house on Martha's Vineyard. I demand to speak with her. Now."

Silence.

Vivian gripped the edge of the island so she wouldn't fall off her stool. Will's clenched jaw told her that whatever he heard on the other end wasn't good. She braced herself for yet another blow, not sure if she could take it. Not like she had a choice.

Will dropped his arm to the side, his phone dangling loosely from his fingers. His mouth went slack and he held her gaze. "My mother isn't in Martha's Vineyard. They had no calls to prepare the house. No one has heard from her. Vivian, we have no idea where our son is."

And just like that, the bottom fell out of her world.

19

The words washed over Vivian like a bucket of icy water. She shook her head, refusing to believe James was missing. All this time she'd thought he'd been safe with Lilith and she hadn't even known his whereabouts. "No. That can't be right. Your mother told me she was taking James to Martha's Vineyard. Why would she lie? And if she changed her mind, she would have called you."

Will ran a hand up and down the column of his throat. "Where else would she go? What the hell is she thinking?"

"What about the apartment in New York?" Hope beat against her chest. This had to be a misunderstanding. Lilith and James were somewhere. She and Will just had to figure out where.

"Mother hates New York. She only goes when absolutely necessary. No way she'd choose to stay there."

She bit the tip of her thumbnail. "Call Patrick. He can tell you where he took them. He's probably still with them. Lilith wouldn't want to drive anywhere. No matter where she went."

"What's the point?" Will threw his hands in the air, his

question heated. "If Mother doesn't want to talk, she'd make sure Patrick didn't answer my call anyway."

Swallowing her frustration, she swiped her phone from beside her now-cold eggs and pressed the number for Patrick. He might not pick up for Will, but the driver was the one member of the household staff who had a soft spot for her.

The line rang in her ear, each second that ticked by spiking her anxiety. When Patrick's voicemail picked up, she disconnected. No need to leave a message. "He didn't answer. Oh, God. What if they got in an accident? James could be hurt. In the hospital and all alone." Her stomach twisted along with the endless, horrible possibilities.

"Someone would have notified us if there'd been an accident. No, Mother has a reason for lying. What's her end game? This doesn't make any sense." Will stormed across the room and yanked the orange juice and vodka back out then refilled his glass.

"End game? She stole our son," Vivian shrieked. "We need to call the police."

Will glared, his glass halted in front of his lips. "No."

Her eyes bulged. "No? We have two missing children. We don't know where your mom is or what she plans to do with James. I'll call Detective Olsen. She should know what's happened."

He snorted then took a long pull from his drink. "She's the last person who needs to know about this."

Vivian dropped her jaw and tightened her grip on her phone. Her head spun in large, loopy circles. "She's the first person we should call. What if your mom took Tabby? What if she wanted to take both of my kids from me and knew it'd be easier to do it one at a time. Or if she took Tabitha first, it'd be easier to convince me not to fight her over James."

"You sound ridiculous. Mother wouldn't take my children

away from me. It doesn't make sense." Will arched one light eyebrow.

She rubbed a palm over her face, trying to figure out the logistics of how Lilith could have pulled this off. "Patrick was in his car when Tabitha was taken. Maybe he followed me up the path. Lilith could have used him to spy on me. Detective Olsen said he needed money. Your mom could have paid him to grab Tabby when a window of opportunity arose." Her stomach rolled, and she dropped her hand from her cheek to press against her gut.

"What's her plan then? Take the children and live a life on the run? Never to return again? Come on. Don't be stupid." He took another sip from his glass, and she had to fight the urge to tear it from his grasp and throw it across the room.

"Plan. End game. What the hell does it matter?" She slammed her palm against the cool counter. Pain shot up her arm.

Will widened his eyes and worked his jaw back and forth. "Throwing a tantrum won't solve anything."

A tantrum? He was accusing her of throwing a tantrum like a child because she was upset that she didn't know where her son was? She shoved her hand through the top of her hair, scrunching the roots in her fist. She couldn't talk to him—couldn't make him understand. She swiped her phone to life and pulled up Detective Olsen's number. Thank God she'd thought to input the information after Ellen gave her a business card the night Tabby went missing.

"What are you doing?" Will set down his glass and took a step forward. "Who are you calling?"

She ignored the question. He wouldn't like the answer, and he'd find out soon enough. As long as Ellen answered the phone. And if she didn't—Vivian was all out of options.

"Detective Olsen."

"Detective. It's Vivian Walker." The relief at hearing the

other woman's voice was cut short by the anger radiating from Will's heaving chest and tightened jaw.

A deep growl-like noise grumbled from Will, and he thundered toward her.

She shot up from her chair, stumbling backward. "James is missing. Lilith took him and lied about where they went. We need your help." The words tumbled from her mouth, faster and faster. She needed Ellen to realize how dire the situation was before Will ended the call.

"I told you not to call her." Keeping his voice low, he ground the sentence through clenched teeth.

"Lied? So you knew your mother-in-law was taking your son somewhere? Did she have your permission?" Ellen asked.

Vivian took another step back then skirted around the island, away from Will's outstretched arm. "Lilith wanted to take him somewhere safe. I'll explain when you get here."

Will latched onto her wrist and yanked her close. "Hang up. Now." He mouthed the words, but the lack of volume didn't stop the venom from coating the command.

"I was on my way out of town and just passed your house," Ellen said. "Shouldn't take me long to turn around and get there."

Will ripped the phone from Vivian's hand and disconnected before she could respond. He shook her arm, rattling her brain. "I told you not to call her."

Vivian tried to pull away, but he didn't loosen his grip. "We need to find James. I can't lose him, too." Her breath hitched in her throat. Unshed tears stung her eyes, and she bit the inside of her lips to keep them from spilling over her lashes. She wouldn't give him the satisfaction of seeing her upset.

"We need to keep the police out of this. Especially Detective Olsen. Her job is to find Tabitha. That's it. And she hasn't proven herself too competent with that." He dug his fingertips into the sensitive skin just above her wrist then shoved her away.

The small of her back bounced off the hard marble of the island counter. Wincing, she slipped further from him. "Why are you so adamant you don't want the police involved?"

He pivoted, giving her his back, and squeezed the back of his neck. "It's complicated."

Irritation pulsed through her veins. She was so tired of being kept in the dark. Of no one trusting her. Here was the man she'd vowed to spend her life with, who she'd given children to, and the best he could give her was *it's complicated*. Was it as complicated as a picture she'd found locked in his desk? Or maybe as complex as a missing sister he'd never told her about?

At this moment, she didn't care about the other bullshit that had landed in her lap. Right now, she wanted to know why her husband didn't want to secure all the assistance they could in finding their son. She crossed her arms over her chest. "Then uncomplicate it."

He spun toward her and humor lit the blue of his eyes. "Excuse me?"

She tilted her head to the side, unwilling to back down. Not now. Not when the stakes were so high. "Explain to me what is so complicated about contacting the police regarding a missing child?"

He rolled his eyes and huffed. "You've never been interested in the details of my campaign before."

Campaign. It sat like a dirty word on her tongue. "Your campaign has never involved my children."

"Fine. Because of you, the police are now digging into my campaign practices."

Confusion furrowed her brow. "Because of me?"

"If you had just taken Sylvie with you to the bluff, none of this would have happened. Tabitha would still be home driving us all crazy with her damn crying, you'd still be moping around the house because God only knows why, and no one would be questioning my campaign manager about my bid for the senate."

She winced—partly because of his description of how their lives had been, partly because he was so damn accurate. "Your bid? Why would the police care about that?" True she didn't understand a lot of what went on behind the scenes of Will's hunt for the senate, but his bid only made sense once Senator Woods stepped down.

He chuckled and the noise raised the hairs on her arms.

"What's so funny?"

He waved his hand in the air. "You're so naïve. Always have been. It's part of your charm. At least it used to be."

His words slammed against her chest. "I don't care about your bid or the police sniffing around. I care about my kids. And if you're precious *campaign* is more important to you than your children, then you're not the man I thought you were."

Ding Dong

"You've got to be kidding me." Will muttered under his breath. "Is the speedy Detective already here?"

Vivian held her breath and listened for signs of anyone approaching. She itched to run for the door and answer it herself, but Will would grab her and keep her in place well before she stepped foot out of the kitchen.

A skittering of footfalls hurried toward them, and Mathilda popped into the room. "Detective Olsen's here. Should I show her in?"

"Tell her we'll meet her in the study." Will downed the rest of his drink and stared at her with narrowed eyes. "Don't you dare make this worse."

She straightened her back, ignoring the pain from where she'd hit the counter. "I'll do whatever is necessary to get my kids back."

Not waiting for a response, she hurried from the kitchen. Her knees nearly buckled as she rushed down the hall toward the front of the house and entered the study. She didn't have to turn around to know that Will followed closely behind. His heavy steps announced his fury—as if she wasn't already aware of the thin leash that restrained his temper.

Detective Olsen stood just inside the doorway to the study, her gaze fixed on one of Will's stupid paintings. She didn't understand why he had them scattered all over. They all looked the same to her. Same trees and valleys, just different seasons.

Ellen turned toward her as she entered the room, worry and confusion shining though her eyes. "I was heading out of town when you called. How long has James been missing?"

"Lilith took him from the home the night before last." Vivian scratched her long thumb nail against the side of her hand. Hiding anything from the detective would impede her ability to find James, but it didn't make it any easier to open up about the night James had been whisked away. Even if Dr. Kudrin's words held a hint of truth, blaming herself came so naturally.

"You were home when this happened?" Ellen shifted her gaze behind Vivian's shoulder. "Both of you?"

"I wasn't home. I haven't spoken to my mother since before this incident."

"I was here. She told me she was taking James to our house in Martha's Vineyard. That she didn't think James was safe in this house. She said I couldn't keep him safe."

Ellen scrunched her face. "Why would she say that?"

"I had just suffered another seizure. James fell and hit his head. She was...harsh. I wasn't able to stop her."

"And now you're telling me she isn't where she claimed?" Ellen dipped in her lips and studied them both.

Will sighed. "She won't answer or return any of my calls,

and when I called the house in the Vineyard, the staff haven't seen or talked to her."

"And this isn't normal?"

"Of course it isn't." Will marched to the sideboard and secured a glass of scotch.

Vivian closed her eyes. This was hardly the time to fill his body with alcohol. Or maybe it was. Maybe she was too concerned about keeping her milk free from toxins that would harm Tabby. Isn't that what had gotten her in this mess to begin with? She should just take the medication, drink the wine, down the liquor—hell throw in some anxiety pills to really take off the edge. Maybe that was only way to make it through this life in one piece.

Will swirled the booze in a circle. "Something isn't right, but I'm not convinced your involvement is necessary. My wife panicked and called, and I apologize for bringing you into this family matter when you have more important things to see to."

Her temper surged like high-tide. "I did not panic. Lilith is nowhere to be found, and she has my son."

"And she'd never hurt a hair on his head. She loves that boy. He's perfectly safe." He collapsed into the armchair adjacent to the fire.

"Are you sure about that?" Ellen asked.

The question lingered in the tense air for a beat before Will laughed. "Absolutely."

"I want to know where she is. And I want her to bring James home. Can you help?" Vivian ignored Will in the corner, speaking only with Ellen.

"I'll make some calls. I'm sure she hasn't gone far. She'd probably stay close in case there's news of Tabitha, right?"

Vivian hadn't thought of that. Unless her earlier thought had been more on the nose than Will wanted to admit. She dipped her chin to keep her voice from reaching Will. "Do you think Lilith could have Tabitha?"

"Nothing's impossible. But just know I'm working all angles right now." Ellen shifted her stance. "Why does Lilith think James wouldn't be safe with you? Have you ever hurt him before?"

The memory she always tried to forget rushed back in full force. James' motionless body on the ground. Blood soaking the little rubber pellets. "I would never hurt my children."

Ellen gave a single nod. "Okay. It'd be helpful to know what kind of car Lilith's in as well. Makes it easier to keep an eye out."

"Yes. Of course." Vivian found a pen and scrap of paper stuffed in the drawer of the small writing desk in the corner and wrote down the information.

"Thanks," Ellen said. She took the paper and slipped it in her pocket. "I'll get on this right away. I'll let you know if I hear anything at all."

Will stood. "Now that this nonsense is over, may I suggest leaving and finding the child who actually needs rescuing?"

Ellen faced Will. "One thing first, Mr. Walker. I want you to tell me what you know about the Coast-To-Coast Rifle Group."

Confusion turned Will's head slightly to the side like a child trying to understand new words. "Excuse me? What in the world does the CTCRG have to do with anything?"

"They're the group that could be responsible for kidnapping your daughter."

20

Frustration mounted in Ellen's chest as she maneuvered down the driveway of Senator Woods' house. She'd left the Walker estate with more questions than answers. Will's request to have a lawyer present when discussing his blackmail of Senator Woods didn't surprise her, but the revelation that Lilith Walker had kidnapped her grandson had come out of left field. The desire to ask a hundred more questions kept her at the house longer than she should have stayed. Senator Allison Woods waited.

Ellen had given William until this evening to secure Mr. Derby and schedule a time to chat. If he didn't come through by then, she'd leak all her findings to the press. The national news channels would have a field day with the grenade she'd hand them. Before leaving him to his scotch in his study, she made sure he was aware of the timeline.

She sent off a quick text to Daniels, asking him to look into the medical history of the family. She'd mentioned wanting Vivian's history—wanting a better picture of her epilepsy as well as any indication of depression—but the request had fallen to the bottom of her list with other details proving more important.

Now she wasn't only curious about Vivian, but also the children. Taking a child from the care of his mother, especially when dealing with such a gut-wrenching situation involving a missing child, seemed coldhearted. Not to mention a touch overdramatic.

Unless Lilith had a solid reason for wanting James out of the house. A reason that could include Lilith's thoughts on what happened to Tabitha.

Pushing the mounting questions and suspicions from her mind, she shifted her focus to Senator Woods. Her connection to the Coast-To-Coast Rifle Group couldn't be ignored. After the beans were spilled regarding her forced removal from the upcoming election, Ellen had poured over the woman's achievements while in Congress. She'd looked up her voting record, her allies, and her enemies.

Now, Ellen needed to speak with the woman herself. Only so much could be surmised looking through paperwork and reading about charitable contributions. She needed the dirt, and thanks to Mr. Walker's sleezy campaign manager, she had a big pile of it to use in order to get Senator Woods to talk.

A gorgeous Cape Cod style home complete with dark gray weathered slats and flower boxes in the second story windows came into view. Two wings flanked either side of home, stretching toward the unseen backyard. Not as imposing as the Walkers' mansion, but impressive nonetheless. Stepping up to the door, she pressed her finger to the doorbell and waited.

The door swung open, and Allison Woods offered a warm smile and a sturdy hand. "Detective Olsen. Thank you for agreeing to do this here. I know it was a bit of a drive."

Ellen took the offered hand. She hadn't expected the senator to answer the door, or for the older woman to be dressed down in jeans and a paint-splattered sweatshirt.

"Thank you for agreeing to speak with me so quickly. I would have driven anywhere. Thirty minutes wasn't too bad."

Senator Woods swept a hand through the doorway. "Come on in. Inspiration struck earlier, and I've been busy all day. Do you mind sitting out on the back porch? I'm loving the light and don't want to lose it."

"Lead the way. Anywhere is fine." Warm earth tones clamored together on the walls and furniture, creating a cozy environment as Ellen walked past several rooms to get to the door off the back of the cream and beige kitchen. White cabinets and backsplash made the room look clean and modern while the rich walls and family-themed decorations gave a splash of down-home love.

Something the Walker house only had in the rooms Vivian had decorated.

The stamped concrete patio extended the length of the house. Wicker furniture with floral cushions circled a built-in firepit. Senator Woods dragged a chair beside a giant canvas with slashes of vibrant oranges and deep reds resting on a tripod. "Have a seat. Would you like a drink?"

Ellen took in the expanse of the backyard. Manicured grass rolled along a hill then disappeared at a thick tree line. The same shades of orange and red from the canvas bled into the green clinging to the leaves.

Senator Woods was right. The sun streaming through the clouds was magnificent.

"I didn't know you were an artist, Senator." Ellen chose to stand instead of taking the cushy chair. She wasn't sure how welcomed she'd be after she started asking questions.

"Please, call me Allison." She waved a thick-bristled brush at her then dabbed it in a glob of paint. "And I wouldn't call myself an artist. Just something I like to do to calm my nerves."

"Well, you're good. I like it." She nodded toward the canvas. "Is there a reason your nerves need calmed today?"

Allison smiled and swiped the brush along a section of still-white background. "You tell me."

Dammit, Ellen liked this woman. Not pretentious or pissy—seemed not to play games. Although that was still to be determined. But she just needed to scratch the surface, not uncover all of the senator's demons. Just the ones that could be related to Tabitha's disappearance. "As I told you on the phone, I'm working to locate William Walker's infant daughter, Tabitha."

A slight cringe pinched Allison's face at the mention of William. "I'm sorry for what his family is going through, but I'm not sure what it has to do with me."

"I understand you weren't ready to walk away from your position in Congress. Is that correct?"

A steady hand hesitated, the delicate motion against the painting halted. "I'd say that's right."

Time to cut the niceties. "And that incriminating pictures in the hands of William Walker's campaign manager were the reason you withdrew your bid for reelection."

Allison grabbed a multi-colored rag and wiped off the bristles of her brush before facing Ellen. "I can't say I'm surprised you've stumbled upon this information. What I need to know is what you plan to do with it, and why you think it's something we need to discuss. My family is very important to me, and I don't want to drag any of them into a mess I should have avoided."

"I have no intention of airing your indiscretions for anyone to see." Ellen shoved her hands in her pockets. "I need to know who was affected by your withdrawal. Who'd be pissed?"

Shrugging, Allison studied the explosion of colors she'd skillfully applied. "I'm not sure too many people care about a Democrat from Connecticut. We're a dime a dozen."

Time to go in for the kill. "Not even the higher-ups at the Coast-To-Coast Rifle Group? I'd think having a left-wing senator on their side is something they wouldn't want to let go of."

Allison stiffened.

"I mean, you're right about the Democrats in this state. But what makes you so damn unique is your very quiet stance on gun control. Mainly the fact that you oppose it. With someone like you on the blue side of the aisle, it'd be a tough pill to swallow to just let you walk away. Someone's feathers must be ruffled."

Allison lowered herself on the seat she'd dragged over from the firepit. Propping her elbow on the arms of the chair, she leaned her head against long, slender fingers. "You think someone from the CTCRG retaliated by taking the Walker baby? How would they know William is the reason I'm not keeping my party's bid?"

Ellen shrugged. "You tell me."

She threw up her hands. "No one knows the reason I decided not to run. I announced my plan to leave after this term, and no one batted an eyelash. There's no reason to suspect anything nefarious was behind my decision, and most of the public buys into Walker's bullshit charm. He'd be the last person suspected of blackmailing me."

Ellen rolled her eyes. "Not everyone buys his bullshit."

Allison snorted. "Enough do. He'll get that seat, and it just burns my blood." Anger heated her words.

Was she angry enough to do something stupid like take Tabitha Walker? If William could trick people into believing he was a good person and the perfect guy to represent their needs in the Senate, could Allison be just as manipulative? "How can you be so sure no one knows about the blackmail?"

Bending her elbow, Allison glanced toward the back door then back to Ellen. "Listen, the CTCRG is the only group that'd have something to lose from my not being elected. They won't like losing my support to help squash bills that will hurt them. But there's no way they know William blackmailed me."

"How can you be so certain? I found out pretty damn quick. Someone else might have looked into this as well. Put pressure on the right people to uncover secrets."

Allison sighed and gone was the easy-going woman who liked to paint and wore jeans when greeting a detective in her home. In her place was a stone-faced career politician who was quickly losing her composure. "Because my husband hasn't left me."

"Excuse me?" Ellen had focused most of her attention on Senator Woods and her political career, but she hadn't been so negligent that she'd forgotten to run a check on her family. Her husband was a certified public accountant who worked for a major cooperation. "I don't understand how the two are connected."

"My husband's step-brother is a lobbyist for the CTCRG. If he knew I cheated on my husband, he would have told. And there's no way in hell my husband wouldn't have walked out the door if he knew." Her voice caught at the end of her sentence. She shook her head, and her dark braid bounced across her shoulders. "I love him, you know? My husband. What happened with Pat was a huge mistake. I still don't understand how it happened."

The regret in Allison's voice spun the wheels in Ellen's head. "What do you mean you don't understand how it happened?"

"I never drink, but that night after work..." Allison twisted her lips and slumped her shoulders forward. "It'd been a long day, and he talked me into one drink. Somehow that turned into a night I don't remember. Walker was lucky as hell to bust me on the one night I lost control."

Pulling over a chair, Ellen sat across from Allison. "How many drinks did you have that night?"

"I only remember ordering two, but Pat kept buying more

and I stupidly accepted. And the drinks were so fruity, I didn't realize how strong they were until it was too late. I should have known better."

Intuition tingled Ellen's spine. "Allison, is there a chance Pat got you drunk on purpose?"

Allison widened her eyes, shock tightening the lines of her oval face. "No. I mean, why would he want to get me drunk?"

Sometimes the smartest people could be the most naïve. Even the ones in politics who used mind games and schemed on a daily basis. "He might have set you up. How else would someone get the perfect picture at the perfect time? That's a whole lot of things that had to line up. At just the right moment."

Furrowing her brow, Allison shifted her gaze along the ground then sprung to her feet. "Sonofabitch. You're right. I'm going to kill Pat. And William. I can't believe they'd stoop this low. What was in it for Pat to put me through this? I trusted him."

"You can't go after them. At least not publicly. Walker is still untouchable unless you can get your chief of staff to confess."

"I'll skin them alive. All of them." She ground together her teeth, and for a second, Ellen believed her. "I'll go to the press. I don't need concrete proof for them to run a scandalous story."

Ellen shook her head. "You can't. They still have photos of you that would ruin your career—your reputation. No matter how much truth you have on your side."

Deflated, Allison sunk back down to her chair. "What do I do now? What does this mean for my future?"

Ellen didn't have an answer, so she sat quietly and stared at the unfinished painting. She didn't know what all this meant for Allison Woods, but for her, it meant she was once again tugging at the wrong line. If what Allison said was true, the CTCRG knowing William Walker was responsible for her stepping away from the senate would mean her husband stepping away from her. Whether her mistake was intentional or not, it sounded like her husband would at least demand an explanation. And since that hadn't happened, the sleazeballs behind her downfall hadn't told anyone the real reason Allison chose to walk away from Congress.

Senator Woods and her allies weren't responsible for the kidnapping of Tabitha Walker. So the question remained—who the hell was?

21

Time ticked by with excruciating slowness. Vivian kept a tight grip on her phone, not wanting to miss a call from Ellen or Harper. One woman could give her the news she so desperately wanted to hear, the other could give her the support she needed to boost her through the next few hours.

Hours that crawled by, each minute possibly taking both of her children further and further away from her.

Vivian sat in the middle of James' room. She held his favorite stuffed puppy in her arms—horrified Lilith hadn't taken it with them. He couldn't sleep without his little brown dog. He needed the comfort of his cuddly toy. Especially now, when he'd been ripped from his home and worried about his sister.

Sweet Tabby.

Vivian's insides twisted. James might not be in his room where he belonged, but at least he was with someone he knew. Someone he loved. Tabitha could be anywhere. Cold and terrified of the monster who'd grabbed her.

Frustration and fear pushed her to her feet. Will might be

able to lock himself away in his stupid office and bury himself in work, but she was tired of sitting and waiting. Tired of not trying. Writing in the journal proved painful and had brought to light memories she'd almost rather keep buried, but nothing that gave her any more clues to prove who'd taken Tabitha.

Except the watch. A chill swept over her, and she flicked her fingers along the cold metal secured around her wrist.

No. She hadn't done this. Tabitha was a piece of her soul, and no matter how sad or tired or overwhelmed she'd been, she could never hurt her baby.

She couldn't keep pushing herself to the brink of sanity trying to figure out that day. At least not now when her emotions were raw. Her third seizure had yet to strike, and her body needed rest before dealing with another physical onslaught that weighed down her limbs and made her muscles ache. But that didn't mean she couldn't figure out another location Lilith could have taken James.

With a surge of determination she hadn't felt in years, she marched down the wide hallway toward the west wing of the house. A wing she never ventured into. Maybe she couldn't help the police find Tabitha, but she could attempt to figure out where the hell her mother-in-law went.

Once on the other side of the home, she cracked open the door that blocked Lilith's living quarters from the rest of the house. Vivian had only stepped foot in these rooms a handful of times, and never by choice. The large sitting area held dainty furniture worth more than her childhood home and delicate glass figurines she always feared James would break. A master bedroom and attached bath, kitchen, and half-bath rounded out the space.

Vivian glanced behind her before shutting the door and securing herself in the dark sitting room. Long shadows stretched across the hardwood floors, darkening the colors of the priceless rug. She tiptoed further inside, even though no one was around to hear her. Lilith may be gone, but her presence clung to every fiber of fabric. Vivian couldn't let that bother her.

Swiveling, she studied the space. A desk sat in front of one of the floor-to-ceiling windows. She crossed to it and lowered herself into the soft, leather chair. Her heart rang a constant rhythm in her ear. Two drawers nestled together at the top of the desk. She slid them both out, releasing a sigh when she didn't need a key. She shuffled through the receipts and post-it notes, but nothing stood out.

She shut the drawers and glanced over the top of the desk. Neat as a pin and with nothing of interest, Vivian hurried to the bedroom. Dryness coated her throat, and she tapped her finger against her thigh as she moved swiftly. She may have been in Lilith's sitting room, but never in her bedroom. She licked her dry lips and switched on the light. Like the sitting area, order reigned. A patchwork quilt covered the four-poster bed and the cosmetics on the vanity were all lined in a neat row. Perfume bottles sat on a dresser alongside a few framed photographs. No art or frilly decorations hung on the walls. Not even a single throw pillow softened the look of the bed. Just like the woman who lived here, the room boasted only the essentials and not one ounce of warmth.

The photographs piqued Vivian's interest. She grabbed the closest one, a thin golden frame around a picture of Will as a boy. A wide, toothless grin split his young face. Lilith crouched low beside him. Her hair was blonde and long, and even in a picture joy radiated from her eyes.

A pang of sadness beat inside Vivian. She'd never seen Lilith with such an enchanting smile or exuding happiness the way she did in this picture. She set the frame back down and moved on to the one beside it. Another glowing Lilith, this time with a tiny baby in her arms and a grumpy Will with arms folded across his chest and pronounced frown beside her.

She ran a finger over the smooth glass. James hadn't understood the changes bringing home a little sister would cause in his life. Would he have been upset if he'd been prepared for the constant crying and a mother who could barely keep it together? Would he ever get a chance to get to know his sister as a friend and realize all the wonderful things that come along with being a big brother?

A fat teardrop plopped on the frame, and she wiped it off before pushing aside the moisture collecting on her cheeks. She sniffed back all the turmoil bubbling in her sinus cavity and focused on the last picture. A handsome family of four. A mother with happy eyes beside her husband—Will's father. A petite blonde girl with wild curls and mile-wide smile. And a solemn boy on the verge of puberty with an all-too-familiar scowl on a face that clung to the roundness of childhood.

The picture must have been taken right before Will's father passed away and not too long before his sister went missing.

The realization of the back-to-back losses stole her breath, and she turned away from the photo. She hadn't put that together until she stared into the eyes of the young girl, a tiny thing whose fate was about to twist into the unthinkable. Will's sister couldn't have been more than three when their father died, meaning he and his mother lost two of the most important people to them close to a year apart—if not closer.

Dammit, she couldn't let her sympathy for what Lilith had been through get in the way of figuring out where she was now. The pain of the past didn't give her permission to inflict pain now—pain Vivian didn't deserve. The top of the dresser might not give her more than a glimpse into the broken past but something inside the ornate furniture might show her what she needed to solve the problems of the present.

Yanking open the drawers one-by-one, she sifted through undergarments and night clothes. She patted down the velvet lining of every single drawer to no avail. Nervous energy vibrated her core. She wasn't sure how much time had gone by, but the longer she was here, the higher the chances someone would find her.

Putting everything carefully back in its place, she eyed the last spot in the room to search. A nightstand beside the bed. An alarm clock, small lamp, and box of tissues sat on top with a lidded decorative basket resting on the floor underneath the stand. Dropping to her knees, she yanked out old copies of magazines and a worn Bible from the container. Wadded up tissues huddled in the corner at the bottom.

She wrinkled her nose. A wastebasket was on the other side of the bed. Why would Lilith toss a dirty tissue in with her bedtime reading material? As much as she didn't want to, a tiny voice in the back of her head told her she had to check.

Cringing, she swooped in her hand and grabbed the tissue. The thin paper crinkled at her touch. Not a Kleenex but decorative paper used in gift bags. Something hard was nestled inside. Making sure not to tear the paper, she unwrapped a white patent leather shoe. Or, at least it used to be white. Age had weathered the leather, turning the white a yellowish hue. A lock of blonde hair tied in a yellow ribbon nestled against it.

"What the hell do you think you're doing?" Will's voice shook with rage from behind her.

Vivian dropped the shoe and spun around. Terror squeezed her throat, stealing her ability to respond.

Will stormed across the room and yanked her to her feet. "I asked you a fucking question. What are you doing in my mother's room? Going through her things? Are you insane?"

She gulped a shaky breath, fighting to keep her composure. Unwanted memories of his hands to her back froze her in place, but she had to push away the fear. "I'm looking for where your mother went."

"In her room? In a box by her bed?"

Vivian jerked away, tearing from his grip. "What else am I

supposed to do? Keep waiting and hoping someone calls and lets me know what the hell is going on? I can't do that anymore."

He dipped his chin toward the ground. "And how is that going to point you in the direction of Mother? You think some random shit in the bottom of a box will be the crystal ball you need?"

She shrugged and scooped the shoe she'd dropped from the floor. "Probably not. I think this must have been your sister's. It breaks my heart to think of your mom keeping one little shoe and some hair to remember her daughter by, yet she's unwilling to actually talk about her."

Narrowed eyes dropped toward her open palm. "Let me see that."

She handed over what she'd found and watched his face transform from anger, to bewilderment, to something she couldn't quite put her finger on. Regret? Sadness? "Why didn't you tell me you had a sister? I'm not dumb, I know we aren't the same people we once were, but there was a time when we loved each other. When we told each other everything. Why didn't you ever tell me about Daphne?"

His gaze shot up and met hers. "How do you know her name?"

"Your mom told me. She also told me it was better to keep some things buried in the past, but why? Why forget this person you both loved so much?" Lilith claimed to want to put that awful nightmare behind her, but the hidden articles of the daughter she'd lost proved she'd never fully let her go. A mother could never wipe away all traces of her child, even if once-joyful memories would always carry a punch of sadness.

Will turned the shoe over and over in his hand. "Losing Daphne was hard. Mother fell apart, and I was the only one around to keep her together. Father was gone, and she'd never had close friends. I was just a child myself, but I was forced to put away my feelings in order to keep the family moving in the right direction. It's a time better forgotten."

His words pierced her heart. How horrible for a kid to be put in that position. "I'm so sorry. For the loss you had to bear alone, and for having to go through something so awful again. It's not fair. Not then or now."

He closed his fist around the shoe and tightened his jaw. "Fair or not, life happens and I won't sit around and watch everything I've worked hard for be destroyed. Daphne is gone and talking about what happened to her won't bring her back. Mother was foolish for keeping this." He jammed Lilith's keepsakes in his pocket.

"What are you doing? You can't take that away." Her feelings for her mother-in-law were anything but amicable—especially right now—but she didn't deserve to have the last piece of her daughter tossed in the trash.

"Enough." Will pinched the bridge of his nose and closed his eyes, his deep breaths heaving in and out, expanding his broad chest. "No more. Please. Daphne is the last thing we need to be concerned with right now. She's dead. Case closed. Move on."

Blinking, she absorbed his words like blows to the temple. Would he be so callous if Tabitha's fate ended up like Daphne's? Would James forever condemn the mention of his sister?

No. She'd make sure that no matter what, Tabitha was always remembered. Always spoken of with love—pictures shown to anyone who asked. Her memory would always live on. But hopefully it wouldn't come to that. Tabitha would come home and they could put this nightmare behind them. Nothing more than a few lost days in the grand scheme of life.

"Do you miss her?" The question escaped her mouth before she could stop it. She had to know that this poor little forgotten girl had served some kind of purpose. That her legacy and memories of her hadn't vanished alongside her.

Will dropped his hand and opened his eyes. "How can you miss a ghost?"

"But she was your sister. You loved her once. You played hide and seek. Surely a part of you still feels something for the child."

He snorted. "I never played with her. She was such a whiny little thing. Her temperament as a baby was a lot like Tabitha. Always crying and never sleeping. I always kept my distance."

Confusion knit her brows. The articles she'd found on the disappearance claimed Will and Daphne were playing hide and seek when a van pulled up and grabbed the girl. Was the claim false, or did Will choose to not remember such a tragic event from so long ago? Maybe Harper was right and he held more guilt for his sister's disappearance than he'd ever admit. Either way, she'd pressed her luck enough. She wouldn't ask any more questions and simply pretend to forget Daphne just like the rest of her family.

"Leave this alone, Viv."

The use of her nickname almost brought a smile to her face. Something that years ago was so natural for them was now a rarity. A sad reminder of the life they once shared. "Okay." She'd agree, but only because she had more important things to focus on.

"Come on. We've got to go."

She furrowed her brow. "Go where?"

"I set up a meeting with Detective Olsen at Mr. Derby's office. I need to stop by his office anyway. I can kill two birds this way."

She suppressed a shudder. The common saying left unfinished brought to mind too many gruesome scenarios. "Why do I need to go? I thought she wanted to talk to you about something with the Rifle Group?"

"Hell if I know. When I spoke with Detective Olsen to confirm the time and location for our little chat, she insisted you come along. So quit snooping and do something with your hair. You look like shit."

Sighing, she smoothed a hand over the tousled stands flowing down her back and watched him hurry from the room. Uneasiness spiked in her gut. Detective Olsen would only ask for her presence if she had a bomb to drop. And when the impact hit, it wouldn't matter what she looked like.

22

Vivian smoothed a wrinkle out of her skirt as she sat in Mr. Derby's office and pasted a pleasant smile on her face. She didn't even attempt to follow along with the conversation between Will and their lawyer. Her input wasn't necessary, so why let their mundane words penetrate the fog in her brain?

An ache in her heavy breasts had her clasping her hands together in her lap. She'd been able to smooth her hair back, change her clothes, and swipe the little leather shoe from the trash bin in the kitchen before Will forced her from the house. Unfortunately, that hadn't left time to pump before being whisked to the boring Mr. Derby's office where she was certain more bad news would be dumped on her.

A loud knock at the door tightened the muscles in her stomach. No more avoiding the inevitable. Logic told her that if Ellen came bearing good news, she'd hurry to deliver it via the phone. Not make her sit and wait in a lawyer's office for a face-to-face meeting.

"Come in." Mr. Derby swiveled his large frame to face the door, unwilling to stand to answer it himself.

Will straightened from his spot perched by the window. He crossed his arms over his chest and planted his feet in the wide, don't-mess-with-me stance Vivian hated.

Ellen swept through the door with a deep frown and lines pulling at the corners of her eyes. A file folder hung in a firm grip at her side. "Good evening." She connected her gaze with each of them before closing the door behind her.

"Thank you for meeting us at my office, Detective. Mr. Walker and I had other business to attend to." Mr. Derby swept a hand to the empty chair beside Vivian. "Please. Take a seat."

Ellen dropped her glance to the empty chair, her lips twitching to the side. "I'll stand for now, thanks."

"Suit yourself," Mr. Derby said.

"Do whatever you want as long as you get on with this." Will relaxed against the windowsill again and twirled a finger in the air, as if to tell the detective to wrap things up.

Vivian bit her bottom lip, just wanting to get this over with. "Did you find Lilith and James? What about Tabitha?"

Ellen shook her head. "Not yet."

Her heart sank. If this wasn't about finding her children, why did she need to be here?

"I understand you have reason to believe a member of the Coast-To-Coast Rifle Group could be responsible for kidnapping Tabitha," Mr. Derby cut in. "May I ask why you believe this group would target my client's family? He has no previous dealings with this group. No reason to believe they'd be angry with him for any reason."

"You're right. I haven't found any questionable connections between the CTCRG and Mr. Walker. But I have discovered some interesting dynamics between Mr. Walker and Senator Woods. And the CTCRG would be upset by Senator Woods' decision not to reclaim her seat in the senate. Especially if they learned about the person responsible for her decision."

Vivian frowned. "Do you mean Will is the reason Allison

Woods stepped away from her seat? How could that be possible? He what—blackmailed her?"

Will laughed. "I did no such thing."

"That's a pretty serious allegation, Detective. I hope you don't plan to spread such heinous accusations about my client. That could get you and your department into serious trouble." Indignation might have raised Mr. Derby's brows, but a sheen of sweat appeared above his top lip.

"You might want to talk to Jim Ballinger if you don't want word of Mr. Walker's blackmail to get around. He had no problem telling me all about it when Officer Daniels and I questioned him yesterday." Ellen crossed between Vivian and Mr. Derby's desk then dropped into the vacant chair.

Vivian bounced her gaze between her husband and his lawyer, waiting for either of them to refute the claims again. Or to demand the detective not speak about a trusted employee in such a way.

Instead, Mr. Derby rotated his thick neck to face Will, as if he needed assistance in how to proceed from here.

Clearing his throat, Will raised his hands in a small V then dropped them. "I don't know what you're talking about. If Mr. Ballinger is spreading lies about me and my campaign, that's something I'll have to take up with him personally. I won't have a member of my staff creating problems. Not at a time like this."

Ellen locked her gaze with Vivian for a beat, something akin to remorse skittering across her prominent features. In a flash, the look was gone and Ellen's focus was back on Will. "I'm surprised Mr. Ballinger would risk his position, given your personal connection with him and his cousin."

Instinct set Vivian on high alert. She didn't have much knowledge of the people Will employed, but something about the way the vein ticked against his temple told her she'd missed something important.

"Step lightly, Detective." Will's voice brokered no argument.

It was the same voice he reserved for bossing Vivian around, expecting her to always do as told.

The voice she always listened to.

"I don't take orders from you, Mr. Walker. No matter who you are or what you represent. And I will step wherever I damn well please. I regret that the information I've come across will inflict more pain on Mrs. Walker, however, I am under no obligation to hide your indiscretions from anyone. Not when the lies you've been caught in make me question where you were the morning your daughter was kidnapped."

The meager contents of Vivian's stomach rebelled. Was this why Ellen wanted her here? So she could confirm that Will was having an affair? If that was the case, the detective could have been a lot more delicate. No need to drag her from her home to humiliate her in front of their lawyer. Anger surged to life, not only at William for making a mockery of their marriage, but for trusting Detective Olsen to be her ally.

Will snorted. "Please. Tell me what lies I've told."

"You lied about where you were when Tabitha was taken." Ellen ticked the allegation off on her index finger then lifted another. "About your personal connection with Jim Ballinger, the cousin of Jessica Stevens. By the look on your wife's face, you've lied about having a relationship outside your marriage with Jessica Stevens. Then there's the business of ordering the intoxication of Allison Woods and placing her in a compromising situation so you could get the photograph you needed in order to make your run for the senate."

"You don't know what you're talking about." Tight fists hung at Will's side, the ever-shortening leash on his temper close to shredding.

All the moisture in Vivian's mouth evaporated. "Is it true?" She stared at Will, wanting him to tell her that all of it was wrong, but knowing in her gut it wasn't.

He licked his lips and kicked the old-fashioned radiator

churning out warm air beside him. "We will discuss this at home."

She shot to her feet. "No. You'll tell me now. Are you seeing another woman? Some Jessica Stevens?" The name was bitter on her tongue, but at least now she had a name to match the picture of the smiling blonde. "Were you with *her* when our daughter was taken? When I called you, panicked and shaken to my core, needing you?"

She pressed the back of her hand to her mouth to stifle a sob. Deep down, she'd known exactly what that picture meant, but having it confirmed almost broke her in two.

"Answer her. Were you with Jessica Stevens at the time of Tabitha's disappearance?" Ellen asked.

"Yes." Will dropped his gaze to the floor.

"I need her to confirm. Then I can at least drop you to the bottom of my list of suspects." Ellen propped open the file on her lap. "Which leads me to you, Mrs. Walker."

Vivian whipped her head toward Ellen. "Me? What about me?"

"I asked you earlier if you'd ever hurt your children before. You told me no." Ellen held her gaze and any ounce of sympathy she'd shown earlier disappeared.

Vivian swallowed hard and lowered herself back to her seat. She'd just found out her husband was cheating, and now she was expected to just switch gears. She blinked, trying to process the question. "That's right."

"Can you explain to me how your son ended up needing treatment for a broken nose while under your supervision?" Blasts of icy judgement shot from Ellen's cold eyes.

She glanced at Will, but he refused to meet her gaze. "Umm, I was pushing James on the swing when I had a seizure. He fell—face first—and smashed his nose on the ground."

Ellen raised her brows. "And you didn't think that was important to tell me?"

She shook her head. "No. I mean, I didn't hurt him on purpose. When I black out, I can't control my movements. I pushed too hard and he fell. It wouldn't have happened if I'd been aware of what I was doing."

"And what about when he was found unconscious in the pool this summer?" She lifted a page from the folder. "The medical reports show he almost didn't make it. Another accident beyond your control?" Ellen pressed her lips in a tight line and raised her eyebrows so high they almost met her hairline.

"What are you talking about? That never happened," Vivian sputtered. Detective Olsen must be grasping at straws to create some story about James.

"Where did you get those records?" Will asked.

Vivian stared at him with her mouth wide open.

"James' pediatrician. A social worker might have become alarmed to see a small boy hurt so badly twice in such a short time. If Dr. Goodman had reported the incident. Fortunately for me, the subpoena I was issued was for hospital and family doctor visits. Even the ones performed at your home."

Confusion had her shaking her head. "You're both nuts. There aren't any records. James never came close to drowning. We're always very careful by the pool. I'd never let that happen."

Ellen extended a sheet of paper to her, and she ripped it from the infuriating woman's hand. She scanned the paper, James' name and birthday. His diagnosis. The summary of the visit from August. She lifted the paper in the air. "What the hell is this? I don't understand. I didn't take James to Dr. Goodman. Is this some kind of sick joke?"

Ellen stood, disgust twisting her mouth into a sneer. "You can cut the innocent act. Both of you. I'm not buying it anymore. You're both lying to me, and I'm sick of it. Where's Tabitha?"

Vivian reared back at Detective Olsen's unexpected

outburst. Her pulse raced and she searched her mind for any memory of James falling in the pool or of what happened to Tabby. "I assure you I don't know where my daughter is. And I don't appreciate you bringing me here to play some kind of mind game. Is any of what you've said today true? Because from where I'm sitting, you're the one spewing ridiculous lies."

"Really? This signed document from your son's doctor is a lie?" Ellen laughed. "You're all crazy."

"Don't call me crazy." Vivian rose to her feet, all the emotions of the past few days pushing her to her limits. "I'm a mother who is barely holding it together because I don't know where my kids are. How dare you accuse me of...what...trying to drown my son? Lying about my daughter's disappearance?" She thrust a finger toward Detective Olsen's chest. "You've crossed the line."

"Viv. Enough."

The softness of Will's voice made her blood turn cold. "Enough of what, Will? Are you finally going to chime in?"

He raised his palms then pushed them down through the air, as if telling her to calm down. "What Detective Olsen said is true. James had an accident in the pool over the summer. He was treated by Dr. Goodman, and he was fine."

"What are you talking about?"

He reached for her, but she pulled away. "Don't touch me. Just tell me what the hell is going on." Her command came out on a high shriek.

"I'd like to know that myself," Detective Olsen said.

"You hadn't slept in days after bringing Tabby home, but felt guilty for not spending time with James."

The days surrounding Tabitha coming home from the hospital were all a blur. The baby never slept, and Vivian did nothing but cry. Not like that had changed much in the two months their daughter had been home, but the first few days were the worst. "I remember. Kind of. At least the constant crying and me craving quality time with James."

"That's right. So you took him outside to play. Sylvie was with the baby. But you had a seizure, and when Mother went out to check on you, he'd fallen into the pool. We had the doctor come to the house to check on James... after I revived him with CPR."

Horror buckled her knees and she fell into her chair. She closed her misting eyes. She was such a terrible mother that she didn't even remember almost letting her child die. Couldn't recall the moment he'd walked over to the pool and fallen in. If Lilith hadn't come outside, James would have died.

Because of her.

"Why didn't anyone tell me?" She blinked back her tears, unwilling to meet anyone's gaze—Will's remorseful one, Detective Olsen's questioning one, and Mr. Derby's disinterested one. She couldn't handle taking on anyone else's judgement. She had enough self-loathing and condemnation without gaining it from anyone else.

"What was the point? It wouldn't have changed anything, and you hardly wanted to get out of bed anyway. You already cried over every little thing. Adding more stress could have created more issues. Issues we didn't want to deal with."

All the air was sucked from her lungs as the truth of what Will and his mother really thought of her finally sunk in. They didn't want to deal with her. Didn't want to deal with helping her or making her understand the severity of the issues she faced. They wanted to control her and contain her—keep the ugliness of her problems hidden from everyone.

Even from herself.

A light touch to her knee lifted her gaze to Detective Olsen. "Vivian. Have you ever talked to a doctor about postpartum depression?"

Unable to form words, she shook her head.

"The crying, the lack of sleep, the anxiousness. All these are signs. You can get help. You can even talk to the therapist you saw about it. I'm sure he can do something."

"The what?" Will asked, voice raising. "When did you see a therapist?"

"Why do you care? You don't want to deal with my issues." Numbness crept along her limbs, leaking into her mind. She wanted to go home, close her eyes, and escape from all the horrible things she'd learned today. Nothing could make it better. Not now. Not ever.

She stared past Will, watching the birds glide outside the window. "I love my children, even if I can't take care of them. Even if it's my fault they were hurt. I'd never harm them. Not on purpose." But as she watched a robin diving down from the sky, she wondered if that was enough. If the knowledge that she'd never knowingly inflict pain on her children could absolve her from whatever horrible things she might have done.

Gliding her thumb over the watch Will had given her on their wedding night, she kept her eyes on the birds.

I love my baby. I'd never hurt my baby.

But now, the mantra that had kept her going the past few days, was nothing more than an echo of a prayer she longed to be true.

23

The crisp air beat against Ellen's face, chasing away the dregs of fatigue clinging to her psyche. This case was keeping her up, making her follow every damn trail that always ended up at the same place.

Nowhere.

The connection between the nanny and her aunt's previous employment with the Walkers led her to a dead end, the only way the driver was involved was by association with Lilith, and the woman William Walker blackmailed was at the very bottom of her list.

Yesterday, she was certain one of the Walkers was responsible for their daughter's disappearance. She wanted it to be William—if only because he was an asshole she itched to take down—but her gut leaned toward Vivian. A mother climbing out of a giant hole of depression she didn't realize she was in, with a family who didn't care enough to help.

But now she wasn't so sure. Vivian's reaction to James' pool incident seemed sincere. The confusion followed by realization of what had happened to her son while under her supervision struck a chord Ellen didn't want to acknowledge. Ellen had no doubt Vivian loved her children, but that didn't mean she was off the hook if she'd done something to her daughter that morning on the cliff. If only she wasn't at a complete loss as to how to figure out the truth.

She glanced at her phone as she stepped out of her car and waved at Officer Lopez. No missed calls. Irritation simmered in her blood. The only way to find out more about Vivian was to speak with someone close to her, and the only person close to her was Harper Kellington. If Harper would just answer her damn phone, or call back, Ellen might get the answers she needed.

Until then, she had another mystery tugging at her brain and refusing to let go. She marched through the fallen leaves, the crackling sound combining with the rustling wind through the trees. "Hey, Lopez. Thanks for doing this."

Officer Lopez dipped his chin, lips tilted up at the corners. "No problem. Nothing like a walk in the woods first thing in the morning."

She chucked. "That's where you and I disagree. I'd be happy to never step foot on a hiking trail again, but something's bugging me and I need to make it back to the exact spot we found the other day. Even with a map, I don't think I could locate it by myself." She might be good with a gun and have a knack for finding the missing, but her sense of direction sucked.

"Thunder will be upset he missed it." Lopez slipped a map from his back pocket. He studied the markings then glanced around them. "Starting on this side of the property will get us there a lot quicker. What made you think to try from this angle?"

"I came around the back of the property the other day. I can't tell north from south most days, but even I could see the Walkers' estate butted up against this road. Since we made it so far into the woods, it was only logical that accessing that spot from here would be quicker."

When she'd first realized William Walker kept his mistress so close to his home, her first thought was of how much nerve the man had. Now, she wondered if it meant something more. The spot he'd taken a picture of Jessica was the same spot he'd memorialized in multiple paintings in his office. Since he didn't appear the type of guy to be sentimental, something important must have happened.

"Smart. Let's head out."

Ellen hoisted the heavy pack higher on her back and followed close behind Officer Lopez. Without the mud sucking her feet into the ground and cold rain splashing through the trees, the scenery was beautiful. Maneuvering through the outstretched branches and pushing away thick bushes to stay on track might not be something she'd want to do daily—or even weekly—but in this moment it wasn't so bad. This morning, the physical exertion and fresh air helped center her and kept her from pulling out every strand of hair in her head.

Her phone vibrated in her pocket. She stopped to catch her breath and glance at the screen. Excitement pushed against her chest. "Can you give me a minute, Lopez? I need to take this call, and if we get much further into the trees, I'll lose service."

Lopez nodded his consent then let his pack drop to the ground.

She followed suit, answering her phone as she released the strap on her bag and laid it at her feet. "Detective Olsen."

"Hi, Detective. This is Harper Kellington." A slight tremble shook her words. "I tried to call Vivian but she didn't answer. Is everything okay? Did you find the kids? I can't believe Lilith took James, and I'm not there. How can this be happening?"

"Thank you for returning my call. No, we haven't located either of the children. I wanted to—"

"Do you have a solid lead? Any idea who took Tabby or

where Lilith could have gone? That woman has some nerve doing this to Vivian."

Ellen sucked in a deep breath of fresh air. She'd hoped to have a calm conversation with Vivian's friend, but Harper's rapid-fire questions and high-pitched voice announced her fear loud and clear. "I can't discuss the investigation with you. I would like to ask you some questions about Mrs. Walker."

"Oh, I have plenty to say about Lilith Walker. The woman is controlling and mean."

Ellen hadn't needed anyone to spell out the elder Mrs. Walker's charming qualities. They'd been clear as day the moment she'd met the woman. Her daughter-in-law was much more of a mystery. "I'm sorry. I need to ask you questions about Vivian Walker."

"I don't understand. What do you need to know about Vivian?"

"Can you tell me how long you two have known each other?" Clearing away a pile of leaves, Ellen settled on the hard ground beside her bag and took out a bottle of water.

"About five years now."

"In that time, have you ever known her to make irresponsible decisions regarding her children?" She hated the bite of guilt at asking the question, but it had to be done. The safety of James and Tabitha Walker was much more important than preserving the feelings of a woman she pitied.

A sharp huff of breath filled the line. "Vivian loves those kids. They're her entire world. She'd never do anything to hurt them."

Harper's statement matched what Vivian professed. "That's not what I asked."

"I disagree. You asked if she's ever made irresponsible decisions regarding the children. Vivian's never made an ill decision when it comes to James and Tabby." A hard edge made her words comes out tight.

"Let me rephrase that. Are you aware of either James or Tabitha being injured while in Vivian's care?"

Silence dominated the line.

"Ms. Kellington?"

"There may have been an accident or two when Vivian's experienced a seizure. But she can't help that and it shouldn't reflect what kind of mother she is."

"What kind of mother would you say she is?" The picture that was painted in Mr. Derby's office the previous evening wasn't exactly pretty.

"The kind who loves her children more than life itself. Who centers every decision around making them happy."

"Even when she couldn't make it out of bed?" Ellen didn't need a rosy picture from a woman who didn't want to betray a friend. She needed the truth. Whether Harper wanted to spill or not.

"Having Tabitha has been.... difficult."

"How so?" Untwisting the cap from her bottle, Ellen took a swig of the still-cool liquid.

"Tabby is high maintenance. Lots of crying and no sleeping. Complete opposite of James who was perfect from the day he was born. Vivian has had a hard time adjusting. Will doesn't help, and Vivian hates depending on a nanny to care for the kids. She pushes herself—does too much—when she should be taking care of herself."

"Isn't that true of most mothers of infants? Babies are hard. That's a pretty common fact."

"I wouldn't know."

Harper's harsh tone had Ellen lowering the bottle to the ground. "Did I upset you?"

A slowly-released breath muffled against the speaker. "I'm sorry. I've never been lucky enough to have children of my own."

"No apology necessary." Harper's reaction told her that not

having children wasn't a personal choice but a curse. A pang of sadness echoed through her. Even if her time with Sara had been cut tragically short, she'd always cherish the memories they'd been blessed to share. "Let me cut to the chase. Do you think it's possible that Vivian could be suffering from post-partum depression?"

"I... I don't know."

Ellen sighed. "I know Vivian is your friend, but not being honest with me or yourself about her mental state isn't doing Tabitha any favors."

"I guess. I mean, maybe. She's been so upset and always sad. But I figured she was just tired. And the baby blues are normal, right?"

Ellen cringed. She hated that expression. Such a simple and nice way to describe the hormones and emotions coursing through a woman's system at the same time she suddenly is getting zero sleep and is learning to take care of a newborn. "The baby blues and postpartum depression aren't the same thing. Please. Harper. Vivian can't get the help she needs if we don't understand what's really going on."

"Oh my God, how did I not see that? All the signs were there. I'm her best friend. I should have realized what was going on."

"Signs associated with issues of declining mental health is something most people miss. Even those who are experiencing it." Although Vivian's signs were fairly obvious, Ellen's own diagnosis of depression after Sara's disappearance made her more aware of the same symptoms in others.

"Why are you so curious about Vivian? Why ask me all these questions?" Harper gasped. "You don't think she hurt Tabby, do you?"

"I have to explore all avenues." She rolled her eyes at the standard response she gave a hundred times each investigation.

"She'd never do anything on purpose." A hint of weariness drifted through the line.

"But if she was suffering a seizure and repressed emotions floated to the surface, what about then?" An image of a crying Vivian with black hair whipping across her face standing on the edge of a cliff with a baby in her arms replaced the cascade of colorful trees. An image that she feared could be more fact than fiction.

A long pause stretched out before Harper responded. "I don't know. She's been in a bad place. I hope to hell that didn't happen. Vivian could never live with herself. But it's not impossible."

Harper's hesitant confirmation of Ellen's brewing theory made her stomach churn. The best absolute outcome to this situation was finding whoever took Tabitha and bringing her home. The worst meant the child was already dead. Worst turned to unimaginable if that death was caused by Vivian.

The corner of her eye caught Lopez standing and repositioning his pack.

"Thank you for talking with me, but I need to go. I'll be in touch if I have more questions." Ellen rose and grabbed the strap of her heavy bag.

"Detective," Harper said. "No matter what happens, please be kind to Vivian. She's been through a lot and doesn't have a lot of people on her side."

"My job is to locate a missing child, not care about how kind I am while I'm doing that. Trust me, I don't want to cause Mrs. Walker any more pain than she's already endured, but if I find out she's the reason Tabitha's missing, there will be major consequences."

"If Vivian hurt Tabitha, nothing in this world will cause her more pain than she's already caused herself."

Ellen understood the truth of that statement better than most. She hadn't killed her child—or even found out who had

—but if she'd been home instead of at work, nothing would have ripped Sara away. Ellen would have made sure of it. The guilt of not saving her own child when her job was to ensure the countless lives of others was a constant burden heaped on her slim shoulders. "I'm sure you're right. I'll be in touch if I have any more questions."

Pocketing her phone, she secured her pack. "Sorry about that. Let's go."

Officer Lopez flashed a smile before turning in the opposite direction and heading toward their destination.

Each step grew heavier than the last, the conversation with Vivian's friend playing on repeat in her mind. Harper was insistent that Vivian would never purposely hurt her children, and the evidence so far supported that claim. But postpartum depression could make women do all sorts of things they'd never normally do—resort to all sorts of behavior. Add in Vivian's epilepsy, and there was no telling what had happened on that bluff.

And for the first time in her career, she wasn't sure if she wanted to figure it out.

"This is the spot." Officer Lopez pointed toward the tree with the rock they'd moved a few days before. "What exactly are you looking for?"

She dropped her backpack to the ground again, not wanting the extra burden on her back as she explored. "I'm not really sure, but there has to be something special about this place. I can feel it in my bones."

"All right. We'll know when we see it, I guess." He flattened the map on the ground and traced a finger along the thin paper. "We've already been north and south of here. Did anything spark your interest on either hike? I mean, besides the rock and what we found beneath it."

She shook her head. The path here looked exactly like the one they'd traveled before, only not caked in mud. She studied the map, searching for anything nearby that could give her the answers she sought. "Is this a river down here?"

Officer Lopez furrowed his brow and looked closer. "Hard to tell. The map from the county auditor is just an aerial view, but it looks like some kind of waterway a little way to the east. Pretty close really if you want to check it out."

"Might as well."

Not even a shadow of a former trail cut through their path. Weeds snaked up thick trunks and the wind caused branches to slash across the sky. Beams of the morning sun barely filtered through the blanket of interwoven leaves, making the hour appear much later and the day more ominous.

"Watch your footing." He stopped for a beat and glanced over his shoulder. "There's a little drop off right here."

She slowed until she reached the edge of steep incline. Rocks and stones clung to the overgrown hillside. "This might be where the rock from the tree came from."

He grunted.

She continued down the hill, jagged bits of exposed limestone making the descent more unpredictable than she anticipated. Her foot skidded on loose pebbles. Losing balance, she fell to her ass and slid to the bottom. Wincing, she clamored to her feet. "Well, I found the creek."

A narrow stream of water trickled past. She could probably clear the creek in one jump. She glanced upstream, amazed at the different scenery at the bottom of the hill. More exposed stone lined the landscape.

Making it down with much more grace, Lopez stepped up beside her. "It's pretty."

She nodded, squinting downstream. "Looks like a cave or something down there."

Lopez fell into step beside her, but she barely registered his presence. Instinct had taken over, an excited buzz sparking her nerve endings and urging her toward the cavern nestled into the side of the hill she'd just fallen down. The mouth of the cave was narrow and drips of moisture coated slick stone. "Do you have a flashlight?"

"You're going in there? Is that safe?"

"I'll be fine."

Lopez swung his pack to the side and fished inside, pulling out a small flashlight.

Ellen grabbed it and turned it on. She shined the beam into the darkness. God, she hated small spaces. But her gut screamed that something important was inside. "I won't go in too far."

Ducking low, she moved slowly into the space. The air chilled, sending goosebumps shooting up her arms. Dead leaves littered the ground. The pungent scent of musty decay filled her lungs. She forced her feet to keep moving. The walls narrowed further, the cool stone rubbing against her shoulders. She swept the dim beam ahead of her. A dead end stood nearly ten feet away.

Dammit. What the hell did she think she'd find? She needed to be following solid leads, not trekking through the woods on some stupid hunch that probably didn't matter. Frustration swelled inside her, squeezing her lungs and contributing to the suffocating feeling of being trapped in the dark pit inside the earth.

She kicked at broken twigs and God knew what else, shoving a pile of leaves to the side. A little white shoe poked through the litter of debris. Her heart jumped to her throat. It was still attached to the little girl who'd worn it.

Dread settled in the pit of her stomach. She hadn't found Tabitha Walker, but she might have just found Daphne.

24

Sitting at the pretty antique desk in her office, Vivian wrote all her ugly thoughts and emotions in her notebook until the muscles in her hand cramped. How had something so horrible happened to her son and she couldn't remember? Hadn't even known how close James had come to death? Her mind raced with all the other things that might have happened that the people in her life had shielded her from. Not out of love, but because exposing the truth was too much trouble.

She read through the words scattered across the white sheets of paper. Blue pen marks smudged the messy writing. It didn't matter. The sentences were nothing more than the ramblings of a desperate woman trying to make sense of the impossible.

Defeat sucked out all her remaining energy, and she threw the stupid book across the room. A groan of agony ripped through her. She didn't deserve to remember every single moment when she let down the people she loved the most. Didn't deserve to shine a light on anything that could bring justice for Tabitha.

She didn't deserve to be alive.

The urge to drag herself across the hall and climb into bed tugged at her muscles. But she couldn't give up, not yet. She had two children who needed to come home, and even if she could never be the mother they needed, she'd do everything within her power to help them—give her last breath to make sure they were safe.

But how? No word had come from Lilith, and Vivian's search hadn't turned up any clues as to her whereabouts. Writing didn't help. Her options were limited. Standing, she crossed the room and picked her notebook off the floor. Her gaze followed the first words she'd written—the night when she'd remembered the shadow right before disaster struck poor little James again. If writing down memories of her senses helped, maybe it would be beneficial to go back to Lighthouse Point.

A shiver raced down her spine, and she folded her arms around her stomach. The idea of going back to the place this whole thing started was enough to make her dive under her covers and hide away forever. She didn't want to face it, but she didn't have much of a choice. Not if immersing herself into the past could help conjure up memories or find something the police overlooked. And if she wanted to go to the bluff, she'd have to get herself there.

Racing through her bedroom, she hurried toward the bathroom—averting her gaze from the king-sized bed with the fluffy down blanket that beckoned her like an old lover. Cool marble tiles met her bare feet. She tossed open the cabinet door below the sink in the double vanity. Crouching low, she scanned the bottles until she found the medication to stop her seizures in their tracks. If she had to drive, she needed to make sure she was safe. Plenty of milk occupied the freezer for Tabby when she came home. Dumping out a little milk would be worth making sure she didn't wrap her car around a tree trunk

—if she'd need to take the medicine at all. The only reason to take a pill would be if the familiar threat of a seizure took over her body.

She grabbed the bottle then bounced back to the bedroom to throw a sweater on over the t-shirt she'd worn to bed and a pair of faded jeans. Securing the bottle of pills in her front pocket, she ran back to her office, swiped her phone and purse from the desk then ran down the stairs. She had to keep moving, keep willing her feet to run along with the plan forming in her mind, or she'd fall apart. Crumble to the ground until someone forced her to move.

The cool mid-morning air skimmed her cheeks and brought a fresh wave of vigor to her purpose. She fisted her keys in her hand and headed toward the garage that kept her never-used car. So many years had passed since she'd driven. Hopefully it was like riding a bike.

She slipped into the cavernous building that housed several of their cars. The scent of oil and the faint smell of gasoline permeated the air. She wrinkled her nose, hitting the button to lift the large door. Beams of light spilled across the concrete floor and over the little red sports car she'd loved to drive before becoming a mother. Even if driving herself and the children was an option, the sparkling BMW would be far from accommodating of two car seats and whatever other crap she carried. Now, the speedy car Will gave her before they'd wed was just enough space for her small frame and the purse she threw on the passenger seat.

After adjusting the mirrors, she strapped on her seatbelt and started the engine. The leather wheel vibrated under her hands. At least someone on the staff had made sure the car remained in pristine condition, regardless of its lack of use. She shifted into Drive and bolted from the garage. A time once existed when she'd loved nothing more than putting down the top of the car and driving through the country, letting the wind lift the strands of her hair. The breeze on her face and the sense of control she'd had when pressing her foot to the gas and speeding down a winding road gave her a freedom she'd craved.

Yet another avenue of fun and joy she'd lost when the constant threat of a seizure took over her life.

Taking the turns toward James' favorite walking path had her tightening her grip on the wheel. Each landmark they passed was like a punch to the temple, bringing with it the horrible memories from just a few short days ago. Memories that would forever haunt her.

She pulled into the parking lot at the state park, and her breath caught in her throat. Only two vehicles took up spots, and she maneuvered her car into a space closest to the trail that led to the lighthouse then cut off the engine. Trembling legs carried her out of the car and toward the familiar path. Her purse slung across her chest, and she closed her fists over the thin strap. Her hands ached for the feel of James's palm in hers —for the smooth handle of Tabby's stroller.

Keeping her pace slow, she searched every inch of the trail, along with the stretches of grass and beyond. The police had scoured the area the day Tabitha was taken, but something might have been overlooked. The smell of the ocean tickled her nostrils and filled her lungs, and the fierce wind coming off the sea stung her eyes. She pressed on, her gaze to the ground until she reached the top of the bluff.

Her steps faltered. Tears burned her retinas. The lighthouse stood tall, its red and white stripes bright against the blue sky. The sound of the waves crashed against the shore. Everything was exactly the way it'd always been, yet so different. She should be here with her kids—James with his wide smile staring out in the great expanse of the sea and Tabby crying in her stroller. She shouldn't be here all alone with nothing to hold onto but her damn purse and memories of two children so far away.

Needing to continue her search, she circled around the spot where tragedy struck. She veered off the path and trudged into the thick weeds. Long blades tickled her exposed ankles. She used the toe of her shoe to push away leaves and acorns. Nothing loosened from piles or stood out.

She sniffed the air, trying to find the source of the smell she'd remembered in Dr. Kudrin's office. Lilacs or lilies or something floral. It had mixed with the salt and the sweet-clinging scent of James' car-ride snack. Bushes clustered on the ground in small mounds. Some sprouting greenery, others with leaves turning orange or red. None had flowers still clinging to life in the cool fall air. Maybe she'd imagined it, or her mind was playing another one of its sick games with her.

She doubled back to the lighthouse. The memory of her retching at the base of the structure made bile swim in her stomach. She licked her lips and approached the bright red door that hadn't been opened in years. At least that's what she assumed by the rusted hinges and padlock on the handle.

A gust of wind rustled the overgrown grass, shuffling the vibrant green blades. A piece of clear plastic caught her attention, and she squatted to get a better look. A candy wrapper with bold white, foreign words was wedged between a thicket of weeds at the white base of the lighthouse. Great, she'd made the trip all the way up here and a piece of trash was all she could find. She swiped it off the ground and shoved it in her pocket. Never leaving litter on the ground was a habit drilled into her from childhood.

Slowly, she stood and made her way to the edge of the cliff. A siren's song called, but it wasn't the beautiful singing of a woman beckoning. No, it was the sound of the waves smashing against the rocks at the base of the cliff. Luring her to take a closer look, another step forward. She closed her eyes and inhaled deeply, letting the cool breeze skim over her cheeks. It'd be so easy to lift her arms and fly toward the waves. To let the icy water carry her away to a place where she could never burden anyone.

Tears slid down her face. If she didn't have her children, she didn't have anything left to live for. It'd be so easy to lift her foot, step forward, and fall.

A tiny voice in the back of her head told her to lift her heavy lids and tear herself away from temptation. Sighing, she opened her eyes and roamed her gaze along the open expanse of blue, then scanned the side of jagged rocks plummeting to the bottom of the cliff.

A sliver of pink stood out against the gray rock. Her heart stopped beating. Tabitha had worn a pink sweater the day they'd taken their walk. Leaning forward, she squinted and tried to figure out what had washed to shore. Her pulse beat a rapid rhythm. She searched for a way to descend the side of the cliff, but no way she could repel the slippery stone that crashed straight to the sea. The waves beat against the rock, the vibrant blue churning into a white froth of fury.

There had to be another way to get her close enough to make out what the hell was down there. Turning, she ran down the trail. Her lungs burned with each footfall against the hard ground. Another trail forked toward the water. Pivoting, she slowed her pace on the unfamiliar path. The scenery resembled the sights she'd just surveyed, but the incline steepened as it zigzagged toward the ocean.

The grove of trees opened, and the smashing waves rang in her ears. The sound almost deafening, yet unable to replace the din of questions clamoring in her head. The dirt trail gave way to soft sand. A narrow beach stretched a few yards before meeting the outcropping of rocks from the cliff that stretched up to the lighthouse She ran over the sand and tiny grains flew up to coat her jeans. The uneven terrain made her gait awkward and slowed her pace, but she hurried forward until the sand melted away into a ground of rough rock.

Stepping lightly, she picked her way toward the pink mystery item now churning in the water a few yards away. Her feet slid on the slippery surface and sharp shards of rock penetrated the rubber of her shoes. She kept pushing, kept moving forward. Waves splashed and water sprayed on her, soaking her clothes. Her teeth chattered.

The jagged ground came to an abrupt stop, the water rushing to meet her feet. The white froth from the violent whirlpool at the base of the cliff spun and tumbled among the surf. She dropped to her knees, wincing as pain scraped her kneecaps, and lunged forward. She stretched her arm as far as she could and wiggled her fingers, willing the pink scrap to come to her.

Her knee slipped, and she fell. She stopped herself from tumbling into the water with one hand. The icy water splashed against her face. She stretched farther, pushing the bounds of gravity to not fall into the ocean. Something brushed against her finger, and she cupped her hand and scooped it through the water then pulled it toward her.

Water-logged fabric weighed down her hand. Vivian dropped to her butt and smoothed the material out on her lap. Loose threads spiraled from the frayed hem and slits tore through the back. But there was no mistaking it was Tabitha's sweater that lay battered and broken on her lap.

Lifting the tiny sweater in her flattened palms, Vivian pressed it to her face and wept.

25

The scene that unfolded before Vivian was eerily similar to the one she'd barely survived less than a week before. Police officers combing the area. Wide-eyed stares from strangers stealing a peek into someone else's misery. The distrusting eyes of every officer skittering her way as they passed.

But this scene was so much worse. Before, she'd clung to a desperate hope that Tabby would soon be found and come home. Now, the officers scoured the beach and the Coast Guard boarded a boat in the water nearby to search for the lifeless body of her child.

No coming home. No cheerful reunion with her daughter. No hope.

She sat on the beach with her arms huddled around her shivering frame. Sand coated the moist denim clinging to her legs. As much as she didn't want to witness whatever was found, she couldn't tear away her gaze.

"We should go home. There's no reason for us to be here." Will stood behind her, his voice barely audible above the roar of the sea.

"I have to stay. If they find her, I want to be here." Tears flowed down her face. Her heart knotted, twisting like a pretzel. She'd thought not knowing where Tabitha was, or who had her, had been the worst feeling in the world. This moment was so much worse. She'd give anything to go back to those moments —moments when a chance still existed that she'd see her baby's smiling face again.

Now she waited for Tabby to be pulled from the frigid ocean—no chance she was still alive.

Will lowered to her side, crossing his legs under him like a child at story time. He wrapped an arm around her shoulder and molded her against him.

She tensed. As much as she'd craved his support, now his touch caused her stomach to pitch with the nausea that hadn't gone away since securing Tabby's sweater in her hand.

"Listen. I don't blame you for not wanting me close. I've been an ass. But right now, I need you and you need me." His voice caught. She glanced at him through her lashes, and fat tears slipped over his cheeks. "Please. Just for a minute. Can we forget all the bullshit—all the mistakes I've made? Can we sit together? Support each other for just a minute? Please."

Her heart shattered all over again. A moan of despair erupted from her aching chest, and she collapsed against him. He engulfed her in his arms and held her too tight, squeezing all the air from her lungs. She longed for him to squeeze tighter, to force every breath from her body so the pain eating her alive from the inside out would go away and she could maybe find just a shred of peace.

Not like she deserved it. She deserved the agonizing pain. She did this. She was the reason the Coast Guard searched the choppy waves for her daughter. A daughter she loved. Vivian had let her frustration and depression and every other feeling of inadequacy swallow her whole and she'd done something so unthinkable and twisted she still couldn't believe it.

A young officer with a familiar face trudged up the beach toward them. Will sniffed back the emotions contorting his face and stood. Vivian couldn't move, the numbness sweeping up her body gluing her limbs into position.

"I'm Officer Scott. We spoke the other day."

Vivian didn't even glance up to acknowledge the woman's words. She remembered the woman—the judgement in her tone as she'd asked questions about what Vivian had done that morning. Turned out, the judgement was warranted. Officer Scott should have slapped a pair of handcuffs on her and hauled her to prison the moment they met.

"Yes, Officer," Will said. "What can you tell me?"

"I'm afraid we haven't found anything else. The sweater your wife found has been taken into evidence, but nothing more has turned up."

Vivian kept her blurry gaze forward. She should be the one in the churning waters. Whose body was blue and unresponsive, waiting for someone to rescue her from sinking into the dark abyss.

"What happens now?" Will asked. "Is Detective Olsen here?"

"The detective was detained at another scene. I'm sure you'll hear from her soon. Until then, it'd be best to go home. We'll contact you if…"

Vivian shut her eyes as the officer's voice trailed off. The words left unsaid but her meaning loud and clear. Someone would call if Tabitha's body was recovered.

"Thank you, Officer." Will crouched in front of Vivian. "We should go home. You need to get out of those wet clothes. We'll hear if anything happens, and I'd like to speak with the detective whenever she's deemed us important enough to visit." A hint of resentment bit into his words.

Vivian stared past him, her focus locked on the crashing

waves against the shoreline. She couldn't move, couldn't speak, couldn't think. Tabitha's name was the only thing that echoed through the hollowness inside her.

Will grabbed her hand and helped her to her feet. She didn't protest. She didn't have the energy. She let him lead her to his car in the parking lot and tuck her into the passenger seat, securing the seatbelt around her. Her head fell against the back of the seat and the world went by in a blur. Time didn't register as trees and houses and cars whizzed by.

When Will pulled through the gates of the estate and parked, she waited in her seat until he opened her door and peeled her out of the car. He ushered her up the front steps and into the house. "Why don't you clean up and rest for a bit?"

She tried to lift her shoulders in response, but her muscles wouldn't move. She didn't care to wash the dirt and sand from her body. Hell, she doubted her ability to make it up the stairs. But the sooner she could put one foot in front of the other, the sooner she could climb into bed and shut away the world for a little bit.

Without muttering a word, she trudged up the stairs and made it to her room. An image of Tabby was stamped in her brain, and her fingers longed to trail over the soft skin and inhale the sweet baby smell one last time. But she'd never get that chance. Not an ounce of energy remained in her body. She collapsed onto her bed and curled into a tight ball.

She squeezed her pillow to her chest and let the turmoil building inside her spill out. Pain pulsed through her veins and took over every square inch of her body. How was she supposed to live like this? How could the agony consuming her soul ever go away when her daughter was dead, and she was the reason it'd happened?

Sobs tore through her, her breaths coming out between staggered bouts of expelled emotion. Pressure slammed against her nasal passage. Tears soaked the satin pillowcase. She squeezed her eyes shut and prayed this was all a bad dream and she'd wake up to Tabby's piercing screams.

A burning sensation seized her lungs, making her bolt upright. Tabby might not be here, but Vivian needed a piece of her child. Needed to hold something in her hands with Tabby's scent—her essence. She staggered off the bed and ran to the nursery. Tabby's white bear sat in the crib, right where she'd placed it the night Tabitha disappeared. Grabbing it, she clutched the stuffed animal to her chest and fell into the rocking chair.

The shifting shadows on the shaggy rug was the only indicator of the passing hours. Vivian rocked back and forth, raking her gaze over the frilly decorations and cute toys Tabitha would never enjoy.

Fast footsteps pattered down the hall. She sat, burning eyes staring into space. A squeal sounded, and her heart rate picked up. She straightened, but couldn't tear herself off the chair.

James ran through the door and vaulted himself into her arms. "Mama!"

Joy so swift and fierce burst inside her, and she immersed him in a giant hug. Happiness beat back the sorrow and grief for an instant, before it returned again, stealing her breath. But she couldn't dwell on the sadness now. Not with the mop of her little boy's blond hair nuzzled under her chin. "James, honey, Mommy is so happy to see you. I missed you so much."

James snuggled closer, as if trying to make her absorb him into her skin.

"Hello, Vivian." Lilith entered the room and ran her hand along the slight curve at the front of the ornate crib that'd never be used again.

Vivian tightened her hold on James. So many harsh words sat on the tip of her tongue, but she couldn't unleash her fury in front of James. "Why did you come back?"

"Will left a voicemail about Tabitha." A glimmer of tears touched the corners of Lilith's eyes. She kept her gaze on the crib, due to shame for taking James or a desire to see her grand-daughter resting on her sweet bed Vivian couldn't be sure.

"I can't believe you lied to me. Taking James was bad enough, but then to not know where he was. On top of every-thing else. How can you be so cruel?" She tried to keep any anger from words, but it was damn hard.

Lilith finally met her gaze. Soft light from the afternoon sun streaming in through the window highlighted the deep wrin-kles lining her forehead. She lifted her hand to her necklace and rubbed the brilliant diamond between her fingers. "I did what I had to do."

"You had to lie? You had to leave me wondering where my son was?" The audacity of this woman astounded her. Even now—with one child lost forever—Lilith still stood by her decision.

"I couldn't lose another child by refusing to see what was in front of me. Not again. Not after—" She pressed her palm to her mouth and shook her head.

Vivian swallowed past the hard knot at the base of her throat. "We didn't know what had happened to Tabby. Not then."

A soft whimper fell from James' lips.

She ran a soothing hand over his back. She didn't know what all Lilith had told him about his sister, but there was no way he couldn't pick up on all the tension and heavy emotions in the room.

"Not Tabby." Lilith's voice trembled.

Awareness sucker punched her in the ribs. "Daphne? But you couldn't have stopped that from happening." She longed to say more, but didn't want to traumatize James any further. The days ahead would be hard enough on him.

"You don't understand. No one did. No one but me."

Vivian sighed. The weight of the conversation too heavy to carry. "You're not making any sense, and I don't have it in me to figure you out right now. I'm just happy to have James home." Her arms were full even though her heart was empty.

Lilith deflated, her slender shoulders drooping forward. "Just know. I did what I thought I had to, but it won't happen again."

Silence hung heavy in the air. The gentle motion of the rocking chair gliding back and forth hummed. As much as Vivian would never understand her mother-in-law, she did understand desperate attempts to keep loved ones safe. And now, like Lilith, she understood the pain that cut so deep when a mother lost a child. "How did you get through it? How did you move on?"

Lilith moved further into the room, reaching out and touching everything she passed—the top of the dresser, the soft rocking horse, the basket full of blankets. "I didn't. For a while at least. I was paralyzed with guilt and despair. But one day." She shrugged and faced Vivian. "I just did. I had Will. He had lost a father and a sister. He couldn't lose his mother, too."

Vivian thought back to Will's description of the time after Daphne went missing. How Lilith had fallen apart and he was forced to take care of his grieving mother. If Lilith didn't want to elaborate, Vivian couldn't blame her. But it was funny the way the mind created its own illusions of the past.

A sudden bout of dizziness swam in Vivian's head and she planted her feet to the ground to stop the motion of the chair. Her heart rate accelerated and the nausea in her stomach pitched all the way up her throat. Sweat collected along her hairline and down the back of her neck.

Her third seizure was about to strike.

Shifting James to her side, she reached into her front pocket and grabbed the pills she'd located before heading to the bluff.

Quickly, she unscrewed the top and popped a pill in her mouth, washing it down with the burst of saliva coating her tongue.

Closing her eyes, she inhaled large gulps of air before releasing the breath with a gust of force from her open mouth. She counted to twenty, waiting and hoping the medicine worked as well as she remembered.

Her heart rate slowed and the nausea returned to the constant state of unrest she'd experienced all day. A sigh of relief slipped from her lips, and she shifted James back on her lap.

The sound of crinkling plastic caught her attention. She squinted at James' little hands, fisted together and rubbing something between his fingers. "What's that, baby?"

James grinned up at her and excitement lit his eyes. He held up the candy wrapper she'd found by the lighthouse. It must have fallen from her pocket when she'd grabbed her pills. James waved it in the air, and his bottom bounced against her thighs.

She grabbed the wrapper and studied the bold letters.

James lunged for it. "Mama! No!"

Recognition dawned on her and she shook her head, a tiny tickle of laughter scarping her raw throat.

"Whatever he found, he's very excited about it," Lilith said.

"It's a candy wrapper."

Lilith drew down her brows. "How does he know that? You don't like giving him sweets. Especially processed candy from the store."

Lilith might cross boundaries, but at least she stuck to the few steadfast rules Vivian had put in place once James was born. Next time she'd add 'Don't kidnap my child' to the list. "I don't give him sweets, but Harper always sneaks him candy when they see each other. She's given him this kind of candy before."

Vivian took the trash from James and shoved it back in her pocket. She held on tight to her little boy as a giant hole continued to fester in her soul. She might have one piece of her heart back in her arms, but the other was lost to her forever.

26

E llen rubbed at the pounding ache behind her temples and collected her thoughts before stepping into the lion's den—also known as the Walker Estate. The day had been long and brutal. Finding missing children was her job, but finding one who'd died cold and alone on her family's property was one of the most horrendous experiences of her life.

Right next to a phone call to inform her of Tabitha Walker's sweater being found tossed in the vicious ocean waves.

She'd wanted to be at the scene, but first she owed it to Daphne to see her tiny body taken away respectfully. Tests would be done to confirm her identity, but the tattered clothes matched the description and no doubt existed in Ellen's mind that the child had finally been recovered.

But discovering Daphne Walker led to many more questions. Questions she needed answers to, even though the family was dealing with another devastating blow.

She rang the bell and waited.

William answered the door with a pungent glass of alcohol in his hands and blood-shot eyes. "It's about time you showed up. We've waited hours to hear something." He shoved the door open wider and walked away.

Well, this would be a fun conversation, she thought. She stepped inside, closing the door behind her.

William glanced over his shoulder as he marched up the stairs. "Vivian's upstairs. Might as well head her way for this."

Surprise halted her motion for a beat. Her last encounter with Mr. and Mrs. Walker left her questioning his controlling behavior of Vivian. Beyond that, in every meeting she'd had with the two, William had never shown any consideration for his wife, but she supposed there was a first time for everything. Too bad it took such a tragic turn of events to soften his hard edges. Regaining her wits, she followed him up the winding staircase and down the wide hall to a room beside the nursey.

If William's suggestion to meet Vivian upstairs surprised her, the scene in the room shocked the hell out of her. James laid sleeping in his bed with Vivian beside him. Her green eyes stayed on the little boy's face, and she ran a hand up and down his back while he rested. Lilith sat in an armchair in the corner with red-rimmed eyes and the aura of a broken woman. William crossed the room and sat on a cushioned bench situated below a low window.

Ellen stood in the threshold, blinking and bringing the picture into better focus in order to make sure it wasn't imagined. "Lilith. I'm surprised to see you here." In one sense, it made her job much easier. She wouldn't have to track the elder Mrs. Walker down to tell her about finding her daughter, and hopefully she'd have some insight to make her understand why the case file she'd read had been full of incorrect information.

But on the other hand, she now was forced to inform a mother about the cruel twist of fate that led to locating her child.

"I came home to be with my family, Detective," Lilith said.

Since her family didn't argue or attack the older woman for

taking James, Ellen would just let their earlier accusation of kidnapping go. She had bigger issues to address right now, and with James safely napping in his bed, the issue must have been resolved. "I'm sure they're happy to see you."

"Enough small talk," William said. "Did you find her?"

Vivian closed her eyes, preparing herself for the blow.

Ellen's gaze flitted across the sleeping child. "Should we discuss this in another room?"

"No," Vivian said. "I don't want to leave him alone. He's a deep sleeper, so there's no chance he'll hear a thing."

Ellen nodded. If they were fine speaking in front of the boy, who was she to argue. "Nothing more has been recovered from the scene." Ellen shifted her stance, planting her feet on the soft rug and taking a deep breath. "At least not at the scene you were at earlier today."

Vivian sat, keeping a steady hand on James, and frowned. "What does that mean? Did you find Tabitha somewhere else?"

"Nothing regarding Tabitha or her disappearance has been found besides the sweater you recovered from the ocean." She licked her dry lips. She couldn't let her mind venture to what it meant for the baby that her sweater was found but no body. Her focus needed to remain on Daphne for the moment. "But remains have been found and identified as Daphne Walker."

"What?" William asked, setting down his glass on the windowsill and standing. "Where? Why were you even looking for her? You're supposed to find Tabitha."

Lilith might not be her favorite person, but Ellen was about to deal a blow so low, most people would have a hard time recovering. Even a woman with steel in her veins. "Her remains were located in a cave at the back of your property." She faced Lilith and kept her voice low and steady.

A sharp inhale of breath sounded from Vivian, but Ellen remained focused on Lilith. She sat stock-still, but a myriad of

emotions shone through her blue eyes and furrowed brow. "I...
I don't understand. How is that possible? I mean, are you sure?"

"I'm afraid so."

Lilith shook her head. "That can't be right. She was taken in
a van. By the front gate. How did she end up at the back of our
property?"

Vivian scooted from the edge of the bed and hurried to
crouch beside her mother-in-law. Vivian placed a hand on top
of Lilith's, and the older woman squeezed her fingers around it.

A pang of regret for the life Vivian found herself in rang
loudly in Ellen's ears. Vivian was stuck with a family who
treated her with no respect or kindness, yet she sat beside
Lilith, offering comfort.

Ellen cleared her throat, removing unneeded emotion. "I'm
sure, but I have the same questions you do. I looked over her
case file. It stated William saw his sister abducted while they
played hide and seek. I'm sure your property was swept, just as
it was after Tabitha went missing, so I'm not sure when she was
placed back on the property. If she ever left at all."

"What does that mean?" William asked. "You think
someone took her directly to our fucking backyard? That
doesn't make any sense. Besides, after all these years, how can
you be sure it's her?"

"Further DNA testing will be done, but the body, as well as
the clothes worn by the victim, are identical matches for
Daphne the day she disappeared. Right down to her white
patent leather shoes. Well, at least one of them. We couldn't
locate the other shoe near her location." Chances were the girl
lost the shoe during a struggle or while trying to make it out of
the woods. At least that's how it played in Ellen's mind. What
she couldn't figure out was why she was back in the woods in
the first place.

"Wait. A white leather shoe?" Vivian glanced at Lilith. "Like
the one you keep in the lidded basket by your bed?"

Alarms blasted in Ellen's head. "Excuse me?"

"Viv." The single syllable from William's mouth spoke of years of commanding his wife to obey.

Vivian stood with her hands fisted on her hips. "Viv, what? Viv don't ask why a shoe matching the description of the one your sister wore when kidnapped was found in the house?" She rested her hand at the base of her throat and took a step away from Lilith. "I'm tired of not asking questions and everyone keeping me in the dark about every damn thing. I will ask questions. So tell me, Lilith, why do you have that shoe wrapped in tissue paper and hidden under a stack of magazines by your bed?"

"I'd like to know that myself." Ellen's blood pumped furiously through her veins. If the family had found a missing shoe—the one the missing child had worn—the case file would have made mention of it. She'd dreaded telling another mother about the death and discovery of her missing child. But had Lilith known all along that her daughter was cold and lifeless in her own backyard? Disgust swirled in her stomach.

"It's not what you think. The shoe." Lilith raised her hands in a shrug then dropped them back down to her lap. "It was a part of my child. A child I loved and wanted to come home more than anything. That shoe was proof she existed. I needed to keep it by me. Needed to have something to hold on to." Tremors shook her words until she dissolved into tears.

"Did you take the shoe off of Daphne before or after she died?" Ellen asked, not sure if she wanted to know the answer. Either would provide her a horrible visual she'd never be rid of.

Lilith snapped her gaze up to meet Ellen. "What? No. I didn't take it from her. I would never. How could you even think such a thing?"

Ellen tilted her head and studied the horror etched on every line on Lilith's face. Either she was the world's best liar, or something else had happened in order for her to get the missing shoe. "What am I supposed to think?"

Lilith shrugged and dropped her gaze.

"Lilith. I need to know. Is the shoe the same one Daphne wore the day she disappeared?" Ellen asked.

Silence.

Ellen ground together her teeth. "I need to see the shoe."

"You need to stop pestering my mother," William snapped. "She's obviously upset. Give her a second to digest all this. I mean, hell, my sister has been missing forever and we find out she's been on our property this whole time." He shoved a hand through his hair. "Dammit. How the hell is this happening? And now, of all times."

Vivian lifted a finger to indicate she needed a moment and fled from the room.

Ellen turned to Willian. He'd demand to have his lawyer present at any moment. She should hit him with a few questions while he was knocked off balance. Maybe he'd accidently let something slip. "In the file, you stated that a man grabbed Daphne close to the front gate."

His jaw tightened. "That's right."

"But you were unable to get a look at the man? No discerning features?"

"No. Look, I was just a boy myself and it all happened so fast. Here I was, playing hide and seek with my little sister one minute, the next she's nabbed right in front of me. I ran, trying to get to her, but I couldn't get there fast enough."

Vivian returned and stopped in the doorway, inches away from Ellen, with a small shoe in her hand. "You said you never played with your sister. She cried all the time. Just like Tabitha." She widened her eyes and a tiny gasp sounded from her barely opened mouth. She pointed a shaking finger toward Lilith. "You said you couldn't refuse to see what was in front of you again."

"Vivian. Stop," William said.

"You said no one understood but you. That you couldn't lose another child."

"Vivian, let me see the shoe." Ellen extended her palm and waited for her to place the small leather shoe in her hand. She studied it. Same size. Same look. Same shoe. Her heart hammered against her chest. What the hell had she stepped into? "Where did you get this?" She shook the shoe in Lilith's direction.

"What was right in front of you, Lilith?" Vivian asked. "You made it sound like you should have been able to stop what happened to Daphne. How? What did you refuse to see?"

Lilith kept her gaze latched on her tightly clasped hands on her lap.

She wasn't budging. Ellen needed to push a different button. One that belonged to someone else. "William. Why did you tell Vivian you never played with your sister?"

William waved away the question. "She misunderstood."

"Like hell I did." Vivian stormed forward with fire in her eyes. "I asked you specifically about the game you claimed to play with your sister. The words you used to describe her were so cruel. So distant."

"Why are you putting your nose in this? It has nothing to do with you." William glared and tightened his hands to fists at his side.

Vivian reared back her head. "Why do you always push me away? How can you shift so damn fast? One second you're holding me in your arms, comforting me over Tabitha. The next you're tossing out your demands and expecting me to fall into line. I'm done with it. Now tell the truth for once in your life."

"I'm not on trial here." He threw his hands in the air. "I want Mr. Derby present for this. You shouldn't be asking these questions without him here."

Ellen bit back a sigh. She'd hoped to put him on the ropes. Make him falter enough to give her a glimpse into what had happened.

"To hell with Mr. Derby," Vivian spat. "Enough hiding. Enough lying. Did you lie about your sister? What really happened that day?"

Lilith pushed herself to unsteady feet. She braced a hand on the top of the chair. "I can't do this anymore. Vivian's right. There can be no more lies. Detective, I found the shoe and a lock of Daphne's hair in William's room after she disappeared."

"Mother." The word came out on a growl.

Lilith lifted sad, tired eyes toward her son. "I've protected you for too long. I can't do it anymore. I knew—the minute I found her things stuffed in you drawer—I knew you were to blame. I never asked, never demanded the details, because I didn't want to know. Didn't want to fully commit to the fact my son would do something so horrible. And selfishly, I couldn't lose you, too."

"You did it. You killed your sister." Vivian crossed her arms over her stomach. "Oh, my God. Did you hurt Tabby, too? Did you follow me on the walk and toss her to the sea, knowing I'd blame myself? Wanting to set me up for her death? You said Daphne reminded you of Tabby. Is that why you were always so distant?"

Ellen's head spun as she tried to keep up with the unraveling tangle of lies. Pieces started clicking into place. The landscape pictures William surrounded himself with. Taking his lover to his special spot. Even the ribbon buried beneath the rock. "The ribbon I found. Did you bury it? To memorialize the place where...what? You stranded the poor girl? Did you know she was in the cave down the hill?"

"I said I want my lawyer." Each word was forced through clenched teeth.

She'd heard enough. Between Vivian and Lilith's statements, she was fully within her rights to take William down to the police station. He could wait for the pathetic Mr. Derby in a cell. She might not be judge and juror when it came to the law, but in her mind, there was no doubt William Walker was guilty of killing Daphne Walker. Hopefully, the legal system didn't let the poor little girl down the same way her family had and justice would be served. "You can call your lawyer when we get to the station. I'm placing you under arrest for the death of Daphne Walker."

27

Not a single word formed in Vivian's head as she watched Detective Olsen escort her husband from their home in handcuffs. Thankfully Ellen had the decency not to cuff him until they'd left James' room. Her son might have slept through the entire, horrible exchange that shone a blinding spotlight on Will's past sins, but he could've woken at any moment. The last thing he needed to witness was his father placed under arrest.

Lilith stood by the window in the foyer, arms crossed tightly over her middle and gaze fixed on the empty spot in the driveway where Ellen's car had been.

An internal struggle warred inside of Vivian. A part of her wanted to comfort her mother-in-law, but another part couldn't believe Lilith had known—or at least suspected—what Will had done and never uttered a word. How could a mother stay silent, letting the person responsible for the death of her child go on with their life without punishment?

A punch of guilt stole Vivian's breath. If she was responsible for Tabby's death, she'd need to make sure justice was served. She couldn't pretend she hadn't ended her daughter's life. But what if it wasn't her? What if Will's alibi was bullshit and he'd gotten rid of Tabitha too? Her mind spun as she tried to think of any way to uncover the truth.

But did the truth matter? Lilith had known what a monster her son was—that he'd killed her daughter. The knowledge had made her cold and controlling, doing everything in her power to keep the monsters around her from striking again. A hard knot of resentment formed in Vivian's throat. Maybe if Lilith had told someone about her suspicions of Will, none of this would have happened to Tabitha.

Nervous energy zipped through her veins. Her body itched to move, to leave, to do something. Anything but stay here in this house. Too much buzzed in her brain. Too many emotions stirred in her gut. "Lilith?"

Lilith glanced over her shoulder before returning her focus out the window.

She rested a hand on Lilith's shoulder. "Do you want to talk?"

Lilith shook her head.

"I understand." Soon, Lilith wouldn't have a choice about what she wanted to discuss. Will might be the one responsible for Daphne's death, but they'd want to speak with Lilith as well. The Walker money and reputation might go a long way in politics, but not enough money existed to get Will out of this mess —and possibly Lilith.

But Vivian couldn't waste time caring about that at the moment. Now, she needed to get the hell out of this cage. A week ago her life had seemed so cut and dry, but now her eyes were forced open. Nothing was as it seemed. Monsters didn't lurk in the shadows, they walked around freely up and down the halls of her home. She couldn't live here anymore, and she certainly couldn't trust these people with James. She swallowed down tears. It may be too late to save Tabitha, but she wouldn't let her son get caught up in whatever twisted games this family played.

Steel formed in her spine, and she turned away from the broken woman in front of her. She fled up the stairs to her room, grabbed a bag, and stuffed essentials for a few days inside. Satisfied she had what she needed, she ran to James' room and did the same. Clothes, toothbrush, and his little brown dog were all shoved into a second bag.

"What are you doing?" Lilith asked from the doorway.

Vivian faced her and zipped the bag shut. "I'm taking James. We can't stay here."

"You can't mean that. You don't have anywhere to go. This is your home. James' home. You can't just take him away." Lilith pressed her palms to her stomach, as if her trembling hands were the only thing keeping her upright.

"Funny. Those weren't your thoughts when you stole James from his mother. You couldn't have cared less this was his home. But that doesn't matter. What matters is you were right. This is a toxic environment for him. You and Will. You're toxic." The hushed accusations burned her tongue as the truth finally set in. She jabbed a finger at Lilith. "You've kept so many damn secrets locked up in this house. And for what? To protect a killer! William killed your daughter. Didn't you even care? Want to know what happened?"

Lilith closed her eyes and shook her head back and forth, back and forth. "I can't live with knowing. I've told myself for years it was just an accident. Daphne slipped or got lost and William panicked. He couldn't have purposely hurt her."

Pity swam in her veins, and for the first time since she'd married into the Walker family, the pity wasn't aimed at herself but at Lilith. "Well then you've lied to everyone, including yourself, all this time. He took her shoe, Lilith. Cut a piece of her hair. What kind of a sick kid does that? What kind of a man did you really think he'd turn into?"

"I...I don't know. Please. Stop."

She sucked in a deep breath as fury shook her core. "I will stop. I'll stop trying to be who you want me to be. I'll stop letting you walk all over me and control me. I'm done with you and this family. I will not let William hurt me or James. And I won't sit back and let you cover up his bullshit." She narrowed her eyes and studied the now-small woman in front of her. "Did he hurt Tabitha? Are you covering for him again?"

Lilith's eyes flew open. "No. I promise. I don't know what happened to Tabitha. The thought crossed my mind—that he could have done something to hurt a child again—but I couldn't be sure. And you...with what's happened in the past. I just didn't know. Couldn't be certain. That's why I took James. I wanted to protect him."

Vivian snorted. "Well, you don't have to worry about protecting him any longer. We're leaving. Now."

Lilith reached for her, but Vivian backed away from her grasp. "But where will you go? What will you do? You can't possibly take care of yourself."

Vivian hooked one bag over her shoulder and shrugged the other on her back before scooping up the still-sleeping James. She didn't have any answers to Lilith's questions, but it didn't matter. The weight of her sleeping child sat heavy in her arms, but it filled her heart. She had James, and that's all she needed to push herself forward—even though the pain of losing Tabby threatened to drown her in misery. She'd figure the rest out. She had to in order to keep James safe. "I'm stronger than you think, Lilith. Now get the hell out of my way."

Pushing past her mother-in-law, she hurried toward the stairs. She hesitated at the first step as memories of Will shoving her in the back and watching her tumble to the marble floor seized her muscles. He'd let her blame her miscarriage on her seizures—heaped more guilt on her already frail shoulders to cover what he'd done.

What other calamities was he responsible for? Had he let James fall in the pool, standing by to watch him drown until his mother interrupted his plans and called the doctor? What else had she accepted blame and guilt and responsibility for because her seizures stole her memories, and her husband used her vulnerability to further his sick agenda?

A shiver tore down her spine, and she ran down the stairs. Mathilda stood by the door and opened it wide, allowing Vivian to escape with her arms full.

The sun streamed down and softened the bite in the air. She hurried to the garage and hooked her fingers under the back-door handle of the black SUV Patrick always drove her in. She didn't need Patrick anymore. Hell, she didn't need any of them. Her pills rested in her pocket, and she was capable of taking care of herself and her son.

She placed the bags on the floor then slipped James into his seat, buckling him into place.

He yawned and blinked sleepy eyes. "Mama?"

She smiled and skimmed her knuckles over his chubby cheek. "You and Mama are going on an adventure. We're going to be all right, okay?"

He nodded and smiled then let his eyelids drift back down.

She pressed a kiss to his forehead, closed the door, then jumped into the driver's seat. She sat for a second, willing a destination to come to mind. She didn't want to be far from town in case more information was uncovered about Tabitha. A hotel maybe, but would Will or Lilith track her credit card and drag her back home? Harper was her only friend in town. Maybe she could crash at her place for a night or two while she figured out a more permanent solution.

She dug through her purse for her phone and called Harper. Voicemail. Again. Sighing, she tossed her phone on the passenger seat and started the car. She drove away from the place she'd called home for the last seven years. A place she never wanted to return to. At the end of the driveway, she turned toward town. A key to Harper's house dangled from her keyring, even though she hadn't used it since James was born. Before his birth, Harper's place had been her refuge when Will started getting aggressive or argumentative. Back when those times were few and far between and Vivian hoped it was just a phase.

Years of mental and physical abuse had proved otherwise.

The tree-lined country lane soon led to the small downtown of Hollow Cove. When she'd first moved to this sleepy little town, she'd been so charmed by the towering brick courthouse in the middle of the town square. Shops and cafés clamored around the square, pride for the town colored on storefront windows and waving flags.

She passed by the library she'd taken James to for story hour and the park bustling with little ones and their caregivers enjoying the sunny afternoon. Her visits into town had become almost non-existent when Tabby was born. No one cared that she stopped showing up. Stopped trying.

A twinge of regret pierced through her frazzled state of rage and sadness. She'd wanted nothing more than to fit in and make friends after marrying Will and moving to a new place. She'd longed to become a member of a close-knit community. It hadn't taken long for her to realize that dream would never come true. Will hated being around anyone from town, preferring to keep his distance. He'd made it clear she was to do the same. No friends or family to keep her company or soothe her sorrows when each pregnancy led to another miscarriage. When her husband stopped showing interest in her.

Until she'd met Harper. Her time in the support group for grieving mothers hadn't lasted long, but her friendship with Harper had stayed an important part of her life. A deep longing to see her friend set in as she made the next right turn toward Harper's bungalow on the edge of town.

A bite of resentment tightened her grip on the wheel. She'd sent countless texts to Harper with no response. Harper was focused on finding the right place for her mother to call home for the next few months while receiving therapy, but Vivian had never needed a friend so bad. Just a phone call would've been enough to sustain her through the countless hours of agony she'd endured over the past few days. Anything but silence from the one person she could count on.

Harper's home came into view. Being near her house made some of the tension drain from Vivian's neck. She pulled into the empty driveway and cut the engine. Lights blazed inside the house. A flutter of movement stirred the drapes by the front window. Relief seeped into her pores. Harper was home. Finally, she'd get a chance to talk to her best friend and unload all the emotional baggage that had piled up.

Jumping from the car, she rushed to unbuckle James from his car seat. "Honey. We're at Aunt Harper's."

James opened his eyes, and a wide grin split his face.

"Can you walk?"

He nodded.

She lifted him out of the car and held his hand as they walked to the front door and knocked.

The door opened, and Harper stood in the doorway with dark bags under her eyes and hair piled in a messy bun on her head. "Vivian. What are you doing here?" She glanced down at James and gasped. "James! You're home."

James threw his arms around Harper, who squatted down and squeezed him hard.

Standing, Harper peered over Vivian's shoulder. "Did you drive?"

Vivian lifted her shoulders and smiled. "I did. When did you get home? Why haven't you returned any of my messages?"

"I'm sorry. So, so sorry. Things have been crazy with my mom. Nothing has gone as planned. I've been at my wits end trying to make everyone happy." She sniffed and lifted tearful eyes to meet Vivian's. "And then things went from bad to worse."

Guilt gnawed at her. Harper was one to keep her emotions locked in tight. Something serious must have happened to bring her home so quickly and to be so visibly upset. "Why didn't you tell me?"

"I didn't want to burden you. Not with everything you have going on. I wanted to call, really, I did. Especially after I found out about Lilith taking James and lying about where they were. But I knew the moment I heard your voice I'd crumble. I couldn't put that on you." She ruffled James' hair. "Not sure how it happened, but I'm happy to see this guy. Have you found out any more about Tabitha?"

Vivian sucked in a breath. While her world crumbled around her, Harper's hadn't been any better. "Lilith brought James home. Tabby...." She shook her head, unable to say the words again. Unable to go over every detail that would scar her for the rest of her life. "But what's wrong? What hasn't gone as planned? Is your mom okay?"

Tears fell over Harper's face. "Finding a home has been impossible. My brother has been such an asshole, and then I got a call this morning. My mom's gotten worse. She might not make it."

"That's horrible. I'm so sorry." Keeping a firm hold of James's hand, she pulled Harper in for a hug. A cloud of lavender perfume engulfed her. Such a familiar smell. One that always reminded her of sunny days and friendship and...the bluff.

Vivian stiffened and inhaled slowly. Yes. The floral scent but not completely earthy and natural. A punch of alcohol that always lingered in a perfume.

Harper cried harder, her body shaking.

Vivian glanced past Harper inside her living room. Boxes

were stacked in the middle of the room and all the decorations that usually cluttered the walls were nowhere to be found. She pasted a smile on her lips as questions tumbled in her brain. She pulled back, sliding her hands down Harper's arms until they circled her wrists. Her fingers rested on the cool metal of Harper's watch.

Panic pitched high in her chest, but she couldn't let it show. "Do you mind if James and I stay here for a night or two? I'll fill you in on what happened earlier. But being home is not an option."

Harper wiped at her eyes. "I'm not sure. I mean, I need to go the hospital to see my mom. I don't want to be rude and just leave you two here alone."

Vivian waved a hand in the air. "Oh, I don't mind being here alone with James. Really. It's no big deal. And it would be a huge help."

"What about a hotel? You and James can have some quality time together and enjoy yourselves."

The soft cry of a baby floated through the previously silent house. A cry that Vivian would know anywhere.

Shock stole her ability to breathe, and horror made her blood turn to ice. Tabitha was inside the house. Harper had kidnapped her baby.

28

The stone cottage tucked in the woods sat like a picture from a fairy tale—manicured lawn with toys scattered about, cheerful mums cascading around the home, and a fat cat basking in the sunshine on the front porch. The vibes given off by the property were night and day from the Walker Estate. Not like it mattered. All that mattered to Ellen was getting as much dirt on William as she possibly could.

Right now, his lawyer was trying to secure bail for his bastard client. William would be walking away from the cell she'd thrown him in, strutting around with the confidence that the charges against him would go no further. Since he'd committed the crime against Daphne when he was a child himself, she couldn't be sure he'd be tried as an adult—if at all. So she needed to do whatever she could to make sure he was locked away for as long as possible.

That started with speaking with his mistress about his alibi. Vivian had raised a good point. Could Jessica Stevens have lied about where William was the morning Tabitha was taken in order to cover for him? There was only one way to find out.

The white and gray calico arched his back then weaved

between her legs as she approached the front door. She resisted the urge to bend down and scratch his ears, instead pressing her finger to the doorbell.

A wail sounded behind the thick barrier. The same cry she'd heard the day she'd followed William back here. The door opened to a woman with tired eyes and a baby cradled in her arms. The television droned in the background. "Hello. Can I help you?"

Ellen presented her badge. "Hello, Ms. Stevens. My name's Detective Olsen. I need to ask you a few questions about William Walker."

Sighing, Jessica bounced up and down to calm the screaming baby. "Can't say I'm surprised. Come on in. I need to get a bottle for the baby."

Ellen caught a quick glimpse of the blonde-haired baby in Jessica's arms before she turned and headed for the kitchen.

Definitely not Tabitha Walker.

"I won't take much of your time." Ellen followed Jessica through the living room into the connected kitchen. "I need to confirm William was with you the morning his daughter went missing."

Jessica wiped the back of her wrist across her forehead, sweeping a stray piece off hair behind her ear. "He was here when he got the call. Had been all morning." She grabbed an empty bottle from the cabinet and pulled a container of formula from its spot on the counter. "Shhh, baby, it's okay. Mama's trying to get you fed."

The baby squirmed in her arms, his cries growing more and more frantic.

Tears filled Jessica's eyes, and she struggled to measure the correct amount of powder in the little scoop.

"Would you like some help?" It'd been years since she'd prepared a bottle, but the woman was obviously struggling. Making the bottle couldn't be too difficult.

Jessica thrust the tiny bundle toward Ellen.

Without much choice, Ellen took the baby. Her body tensed. It'd been so damn long since she'd held a little one. She cradled his head in the crook of her arm and stared down into big, blue eyes. No doubt this was William's son—the child looked so much like James. Like his brother.

Tearing her gaze from the beautiful boy, she glanced up at his mother. The woman flew around the messy kitchen, snatching a burp rag from the back of a chair and heating water to combine with the powdered formula.

No housekeeper. No nanny. No help.

William might not assist Vivian around the house, but at least he provided her with support. This woman had no one but a man who would hopefully soon be in jail.

Ellen swayed back and forth, attention back on the child in her arms. Warmth spread through her core. The baby's cries turned to soft whimpers.

Jessica threw a rag over Ellen's shoulder, popped the bottle in the baby's mouth, then fell into one of the four chairs around the kitchen table. "Thanks. It's been a hell of a day."

Ellen poised the bottle in her hand. The little mouth moved against the rubber nipple. Tiny droplets of drool streamed down his chin. Ellen was entranced, captivated by the silly gurgles and blind faith in her ability to feed him. A tiny chunk of the wall she'd built around her heart slid away. Maybe...just maybe...she was ready to finally pick up the pieces of her broken life and find a way to move forward. To allow more than just work into her life.

Emotion squeezed her windpipe. She might be ready to take steps toward a new life, but where would Jessica be with hers? What would happen to William's two other children? His destructive and selfish behavior continued to mow down everyone in his path.

"Do you have any more questions? I mean, I can't exactly

prove Will was here, but I promise he was. He tries to stop by most mornings. He was devastated when he got the call."

Her gut told her to trust Jessica, but she still had more to ask. "Can you tell me about your relationship with Mr. Walker?"

Red invaded Jessica's cheeks. "I know how it looks. What you must think of me. But Will and I..." She shrugged and a small smile turned up full lips. "We've always been meant to be. If things would have been different, I'd be the one in the big, beautiful house."

"You mean if your father hadn't been arrested?" Ellen asked.

Jessica nodded. "I never needed the material things. I just wanted Will. A life with the man I love. I have that, just not in the way I expected or even wanted. But it's all he can give me."

"How does he treat you?" The way she spoke about him, it was clear she loved him. Ellen couldn't help but wonder how this relationship compared to the one he had with his wife. If he gave all his love and affection to the woman behind the big house, leaving only scraps of affection to toss to Vivian.

The smile widened. "Wonderfully. I just wish I could have him all to myself."

Ellen watched the baby eat. If she had it her way, the only way Jessica would have William was with him behind bars. Maybe it'd be for the best. Jessica could find a man who didn't keep her tucked away because of the wife he had at home. No matter how much she claimed they loved each other, their relationship was still based on lies and secrets.

Like everything else about William Walker.

The baby squirmed and spit out the bottle. Ellen propped him on her shoulder and gently circled her hand on his small back. "I'll be honest with you. I don't know what the future looks like for Mr. Walker."

"Whatever it is, I'll be here for him. We're his family, too." A firmness set her mouth, as if she were ready to fight anyone who'd say differently.

"Yes, you are, but things have been uncovered about him today. Things that won't just go away because of who he is. You need to make sure you can take care of yourself and your children without him." She couldn't say more—at least not now—but the need to warn the other woman about the coming hardships weighed heavy on her conscious.

Jessica's smooth forehead rippled with wrinkles as she scrunched together her face. "What do you mean? What happened?"

"I'm sorry. That's all I can tell you." She erased the space between them and settled the little boy in his mother's arms. "He's a beautiful baby. Thank you for letting me feed him." Ignoring the questions in Jessica's eyes, she made her way back through the living room to the door and let herself out.

Her phone vibrated against her leg, and she pulled out the device. She gave the cat a pet before answering the call then climbing into her car. "Hey, Daniels. What's going on?"

"Walker just posted bail. No surprise there. I'm not sure how this will play out." Weariness made him sound beaten down.

She didn't blame him. Nabbing a criminal just to watch him walk, not knowing if he'd be punished for his crimes, was a slap in the face. "Get Jim Ballinger down there. Also Allison Woods' chief of staff, Pat something or other. Let's get some other charges to stick on this bastard."

"I'm on it. Are you on your way to the station?"

"Yeah. I'm going to call Vivian's friend again on the way. See if she has any more dirt on William that Vivian's let slip over the years. I also want to ask her about his treatment of Vivian. I wouldn't be surprised if he's physically abusive. She might help us sway Vivian to press additional charges."

"Sounds good. I'll see you soon."

Ellen disconnected and rested her head against the back of the seat. She needed just one second to reel in her emotions. After a minute, she cranked on the engine and tore down the gravel lane. She wanted distance between herself and the happy life Will had made with another woman. If life had been different, this could be his only family, a life most people would be jealous of. No frills, no political spotlight, no massive ego that destroyed everyone in his path.

But life wasn't different, and William had made bad choices every step of the way. Choices that led to the death of an innocent little girl.

She braked at the end of the lane and scrolled through her recent calls until she located Harper Kellington's number. She pressed the call button and high-pitched beeps sounded on the line followed by a recorded message informing her the line had been disconnected.

That couldn't be right. She'd just spoken with Harper the day before. Maybe she'd pressed the wrong listing. Wading back through her call log, she found the correct number and made the call again.

Same annoying beeps. Same robotic message.

Irritation hummed in her veins. Maybe Harper hadn't paid a bill or lost her phone so had cancelled her service. The only other number she had for Harper was her work number at the hospital. She could be back to work today. Finding the number for the events department where Harper worked, Ellen called and tapped her finger against her steering wheel as the line rang in her ear.

"Hello, events department. How can I help you?" A familiar male voice cheerfully greeted her.

"Hi, I'm looking for Harper Kellington." She didn't want to acknowledge she'd spoken with Jeff before, or he'd ask her about the event she'd claimed to want to sponsor when they spoke the other day.

"Harper no longer works here, but I'd love to help you."

Ellen frowned. Harper had gone from taking a leave of absence to leaving her job permanently in a very short time frame. She pulled at her memory, trying to figure out what it was Harper and Vivian had been discussing that very first night. "I'm sorry Harper isn't there any longer. She was so nice to work with. Is this because of her mother?"

"Her mother?" Jeff asked.

Yes! That was it. Harper's mother had fallen and broken her hip. "I understand her mother's in the hospital due to a broken hip. Would Harper happen to be in her mother's room today? I've grown somewhat close with her, and would love to reach out personally and express my concerns for her mom. And wish her luck in whatever her next step is."

A beat of tense silence filled the line. "I'm sorry. I'm not sure you're remembering things correctly. Harper's mother passed away about four months ago."

Shock stole any response from forming in Ellen's mind. Without a word, she disconnected the phone and logged onto her browser. She quickly found Harper's address and plugged it into her GPS. Harper hadn't only lied to Vivian about her mother getting hurt, but apparently hadn't even told her best friend her mom had died. Nothing was adding up. She only hoped Harper would be home to explain why she'd lied.

29

With her heart lodged in her throat, Vivian swept James into her arms and pushed past Harper. She ran into the packed-up house and down the hall toward the gut-wrenching cries of her baby. James clung to her neck as he bounced on her hip with each hurried footfall. Swinging into the guest room, she spied a small, portable crib on the far wall. She flipped on the light. Flashes of pale skin and flailing limbs peeked through the mesh siding.

Tabby!

With James still on her hip, she slammed and locked the door before hurrying to the crib. Tabitha's red face pinched together in fury. Tears poured from the corners of her eyes. Vivian set James on his feet and scooped her baby into her arms.

Joy seized her soul. She'd thought her child was lost to her forever—that she'd never again press her precious daughter to her chest and inhale the sweet scent that was distinctly Tabitha. But here she was. Alive and perfect in her arms. Tears sprung to Vivian's eyes as Tabby continued to wail—the most beautiful sound she'd ever heard.

James hugged her legs. She lowered herself to eye level with her son. "Everything's okay, honey. Look. Tabby is fine and we're all going to be all right."

James smiled at his sister, his little hand closing around her small fist.

Her heart swelled. She had her children—both of them. Now she just needed to figure out how to get them to safety.

Loud banging echoed through the mostly empty room. "Vivian. Let me in." Harper's frantic pleas sliced through the air, piercing the thin wood.

Vivian reached for her pocket and froze. She didn't have her phone. Her pulse thundered in her ears. If she couldn't call for help, how in the world would she get a toddler and an infant out of the house? She glanced around the room. A window looked out to the back yard, but there was no way to get all three of them through it without risking injury to one of the children.

More banging shook Vivian's already strained nerves. The hinges on the door jumped from the force. Harper might be tall and willowy, but it wouldn't take much effort to bust the flimsy lock. "Please. Vivian. You know me. Let me explain."

Standing tall, she searched for anything she could use as a weapon. An opened carboard box with clothes spilling from the top and a pack of diapers were at the end of the crib. A few more taped up moving boxes were stacked inside the opened closest.

Keeping James close, she hurried to the boxes and struggled to rip one open with Tabby in her arms. "Explain what? How you stole my child? That you let me cry about not knowing where she was or who had her? Lied about being my friend?" Her anger surged with each accusation she threw. Betrayal twisted like a knife in her gut, but she couldn't dwell on the pain of losing her best friend.

"You have to open the door. There's no other way out."

The tape finally peeled loose. She shuffled through the contents. Nothing but clothes and a few books. Although she'd love nothing more than smashing a heavy book over Harper's head, she needed a better weapon.

She pushed the top box to the ground and started over with the second. She ignored the pounding against the door and the words tumbling out of Harper's mouth. Nothing she said could make this better. No excuse could make sense of what she'd done. Tearing the lid open, she threw out sheets and towels. A growl of frustration threatened to erupt from her, but she had to appear calm for James, who clutched the fabric of her pants and pressed his face to the back of her legs.

Tabitha's woeful cries grew more frantic, and Vivian bounced her up and down while sifting through the pile of crap on the floor. A dull gray handle caught her attention in the corner of the closet, the muted color blending in the carpet. She kicked away the pile of clothes and god knew what else and grabbed a box cutter from the floor. She shoved up the pointy blade. It wasn't big, but it'd do enough damage if Harper got too close.

"Vivian! Open the damn door!" Harper's frantic pleas morphed into angry demands.

Vivian licked her lips, trying to figure out the best way to position herself and the kids to keep them safe, but close enough to grab them and escape if the chance presented itself.

A loud crash sounded, and the door banged open. Harper took a step into the room.

Vivian grabbed James' hand and hid him behind her. She clutched Tabby close to her chest.

A twisted smile transformed Harper's face from a tired, overwhelmed woman to a creepy lunatic. She held out her arms and crooked her fingers back and forth. "Give me the baby. Just give me Tabby and you and James can leave and pretend like you never walked in here."

Vivian's mouth dropped open. "You can't be serious. You can't possibly think I'd just leave my child here. Are you crazy?" The answer to that question was obvious. Vivian cupped the box cutter into the palm of her hand, making sure the sharp edge pointed outward.

The smile morphed into a sneer, and Harper's hazel eyes narrowed to slits. "You don't really want her. All you've done is complain about how much she cried and how you never slept. You never appreciated what a gift you'd been given. I can love her in a way you can't. I can be the mother she deserves."

"I am her mother, and I love her." Vivian gritted her teeth as the truth of her statement washed over her like warm water. She was done with people using her weaknesses against her. Tired of believing the lies and doubting herself. She loved her children fiercely. No one would take them away from her again. "Just leave us alone. Let me take them home."

"You know I can't do that. I have to get out of here. I'll take Tabby and start a life with her—be the mother I was never able to be. With a child I've never been able to have." She interlocked her fingers and pressed her hands against her stomach.

At one time, Vivian felt nothing but sympathy for her friend's struggle with infertility. But that didn't mean she'd hand over her own child to benefit Harper. "That'll never happen. The police won't stop looking for you. For both of you."

Harper frowned. "Then I'll have to make sure you aren't able to tell them what you saw."

Bile filled Vivian's throat. If Harper was capable of biding her time and pouncing on the perfect moment to kidnap her baby, she had no doubt Harper wouldn't hesitate to hurt her. But what about James? Harper wouldn't lay a finger on him, would she? His disappearance would be splashed all over the news.

Alarm dipped deep in her stomach. She'd taken James and

told Lilith she wouldn't be back. Hadn't told her where she planned to go or what she planned to do. If she and James were wiped from this Earth, would anyone bother to search?

No. She couldn't let that happen. She had to make Harper doubt whatever plan had twisted her brain. "I spoke with Detective Olsen today. She doesn't think Tabitha was thrown in the ocean. She's still searching for who took her."

Harper shook her head. "That's not possible. The sweater. I made sure to put in the water after I spoke with her. After I confirmed her suspicions."

Another ugly truth revealed. Tabitha's sweater hadn't been torn off her lifeless body as she was tossed through the waves. Harper planted it—wanting it to be found. "You talked to Detective Olsen? When? Why?"

"Yesterday. She wanted to know about your mental state." Harper shrugged. "I didn't have to stretch the truth to agree you could be suffering from postpartum depression. But when she asked if I thought it was possible that you threw Tabby off the cliff, I couldn't believe my luck. Everything came together so perfectly. Like fate. Tabby was meant to be mine."

Vivian tightened her jaw. She longed to hurl insults and spew her anger, but that wouldn't get her or the kids anywhere. Harper was unhinged, and upsetting her could land them in more danger. At least keeping her calm would buy Vivian time to figure out a plan. "What about your mom? How can you be there to help her and take care of a baby?"

Tears filled Harper's eyes and she wiped them away with furious fingers. "Mom isn't here anymore."

Vivian kept her face blank, trying her hardest to emote compassion inside of blind rage. "She's at the hospital, but after she gets better, she'll need you to help with her recovery. You can't take a baby to a hospital. Too many germs. You could get her sick."

"She's not in the hospital, you idiot," Harper snapped, fire lighting her eyes. "She's dead. Has been for months and you didn't even care enough to realize she'd been taken from me. You've always been too wrapped up in your own drama to care about me."

Blinking, she absorbed the insults. Was Harper right? Should she have listened more closely, realizing what was happening to Harper?

No. This wasn't her fault. Harper was unraveling and it had nothing to do with Vivian.

"I'm so sorry about your mom. Losing a parent is really tough." She kept her voice calm and steady. She tightened her grip on James. Not a single noise came from him. He must be so confused, wondering why his beloved Aunt Harper was acting this way.

Harper took a step forward. "I don't want your apologies. I want Tabitha. I won't wait much longer. The car is packed and everything's ready. The rest of this crap can stay. I don't need it anyway. Just hand her over." She took another step into the room.

Sweat broke out across the back of Vivian's neck. The room was small, the space made even tighter with the crib. Harper kept her gaze on Vivian's face. She couldn't just stand here, but retreating would put her and James both against the wall.

Taking a step to the side, she kept James close. "Don't do this, Harper. Please. Get in your car and leave us alone. I won't say a word. I promise. You can just start a new life somewhere else."

Pressing forward, Harper shook her head. "I can't do that. It took so long for things to finally go my way. I can't waste any more time. I need my baby."

"She isn't *your* baby." Vivian couldn't control the hatred that coated the words.

"Give her to me!" Harper screamed.

Tabitha's pitiful screams pierced the air, and James trembled against her legs. She took another step to the side. "Never."

Harper lunged forward, a deep growl rumbling from her like a tortured animal.

Vivian pivoted, barely avoiding the force of Harper's charging body. She grabbed James and pushed him to the side. No way she could hold Tabby, keep one hand on James, and fight Harper. But if James could at least get out of the room, maybe he'd be safe. "James! Run!"

James ducked low and scurried past Harper and fled out of the room.

Her heart beat so hard against her chest it threatened to crack her breastplate.

"He won't get far," Harper said.

Adrenaline rushed through Vivian's veins, and she planted her feet into the worn carpet. She clenched her teeth, tightening her grip on her weapon. It wasn't much, but she'd tear Harper's lungs from her body with her bare hands if she had to.

Harper charged again.

Vivian sliced her hand through the air. The sharp blade slid across Harper's cheek.

"Shit!" Harper staggered to the side with her hand pressed to her face. Crimson blood oozed through her fingers.

Vivian ran. She clutched Tabby tight against her chest. James stood in the living room with tears running down his face. "Outside, baby. Get to the car. Mama's coming."

A hard yank on her hair reared her head back. Pain exploded as her long strands pulled against her scalp.

"Give up, Vivian. You'll never beat me. Give. Me. My baby!" Gasps of air floated between each word.

Vivian used one hand to keep Tabby secure then lifted the

other above her head. Angling her body to the side, she slammed her forearm down on the crook of Harper's elbow.

Harper yelped and released her grip on Vivian's hair.

Vivian caught her balance and scurried forward. She had to get to James. If he wandered into the street, she'd never forgive herself for telling him to go outside, but what choice did she have? The hinges on the front door squeaked.

Harper grabbed a fistful of her shirt from behind and pulled.

Vivian fell backward and tightened her hold on Tabitha. Tabby screamed and waved her arms, making it difficult to keep her grip. "It's okay, baby girl. Mama's got you."

Harper hooked an arm around Vivian's neck and squeezed.

Vivian's eyes bulged and her mind raced. How had it come to this? Harper was her best friend, and now she had to fight like hell for her life and the lives of her children. Her throat burned. Tears stung her eyes. "Please, no." She wheezed and black spots obscured her vision. Adrenaline ripped through her body. She tightened her grip on the box cutter and jammed it behind her, cutting into Harper's side.

Harper screamed and loosened her grip then spun Vivian to face her. She reached for the baby.

Vivian shot up her knee, connecting it with Harper's stomach then ran to the living room, leaving the sounds of Harper's coughs behind her.

The front door swung open, and Detective Olsen rushed inside with her gun trained in front of her.

Tortured breaths heaved through Vivian's raw throat. She pointed toward the hallway. "Harper. Kidnapped Tabitha. In the hallway."

"I'll handle her," Ellen said. "James is in my cruiser. I called for backup."

Vivian nodded and hurried outside. She ran to the cruiser and opened the door. James jumped out and flung himself against her. She wrapped one arm firmly around him while the other cradled Tabitha. Relief flooded her system. Her heart swelled and moisture coasted over her cheeks.

Finally, both of her children were safe, and she'd do whatever she had to do to keep them that way.

30

The gentle hum of the baby monitor was like music for Vivian's soul. A noise she'd never heard when she'd been surrounded by the nanny and staff, always prepared to jump in and take care of the children. Two months after leaving all of that behind—including her sadistic husband and overbearing mother-in-law—the last seven years of her life were nothing but a distant nightmare.

A nightmare she'd worked hard to put behind her.

She relaxed against the cushions of the simple beige loveseat in the living room and smiled at Dr. Barns. She'd been sad to leave behind Dr. Kudrin, but the gentle woman with the kind eyes and easy smile was a perfect fit for Vivian's current needs. "Thank you so much for agreeing to do sessions in my home. I don't have anyone to watch the children and bringing them with me to your office would be a circus."

She'd never had to handle both children on her own before and wrangling them sometimes was like keeping monkeys in line. But her new life, circus and all, was a dream come true.

Dr. Barns settled into the ancient armchair and crossed her ankles. "Not a problem. I'm glad we could finally arrange a meeting. How has it been for you being back in your home-town? Have you gotten reacquainted with any old friends?"

Scrunching her nose, Vivian shook her head. "I haven't had much time for socializing. Getting the house ready took a lot more effort than I'd anticipated."

The home she'd grown up in had sat vacant for close to ten years. The deed had gone to her after her parents died, but she'd been away at school and then moved to the Walker estate. She hadn't had the heart to sell. Will had assured her he'd make sure the property was maintained, and it had been to a certain extent, but not enough to live in comfortably with a toddler and infant. A lot of back-breaking days and elbow grease had gone a long way to make the house the home she'd always wanted.

"That's understandable. You've been busy here." Dr. Barns gestured around the cozy room. A fire crackled in the stone hearth, and the colorful lights shone from the artificial Christmas tree in the corner. Handmade stockings hung from Santa hooks by the fireplace. "But I'd like to see you reach out to some old acquaintances in the coming weeks. Try to reestablish yourself in the community."

A shiver shook her body, and she ran a hand up and down her arm. The cashmere sweater did nothing to help with the sudden chill. "I'm not ready yet. Not after everything that happened." Trust was something that would be hard to find with anyone after Harper's betrayal.

"Start small. No need to rush anything. No one would blame you for being hesitant to start friendships. Have you heard any news regarding Harper's sentencing?"

Vivian swallowed the bile that rose to her throat every time she thought of her former friend. After escaping Harper's house, Detective Olsen had arrested Harper. Ellen kept Vivian updated on everything that was uncovered during interviews—each new piece of evidence another slap in the face.

Harper had targeted Vivian from the beginning. She'd struck up a friendship, knowing she had no one else in her life and wanting Vivian to become dependent on her. After Harper's mother passed, something snapped in Harper's brain, pushing her to do the unthinkable. She admitted to breaking plans with Vivian, then following her if she went out, hoping a chance to grab Tabitha would present itself. With Vivian's history of seizures and all the added stress of a newborn and unhappy marriage, Harper knew it was only a matter of time before Vivian's worst case scenario would become her moment of glory.

"The trial isn't until the beginning of the year. Last I heard, Harper's pleading insanity, which might hold up." A pinch of fear squeezed her flesh. If Harper were ever let back into society, Vivian would have to always sleep with one eye open. She'd never feel safe, or that her children were out of harm's away, if Harper wasn't behind bars.

Dr. Barns nodded. "And what about your husband? Have you had any contact with him?"

"You mean my soon-to-be ex-husband." She tightened her jaw, hating the way familiar feelings of inadequacy and despair swooped in at the mention of Will. "My lawyer has spoken with him and that's the only contact I want."

"How do you think your children will feel about not having a relationship with their father?"

Vivian winced and sucked in a breath to steady her nerves. Determined to heal and move forward into a better tomorrow for her and her children. No matter how hard it was to rethink on the last days—hell, the last years—she lived as Mrs. William Walker. "I'm not saying James and Tabitha will never have a relationship with their father. Maybe one day..." She shrugged, not wanting to finish the thought. The idea of Will being anywhere near them made her skin crawl.

"The autopsy report came back for Daphne," Vivian said.

Emotion hit the back of her throat. "Blunt trauma to the back of the head. Will killed that poor little girl, and for what purpose? I don't know what the future holds for him, but I can't trust him with my kids. Not after what he did to his sister—what he did to me." Angry tears burned her eyes.

Dr. Barns reached forward and grabbed a box of tissues from the coffee table. She handed them to Vivian then leaned back in the chair. "You might not have a choice. The autopsy might help build a case against him, but it's not a slam dunk."

Fury made her fist her hands on her lap. "Oh, I'm aware. Will is used to getting what he wants, no matter what the cost. Even with the additional allegations of blackmail, I wouldn't be surprised if he gets a slap on the wrist since he was so young when he murdered Daphne. But he doesn't care enough to chase me all the way to Ohio. I'm not worth it, and he has other things to worry about besides the legal minefield he's wading through."

"What's that?" Dr. Barns arched a thin, blonde eyebrow.

"His reputation. If he's able to spin things his way, he won't be out of the game for long. That's a big if, but it could happen. I'm prepared to come after him with everything I have if he ever comes for me or the kids."

The therapist tilted her head to the side, brow furrowed. "How so?"

Her mind wandered to the large envelope that contained every last piece of dirt Detective Olsen had dug up about Will. From his mistress to his other children to his unethical schemes that furthered his career. Then there were photos of Daphne from the cave and statements given by Lilith. Even if he walked away from this scandal, she could throw him right back into another by leaking it all to the press. It'd ruin him and any political agenda he still had. "Let's just say I wouldn't go down without a fight."

A twinkle gleamed in Dr. Barns' eyes. "Okay. Let's focus a

little on you before our time is up. How are you feeling about the move? Are you adjusting well?"

Warmth flooded her system, chasing away all the bad feelings and memories of Harper and Will. The last two months had been the happiest of her life. After finally finding the strength buried underneath a lifetime of a battered self-confidence, she'd stood on her own two feet. "Well. I won't lie, taking care of two small kids on my own is a lot. But I love it. Even the crying and the whining and the sleepless nights. I wouldn't trade it for anything."

"And your medication?"

She wrinkled her nose, hating how she'd let her guilt and paranoia keep her from taking something her body needed. Something that could have prevented so many bad things from happening. "I take it like clockwork. I still don't like the idea of putting chemicals in my breast milk, so I switched to formula for Tabby."

"You know," Dr. Barns said, pointing her pen at Vivian. "Your physician wouldn't prescribe something that would hurt the baby."

She shrugged. "I know, but when my body and mind tell me something, I need to listen. That's something I've learned the past few months. I need to clear away the clutter and listen to my instincts. Stop letting other people tell me what to do or how to do it."

"I can appreciate that. But let's try to keep an open dialogue about what your body and mind are telling you. I encourage you to keep trusting your instincts, but I'd hate for you to end up in the dark place you once were. I'm here to help, in any way I can."

Appreciation squeezed her chest. "Thank you. Trust me, I never want to be in that dark place again, and I know I have lots of work to continue doing on myself."

Shuffling noise crackled through the monitor. "Mama?"

"Oh, that's James. He doesn't nap long these days. I need to grab him." She stood and curled her toes against the soft rug under her feet.

Dr. Barns followed suit and rose. "I think we've discussed plenty today. Should we set up another appointment for next week? Same time?"

"Perfect." Vivian walked Dr. Barns down the narrow hall to the front door. "I'll see you next week."

Closing the door behind the therapist, she hurried to the bedroom James and Tabby now shared. The two-bedroom house was modest, but plenty of space for the three of them and an acre of land behind the house to play. She didn't need anything more. Her expenses were low, and the child support Will already sent went a long way. The checks might be coming from Lilith, but she didn't care. She'd paid her dues and deserved every penny she was sent. And maybe once a little time had passed, this small show of Lilith's support would allow Vivian to open the door for her children to visit their grandmother. On her terms and nobody else's.

Cracking open the door, she peered through the darkness. Thanks to the black-out curtains she'd found in the basement, the sunlight pouring through the windows in the middle of the afternoon wouldn't be a problem at nap time. "James, honey, Mommy's here," she whispered, not wanting to wake Tabby.

James stood on his tiptoes beside the crib, giggling at his baby sister.

"So you're both, awake, huh?" She flipped on the light and stepped into the room.

Tabby gurgled incoherent baby coos in the crib.

Vivian pressed a kiss to the top of James' head then scooped Tabby from the crib. "How about we get some hot chocolate and drink it by the fire? And a nice, warm bottle for Tabby."

James squealed and clapped his hands under his chin before running from the room.

She grinned, listening to the pitter-patter of his footsteps on the ancient hardwood floors. She quickly changed the baby's diaper then met James in the kitchen.

Another squeal from her son had her following his gaze to the sliding glass door that spilled onto the deck. Fat snowflakes dotted the blue sky. James bounced up and down, excitement beaming from his blue eyes.

"Do you want to go out in the snow?"

James nodded.

Vivian laughed and grabbed his coat from a hook by the door and helped him into his boots. She shrugged into a coat, then placed a warm knit hat on Tabitha's head. She grabbed a chunky blanket from the back of the couch and swaddled Tabby, keeping her pressed close as she opened the door and stepped into the cool, December afternoon.

The wind bit into her cheeks, but the strong beams of sun beat down on her. She closed her eyes and tilted her face toward the warmth. Toward the light. She sucked in a deep breath, enjoying the pure and simple moment with her kids.

Giggles had her opening her eyes and laughing at James as he stuck out his tongue and tried to catch the snowflakes. She nuzzled her cheek against Tabby's. "This is snow, baby girl. One day soon, you'll love playing in it just as much as your big brother. We'll build snowmen and go sledding. We're going to have so much fun."

She hugged her baby close while watching her son in all his innocence enjoy the simple pleasures of life. A life she'd make sure was always filled with laughter and love. The life she'd always wanted.

ACKNOWLEDGMENTS

Much love and gratitude to my mother, Brenda Hill, for sparking this story inside me. This book would never existed without you.

A big thanks to my husband and children. You guys stand by me no matter what, and that means the world to me. Thanks to my awesome critique partners, Samantha Wilde and Julie Anne Lindsey. I couldn't survive a day without your insight and friendship.

Much gratitude to The Editing Soprano for making my words shine, and for the team at Deranged Doctors for designing another beautiful cover.

And mostly, to all my readers. I hope you enjoyed this new adventure and new genre as much I did. Thank you for taking a chance with me!

Until next time!
Danielle

ABOUT THE AUTHOR

Danielle M Haas is a stay-at-home mom turned author. When she isn't writing fast-paced romantic suspense novels with mysteries to live for and romance to die for, she's busy being a taxi driver to her two busy kids and forcing her introverted self to talk to other soccer moms. Her kids and husband are her world, which is also shared with her hyper Bernie doodle, two sassy cats, and one leopard gecko who's happy to chill on a rock all day. Her days are packed with cuddles, kisses, and a brain constantly thinking of new ways to create danger and romance for her next book.

ALSO BY DANIELLE HAAS